"Wakpa Minisota!"

"Wakpa Minisota!"

A Novel By Jerome William DeWolfe

iUniverse, Inc.
New York Lincoln Shanghai

"Wakpa Minisota!"

iUniverse books may be ordered through booksellers or by contacting:

iUniverse
2021 Pine Lake Road, Suite 100
Lincoln, NE 68512
www.iuniverse.com
1-800-Authors (1-800-288-4677)

ISBN-13: 978-0-595-34992-0 (pbk)
ISBN-13: 978-0-595-67185-4 (cloth)
ISBN-13: 978-0-595-79703-5 (ebk)
ISBN-10: 0-595-34992-7 (pbk)
ISBN-10: 0-595-67185-3 (cloth)
ISBN-10: 0-595-79703-2 (ebk)

Printed in the United States of America

CONTENTS

▼

Uŋ Iapi
Word Use

DAKOTA PRONUNCIATION as used in this book is taken from *Dakota-English Dictionary, Stephen R. Riggs, Minnesota Historical Society Press, St. Paul, 1992* as follows:

Ć(ć)   is an aspirate with the sound of English *ch*, as in *chin*.

Ġ(ġ)   represents a deep sonant guttural resembling the Arabic *ghain*.

ħ   represents a strong 'surd guttural resembling the Arabic *kha*.

Ŋ(ŋ)   denotes a nasal sound similar to the French *n* in *bon*, or the English *n* in *drink*.

Ś(ś)   is an aspirated *s*, having the sound of English *sh*, as in *shine*.

Ż(ż)   is an aspirated z, having the sound of the French *j*, or the English *s* in *pleasure*.

MONTHS OF THE YEAR:

Weteȟi	January, the hard moon.
Wićatawi	February, the raccoon moon.
Ištawićayazaŋwi	March, *the sore eye moon.*
Maġaokadawi	April, *the moon in which the geese lay eggs.*
Woźupiwi	May, *the planting moon.*
Wažuštećasawi	June, the moon *when the strawberries are red.*
Ćaŋpasapawi	July, *the moon when the chokecherries are black.*
Wasutoŋwi	August, *the harvest moon.*
Psiŋhnaketuwi	September, *the moon when rice is laid up to dry.*
Wiwažupi	October, the *drying rice moon.*
Takiyuȟawi	November, *the deer-rutting moon.*
Tahećapśuŋwi	December, *the moon when the deer shed their horns.*

FOREWORD

On U.S. Highway 12 on the west side of Webster, South Dakota was a Historical-Point-of-Interest sign with text that read...

> *Following the 1862 Minnesota Indian Uprising where nearly 600 men, women, and children were killed, the U.S. Army at Fort Wadsworth recruited friendly Indians as scouts to restrict the hostile Indians from white settlements. A half-breed, Jack Campbell, led a group to the Mankato area and massacred the Jewett family. Campbell was caught and hung but his companions escaped and fled west. Near the present site of Webster this murderous group were met and recognized by Solomon Two Stars, an Army scout, on May 16, 1865. Solomon and four enlisted scouts: Wahacankaiteton, Kampeska, Tatankawanjidan, and Cankuwanjidan promptly attacked. Three of the hostiles were killed, one escaped, and a renegade nephew of Two Stars was captured. The latter confessed that he and the others were guilty of the murder. Under strict orders to take no prisoners, Two Stars was faced with a terrible choice. Duty demanded his kinsman be killed. Should he order the scouts to shoot him or accept the responsibility? Fifty years later he said "I shot him before my tears would blind me." Can white men produce a better chronicle of integrity?*

By the summer of 2000, the sign had disappeared.

SUNDAY, AUGUST 17, 1862

2   "Wakpa Minisota!"

White Eagle Ghost

Wayuhi could feel the wrenching of his stomach reminding him that he hadn't eaten for two days. He was sitting in the shade of an old elm tree on a hot, humid morning beside the Yellow Medicine River. The westerly wind was searing across the Dakota Territory into Minnesota scorching the tallgrasses and drying the many rivers and lakes that attracted game.

Grandfather he thought, *how you always talked about the Harvest Moon as being a time of plenty. How you talked about the bountiful rice harvests in the northern lakes. How you talked about the Big Woods with herds of deer numbering in the hundreds. The Medicine Lodge celebrations in our village where...*

Suddenly Wayuhi's thoughts were broken by the faint sound of a snapping twig. He rose to his knee and from behind the tree he could see a deer across the shallow river that, like a dream, seemed to come slowly into focus. He reached for his bow and strung it in one easy, silent motion. As he withdrew an arrow from its quiver, the grazing buck perked up and quickly scanned the surrounding area with huge twitching ears. As the wary deer resumed feeding, Wayuhi slowly drew the powerful bow and released the arrow. The flint tipped shaft cut through the deer's body and into the ground beyond. The fatally wounded buck took three leaps up the steep riverbank and fell, drowning in its own blood.

"Ho! Siŋtesapedaŋ!" Wayuhi lamented in veneration to the dying Blacktail. "The sacred arrow that has taken your life has renewed mine. Thank you brother for looking upon me so I will obtain your magical powers." When Wayuhi could see the deer had died, he looked up into the morning sun and said, "All my relations!" in respect to the Great Mystery and releasing the spirit to the Sacred Circle.

He quickly gathered a small pile of dried leaves and branches and removed his fire-steel and flint from his otter skin bag and started a fire. When the crackling flames had begun to ignite larger branches, he returned down the slope to retrieve his arrow. He found the bloodied shaft buried deeply into the soft earth. He carried the arrow to the edge of the Yellow Medicine and, perched on a large flat stone, began to splash it clean with the cold, pure water.

"Hoka!" he said under his breath as he admired the fine craftsmanship of his arrow. It was perfectly straight, as long as his arm with outstretched fingers. It was made of gooseberry with a zigzagging lightning bolt carved along its entire length. It was fletched with striped hawk feathers and crested with one green stripe flanked by two yellow stripes. The finely flaked white flint tip was the size of his thumb above the top joint and secured to the shaft with buffalo sinew.

Impatient for more hot coals to cook the deer tripe, Wayuhi returned to his fire and piled more dry wood on the growing flames. He sprinkled dried cedar grains onto the few coals there and carefully guided the arrow through its purifying smoke. He returned the arrow to its quiver, which held six replicas.

After completely gutting-out the deer, he scraped the lining from the stomach and large intestines with his knife and rinsed them off in the river. He then stretched the tripe out over the hot coals and sat back with his mouth watering at the smell of the cooking food.

While he waited, he unstrung his bow and felt its perfect weight and balance as he slid it into its sheath. The sheath was attached to the quiver and both made of the furry skin of a mountain lion with long pendants—layered with red trade cloth with narrow rows of yellow and green porcupine quillwork along the edges, hanging from both.

Tiowaśte, he thought. *You gave me these instruments as my Wotaye when I passed into manhood. You said this beautifully carved Thunder Bow is from the horns of Heĥaka—bull elk, and the white flint arrowheads from the Big Horn Mountains of the west. And this bow sheath and quiver bring the swift deadly silent hunting prowess of Inmutaŋka. These instruments are sacred, you said, because the Little People who live in the Yellowstone are sacred and made them so.*

Wayuhi sprinkled more dry cedar grains on the fire, and as he passed the sheathed instruments through the cleansing smoke four times, he said aloud, "Father! Big thank you. These sacred instruments have brought me life. I pray to Grandfather Great Spirit, the Four Winds, Earth Grandmother, and Spotted Eagle that our people will live. All my relations!"

After finishing his meal, Wayuhi lifted the carcass of the deer over his bare shoulders, stepped from rock to rock across the Yellow Medicine, and trudged up its steep wooded bank. From the top of the bank, he surveyed the broad, tallgrass prairie to the west for his spotted stallion. He could see the wooded course of the Yellow Medicine slowly winding across the prairie from its source high on the eastern slopes of the Coteau de Prairies to where he was standing. When he found the horse he knew that nearby would be the young mare and her foal. *Find the stallion and the mare won't be far away* he remembered his father saying as he saw the pintos grazing downstream near the tree line of the river where the grass is sweet.

Wayuhi laid down the heavy carcass and noticed he was standing near an old, deep buffalo wallow. In the bark of the tall elms surrounding the wallow, he found buffalo hairs where bulls had rubbed against the trees many winters ago.

Even the old buffalo trails he had followed from the west for the past two days were eroding from disuse. Near the wallow, he found the huge sun-bleached skull of an old buffalo bull. He picked up the skull and admired its symmetrical shape with the curved, shiny black horn shells still attached. As he gazed into the deep, dark caverns that once held its eyes, a strange feeling had suddenly overcome him. He could feel the presence of the great Buffalo Nation that once shook this very ground with the thunderous, rhythmic beat of their hooves. He could feel their melodic baying like beautiful songs that seemed to penetrate his soul with a soothing vibration. He had an overwhelming feeling of peace and understanding as he remembered his Isaŋti Waȟpetoŋwaŋ grandfather when he spoke of the Ancient Ones.

He told stories of how they used fire during the Moon Of The Falling Leaves to clear underbrush and create open, grassy prairies to lure the great herds. How their torches lit up the darkness as great areas of the prairie were burned with the parched earth slowly flooded by a sea of fresh prairie wildflowers and succulent grasses during the Planting Moon. How the Sacred Circle was complete with great herds of buffalo, elk, and deer returning to this country when, at night, you could hear the beautiful hunting songs of wolves. He said rather than putting up fences and barns to nurture a few cattle like the White man, the Ancient Ones would nurture an entire prairie to ensure the tender young shoots so craved by the great herds.

How our ways have changed, he thought, as he looked again to his horses. He blew a long, high-pitched note through his eagle bone whistle. The grazing horses perked up with six brown ears like warbonnets standing above three white faces looking directly at him from across the field of belly-high little bluestem in a bed of purple prairie clover. As he blew his whistle a second time, his hunting horse started toward him in his strange gaited dance with the mare making sure to stay between the stallion and her foal.

Wayuhi thought about how good it always made him feel to see his beautiful horses. He remembered when his father Tiowaśte—Pretty Lodge, gave him the stallion as a colt three summers ago. When he helped him train the horse to run buffalo and named him Three Buffalo.

Most horses, he said, *are strong enough to run down maybe one buffalo in a hunt. That is because the buffalo are very fast runners. That is one of the few horses I have ever seen that can run down three buffalo in the same hunt. A three-buffalo horse is a great gift for a young Dakota hunter, or any man who follows the buffalo. A great hunting horse deserves a great name. You should call him Tataŋkayamni.*

Once his stallion was saddled and haltered, Wayuhi slid a rawhide hackamore up over the ears of the mare and attached his buffalo hair drag rope, the other end of which was tied to the ash wood frame of his saddle. He cinched up his pack-saddle on the mare and loaded a bundled smoke-tanned buffalo hide on each side of it, tied the carcass of the Blacktail over the pack frame, and then mounted the stallion to continue their trip to the village of Iŋyaŋgmani—Running Walker, near the mouth of the Yellow Medicine River. Dark clouds were gathering in the west with the sound of distant thunder as he found the old trail to the east with even the foal seeming to sense the coming storm as he struggled to stay close to the mare.

It was approaching evening with the ozone filled air of the afternoon thunderstorm mingling with the smells of prairie blazingstar, butterflyweed, and cedar smoke as Wayuhi crested a high, tree lined ridge overlooking the deep, wooded gorge of the Yellow Medicine beginning to become one with the southeasterly flowing Minnesota River. Wayuhi thought of the Ancient Ones wisely living in this valley sheltered from the northern winter winds yet open to the warm, life-giving sunrays of the south. With the confluence of the rivers teeming with fish, with great blue herons and pelicans wading in their shallow pools, the nearby prairies alive with great herds, and a fertile Mother Earth enriched with the bones in the mounds of the Ancient Ones sharing her great abundance, he could understand why the grandfathers call this a holy place.

In the valley below he could see the circular patterns of the cultivated fields of the Three Sisters of the Dakota—corn, squash, and beans. On an adjacent level, safely above the flood plain of the rivers was the Waȟpetoŋwaŋ Village of Iŋyaŋg-mani with smoke from several lodges slowly drifting up the ridge.

The trail gradually descended the ridge to the rocky Yellow Medicine below. Wayuhi guided the horses across the river and up its north bank where the trail twisted through the traditional gardens of the village. In honor of the spirits that dwell there and of the strange reverence he felt, Wayuhi dismounted and walked his horses up the path through the tall lush crops. He could see the bean vines winding around the tall corn stalks and the broad leaves of the squash plants providing the cover between corn and the beans. He could hear the soft winsome songs of the Three Sisters in perfect harmony and feel the presence of the entities invoked by his Waȟpetoŋwaŋ grandmothers to protect the crops from rabbits, deer, and crows, from storms, insects, and human raiders, and to give them a good harvest.

Once through the garden area, he remounted and heeled the stallion, with the mare in tow and her foal close behind, up the steep bank to the village. Several dogs began howling a chorus of welcome and a group of surprised young boys began shouting his name alerting the village of his arrival.

After the horses completed their short climb, he entered the village and headed toward his grandparent's lodge with the dogs nipping at the heels of the colt. He could see only a few of the traditional Dakota summer lodges with walls and sloping roofs framed with long poles lashed together and covered with the flattened bark of elm trees. Several relatives shouted greetings to him as the horses trotted down the path.

Near the center of the village he passed the house of Iŋyaŋgmani, a small log house with a mud chimney, as were most of the twenty or so houses there. Since he lived in this village for several winters as a young boy, he recalled memories of Iŋyaŋgmani always walking around scratching himself. Kuŋśi said he scratches himself like a dog because he's full of fleas from living in that filthy Iaśića house. *Our Dakota lodge,* she said, *breathes like people and is easy to keep clean.* He chuckled as he arrived at his grandparent's traditional home, as he knew these Dakotapi would never succumb to living in an Iaśića house. Even leaning in an adjacent tree was a fresh set of tipi poles as they prepared to live in their breathing buffalo hide covered winter home.

"Grandson!" his surprised grandmother cried out as Wayuhi dismounted in front of her lodge with the dogs squealing and running off at the sight of her.

"Kuŋśi, it's good to see you again!" he said as he bent to hug her and lifted her off her feet.

"Ćaske," she called into the house. "Come see who's here! And help our visitor with his horses."

"Wah! Wayuhi! Grandpa said you were coming home," the astonished Ćaske said "as he emerged from the lodge and took Tataŋkayamni's rope.

"Little brother, it's good to see you," Wayuhi said then pointed with his lips toward his horses. "Butcher that deer and you can have the hide. Maybe you can give the meat to kuŋśi or anyone she wants to share with."

As he was enviously admiring Wayuhi's horses, as were several young boys who were gathering around, Ćaske saw the carcass of the deer. "Blacktail buck! You must have strong medicine to even be able to see one of those. Those tanned buffalo hides for me? Aaaa!"

"Don't worry about those!" said kuŋśi loudly. "After you unsaddle those horses, wipe them down. Then put the stallion in the back pasture where he'll be safe. Then put the mare and her foal in our corral. And get these lazy little boys to help you!"

Wayuhi entered the lodge behind kuŋśi ducking his head to avoid the door lintel and hung his bow case with quiver and otter skin bag from pegs on one of the vertical poles near the doorway. The lodge was about ten paces square with a front entry facing east with a rear door out to the west. Along the north and south interior walls were four beds built into the supporting structure—two on each side with sage filled mattresses, pillows filled with goose down, and buffalo robes lying across them. Resting on pegs above one of the beds was his grandfather's well-oiled flintlock Kentucky Rifle and a bandolier bag colorfully embroidered with porcupine quilled floral designs.

Above another bed hung grandfather's Medicine Shield as he had remembered it as a child. The shield was made of thick buffalo hide stretched over a circular ash frame. A narrow strip of red cloth made from the frock coat of a British soldier with four brass buttons still attached overlapped the top perimeter of the shield and hung loosely from each side. On the face of the shield painted in black was the image of Uŋktehi, the Dreadful Ones—the Spirits of the Waters. From the center of the shield hung four center-tail feathers of a black Gyrfalcon—the Thunderhawk of the Dakota, symbolizing his medicine spirit and the four Tribes of the Isaŋti Dakota—Sissetoŋwaŋ, Waĥpetoŋwaŋ, Mdewakaŋtoŋwaŋ, and Waĥpekute.

The earthen lodge floor was swept clean with a circle of hot coals in the center as wide as his outstretched arms brought in from the cooking fire outside. Tanned deer hides with the hair side up lay on the earth and over the ground level seating platform of four triangular willow-reed backrests supported by tripods and forming a seating area around the glowing coals. Wayuhi was admiring the long fringed buckskin pendants quilled in the green, yellow, and orange symbols of the Three Sisters embellishing the tops of the backrest when suddenly rushing through the doorway was his mother's younger sister—Ćaŋomnićawiŋ.

"My boy, Ćaske just told me you were here!" she exclaimed as she grabbed his hand. "Are you alright? We knew you were up on the Sheyenne Oju. Why did you come back by yourself?"

"Ina," as the Dakota referred to their mother's sisters as mother and her children as brother or sister. "I came to talk to grandpa Ćetaŋiyotaŋka."

"Grandpa won't be back until later tonight. He went up to meet with the Soldier's Lodge."

"What are they doing?"

"They're trying to stop that new government Indian Agent Galbraith from giving the traders any more of our money," kuŋśi said as she went about preparing food for her guests.

"This summer has brought hard times around here," Ćaŋomnićawiŋ said.

"So what has happened?" asked Wayuhi.

"That agent Galbraith only gives our annuities to those who do what he tells them to do. He wants us to become Christians and farmers like the Iaśića. He tells us we can no longer leave this little strip of land that he calls our 'reservation.'"

"And it's not even our reservation," said kuŋśi as she headed outside. "Iŋyaŋgmani has told us that we are only here at the will of the Great White Father who thinks he can do with us as he pleases!"

"Then the Iaśića are clearing all the old mature forests and killing and scaring away the game in the Big Woods!"

"Doesn't he understand that those are our traditional hunting grounds?" asked Wayuhi.

"He does! And he still tells us we can't go there anymore! Now we can hear them across the Wakpa Minisota cutting down all those huge ancient trees," Ćaŋomnićawiŋ said as she sat on one of the deerskins and leaned back on the reed backrest pulling her moccasined feet up under her with a sigh of exasperation.

Wayuhi, noticing that the coals were cooling off, went outside and put more wood on kuŋśi's fire under her pot of cooking stew. Kuŋśi was throwing sticks at yelping dogs that were hovering around Ćaske as he butchered the deer. With an old traders shovel he scooped up a load of hot coals and carried it into the lodge. He deposited the coals in the center of the circle of ashes and, with a long stick used for that purpose, carefully spread the hot reddish blue glowing coals over the ashes as Ćaŋomnićawiŋ continued talking.

"And Galbraith wants us to give up our communal village and our Three Sisters Gardens and live like the Iaśića. He said if we do that then he'll build each of us a brick house with our own field and a basement where we can horde our own food and won't have to share with anyone."

"I see what you're saying. He doesn't understand our Dakota ways," said Wayuhi. "That we are all related."

Wayuhi carried the shovel and smoking fire stick back outside as the sun was beginning to set over the ridge from where he had arrived creating a bright fiery red sky from under a huge black thundercloud as an omen of what was coming. As if adding to the prophetic drama of the sunset, he could hear a big drum and plaintive singing from the village as the Waȟpetoŋwaŋ prepared for tomorrow's harvest. Kuŋśi was busy frying pieces of the butchered venison for her stew while Ćaske and the young boys were playfully struggling to get the mare and her foal into the corral. Wayuhi had a strange feeling that this ancient Dakota way of life, the only life he knew and was willing to die for, was coming to an end as he returned to the lodge and sat at the fireplace as Ćaŋomnićawiŋ continued.

"I couldn't any more live like an Iaśića than Galbraith could live like a Dakota. Can you imagine that fat old white man in a breechcloth and moccasins running after deer in the Big Woods? Trying to jump over fallen timbers? Trying to wade in cold, treacherous streams with those white spindly legs? Ohee nephew!" She laughed harder with each hilarious question.

Wayuhi was beginning to enjoy the image of the poor man stumbling through the woods as Ćaske entered the lodge laughing and voicing his "Aaaa" while struggling with the two bundled buffalo robes and setting them near the door and going back outside.

"Ina, you always have lots of food from your gardens. Why is everyone having such a hard time if you have such a good harvest each year?" Wayuhi asked, trying to be serious.

"It's like you said, Galbraith doesn't understand our Dakota ways. He expects our men to plant in the dry, hard soil of the prairie rather than along our river bottoms in good soil. He expects them to plow long, straight furrows in the fields with iron plowshares that we have to buy from him with oxen teams that we have to rent from him even though the plowed furrows won't hold water, it just runs off with the soil after a storm."

"Gardening is women's work! Men are to be hunters and warriors! The Great Mystery has made us different from the Waśićuŋ; if we were to become farmers, the spirits would be offended and destroy us."

"So it's no wonder his farm program has failed at Yellow Medicine and our people are hungry. If it wasn't for our Three Sisters Gardens our relatives would have starved last year like those people down there at the Redwood Agency."

Ćaske and one of the boys entered with Wayuhi's tack—saddles, blankets, buffalo hair rope, and halters, and set them on the bundled robes and went back outside. Ćaske returned with four sticks of split ash as long as his outstretched arms and stacked them v-shaped with their overlapping ends crossed over the east perimeter point of the circle of coals and open toward the door. He then brought in a shovel full of hot coals and carefully dumped them near the apex of the dry wood, which quickly burst into crackling flames as he fanned the coals with an eagle feather. The light and warmth flooding the lodge were welcome as darkness was setting in. Ćaske began spreading the glowing hot coals over the circle of white ashes as the smoke slowly drifted up and out through an aperture left in the roof.

"Where do the Three Sisters come from?" asked Wayuhi.

"When me, your mother, and our sister Wamnuwiŋ were growing up, kuŋśi always used to tell us that a long time ago the seeds for the Three Sisters came to our Isaŋti people from the Ancient Ones paddling great canoes from an island in the Mississippi River named Cahokia. They used to camp at a place that today we call Kaposia in honor of them."

"My mother always tells my sisters that the seeds come from the Earth Grandmother who lives on that island in the Mississippi and she sends the geese each spring to tell us when to plant."

"Has she taught them all the songs?"

"I think so. I always hear them singing out in their garden."

"Kuŋśi told us to treat the Three Sisters like children because the growing plants like to be together and to hear us sing, just as children like to hear their mother sing to them."

Kuŋśi came into the lodge with her pot of hot stew and set it down in front of the fire and went back out. She returned with a basket of coal-roasted corn and a pail of cold spring water and placed them in line to the stew pot. She laid one of Wayuhi's folded saddle blankets on the ground between her food and the east door and sat down. Wayuhi realized he hadn't eaten since early morning and the smell of kuŋśi's steaming squash, bean, and wild onion succotash with fried venison chunks and the hot coal-roasted green corn was almost more than he could bear.

Ćaske stood up holding his black tipped center-tail eagle feather and a beautifully quilled long-fringed buckskin bag. He had changed into his traditional front-seamed buckskin legging with his blue cloth apron decorated with red, white, and orange cut-and-fold ribbonwork. His moccasins were traditional Dakota vamped types with porcupine quillwork while he wore a shirt of white trade cloth with brass armbands and tucked under his apron. He was wearing colorful Hudson's Bay Company sashes as a belt and as a turban with his black hair in long braids to his waist. Wayuhi was surprised at how much he had grown since he had seen him last. Although Ćaske was two winters younger than him, he was already as tall or taller than he was.

"Ahhh brother Wayuhi," he said. "Kuŋśi asked me to help her this way and use this cedar to bless this food. It makes our hearts good to have you back with us again. We think about you and ina Wamnahezawiŋ and our Northern Sissetoŋwaŋ relatives up there. I want to thank you for that deer hide. The old people say those Blacktails are magical and have great powers. I'll use that hide in a good way and treat it with respect. Big thank you, brother." He sprinkled dried cedar grains on the coals and, using his eagle feather, fanned the cedar smoke on the stew, the corn, and the water as he quietly prayed. He then walked over and handed the feather and cedar bag to kuŋśi and returned to where he was sitting.

"Relatives," she said emotionally. "This evening I want to speak from my heart to give thanks to the Great Mystery for bringing my grandson back to me once more." Kuŋśi took a white cloth from her sleeve and began wiping tears from her eyes. "Wayuhi, it makes my heart good to see you so healthy and strong. You look just like your grandpa Ćetaŋiyotaŋka when he was your age. You are tall and dark just like him and have his mystical ways and at the same time you are a hunter and a warrior and have ways with horses like your dad whose name I can't mention." Kuŋśi continued to wipe tears from her eyes and sniffling. "I want to pray that this food and water of life will help you find whatever it is you are looking for during these troubled times."

"Grandfather Great Spirit, Four Winds, Mother Earth, Earth Grandmother, hear me," kuŋśi quietly prayed. "Oh Grandfather Great Spirit, I ask that you pity and help all of our People. Watch over my grandson, Wayuhi here. May this food and water of life help him find his way on his road through life. Our times are changing very fast and I ask that you guide him from harm's way and guide him in ways that will help our people. He's grown into a fine young man with a clear mind and a strong body and I humbly ask that you watch over him as he finds the ways of his grandfathers to live a life of bravery, respect, generosity, and wisdom. And Grandfather Great Spirit, I ask that you watch over his mother, my daughter Wamnahezawiŋ and all our Sissetoŋwaŋ relatives up north. Help them in their hunt to find the buffalo and guide them from harm from our enemies. And help all of our Isaŋti Dakota people walk the good Red Road. I ask you for all of these things so our people will live! All my relations!"

Kuŋśi rose to her feet with amazing agility then walked over and sprinkled dried cedar grains on the hot coals. She turned to Wayuhi and with the eagle feather fanned him with smoke from the crackling cedar embers. She then held his hand and said "Thank you for coming home again, grandson." She fanned cedar smoke on herself and returned the eagle feather and cedar bag to her grandson Ćaske and thanked him for helping her. She then handed out wooden bowls and spoons to each of her guests and began passing around the water, stew and corn, returned the saddle blanket and sat down at the remaining backrest.

"Kuŋśi, big thank you," Wayuhi said as he finished drinking and passed the water pail to Ćaske. "I always think about your good Dakota ways around here and especially your good succotash!"

As he began filling his bowl with the hot stew, he thought about how beautiful he always thought his kuŋśi was, the strong youthfully athletic woman who he could never outrun as a child was not slowing down with age. Her finely featured face with slightly turned up eyes like a she-wolf was inherited by all three of her grateful daughters. How she always had a love of the earth and seemed to have magical ways with things that grow. Even her name, Makadutawiŋ, Red Earth Woman, betrayed her spiritual ties to the earth. How she would tell her grandchildren to remember Mother Earth in their prayers for this great abundance of life they see growing around them. But at the same time, she would tell them not to forget Earth Grandmother in their prayers for her potential to create life. *These seeds of the Three Sisters*, she said, *are from the Earth Grandmother herself and have within them the magical power to create life, which in turn gives us life!*

"Ahhh Brother, what are you going to do with those buffalo hides?" Ćaske facetiously asked nodding toward the door as he sat down after carrying the water pail over to kuŋśi.

"I brought one for grandpa Mazamani over there—pointing east down the Yellow Medicine with his lips, and one for uncle Taoyateduta," he answered.

"Taoyateduta was just up here during the waning moon for some excitement up at Yellow Medicine Agency," Ćaske said. "He stayed over there at grandpa Iŋyaŋgmani's house. Since he's taken all four of his daughters as wives, and since the white people call him Little Crow, I call him Uncle Crazy Crow! Aaaa!"

"That was really some excitement up there," interjected Ćaŋomnićawiŋ trying to hold back a laugh. "We say that the waning moon is the time to dispose of what is no longer needed or wanted. That's why there were about 800 lodges of our people up there during that time demanding that they get rid of Galbraith as our Agent since he refused to give us any provisions."

"They shot an ox belonging to Galbraith and then they broke into the government food warehouse when that young Lieutenant Sheehan, with only twenty-five soldiers, told them to fall back or his troops would blow them to hell," said Ćaske.

"Ohee that guy! They either respected his bravery or his cannon!" Ćaŋomnićawiŋ said.

"Then that soldier told Galbraith, who was too drunk and scared to do anything, to give us some provisions," said Ćaske. "He was hiding in his house while that young soldier chief stood in front of all of us."

"I got a lot of respect for that 'Śihaŋ'," said Ćaŋomnićawiŋ.

"Even his name sounds Dakota. As I understand our language it sounds like 'behaving badly.' Aaaa!"

"What happened?" Asked Wayuhi.

"He gave out some provisions to last a couple of days, but we refused to leave until all the provisions were distributed," said Ćaske.

"Was the annuity money distributed?" Wayuhi asked as he peeled the husks back from his coal-roasted corn.

"No. Captain Marsh came up from Fort Ridgley and ordered Galbraith to issue all the goods and provisions. Then he told us to go home and not return until he called us back to receive the annuity money," Ćaske answered.

"Taoyateduta was there," Ćaŋomnićawiŋ said. "He asked that Galbraith to make the same issue of government provisions down at the Redwood Agency."

Ćaske got up and restacked the fire with fresh wood. He went out and returned with the five hungry boys who were waiting outside. They respectfully entered and sat on the ground near the beds on the south side of the lodge. Ćaske gave them bowls and spoons and passed them the remaining water and food. He retrieved the fire stick and began spreading the fresh coals from the burning fire while Ćaŋomnićawiŋ continued.

"Taoyateduta called a council with Galbraith, the traders, and some Mdewa-kaŋtoŋwaŋ people that were there." She set down her empty wooden bowl and began eating the roasted Yellow Flint Corn.

"How many trading posts do they have down there now?" asked Wayuhi.

"Four," Ćaske answered as he stood up leaning on the smoking fire stick. "He told them that his people were starving while the trading posts down there are filled with food. He asked Galbraith to make some arrangement where they could get food from those stores or else they'd help themselves to keep from starving."

"Then Galbraith started talking to those traders," Ćaŋomnićawiŋ said. "Pretty soon that trader Andrew Myrick got mad and started to leave the meeting when Galbraith stopped him. Then Myrick turned around and shouted something back in their language."

"When someone translated into Dakota that he said 'So far as I am concerned, if they are hungry, let them eat grass or their own dung,' there was a long scary silence, then those Mdewakaŋtoŋ there really exploded and stormed out of the meeting," Ćaske said using the popular shortened version of Mdewkaŋtoŋwaŋ— Spirit Lake Village.

"Captain Marsh was ready to arrest those traders for upsetting everyone," said Ċaŋomniċawiŋ. "He made sure that government rations were distributed down there."

"It was just peaceful when I was down there during the new moon," kuŋśi said. "I was visiting Wamnuwiŋ and my grandchildren."

"Have they given up our ways?" asked Wayuhi.

"Quite a few people down there have and that's why they have lots of potatoes and green corn that's ready for roasting. They've been busy harvesting all week. Even Taoyateduta has taken up Iaśića farming. They said that and I didn't believe it until I saw for myself that he had gone back on our ways and cut his hair and was even wearing White man's pantaloons!"

"Ohee!"

"And then he was even digging a cellar for his new little brick Iaśića house!"

"Ohee that guy! I wonder where he's going to put all his wives and children."

"Probably have them live outside with his horses. Aaaa!"

"Everything must be peaceful around here now because Galbraith left his family alone up at the Agency. They say he went through here three days ago with about thirty young half-breed men on his way toward Fort Ridgley," said Ċaŋomniċawiŋ.

"Why just half-breeds?" asked Wayuhi.

"Because they all talk the White man's language," answered Ċaŋomniċawiŋ.

"They talk Dakota too. I saw some of those boys that morning," said Ċaske. "They said Galbraith had recruited them and was taking them on to Fort Snelling to learn to be soldiers and fight in that White man's war to free the slaves. They call themselves the Renville Rangers. Aaaa!"

"Why do they call them that?" asked Wayuhi.

"Because most of them are from across the river in Renville County."

"It's just crazy," said kuŋśi. "Those White people killing each other just to free those Hasapa! While they force our leaders to sign those treaties to give away our land and our freedom so these disrespectful Iaśića can have the freedom to live wherever they want."

"And after all that they've done to us, they take our boys to fight and maybe die for those slave's freedom? Those boys should stay here and fight for our freedom!" said Ċaŋomniċawiŋ.

"Maybe that's why they're taking them away," said Wayuhi.

Ċaske and two of the boys began picking up the empty bowls and food dishes and taking them outside. The other three boys were standing by the door excitedly talking about Wayuhi's superbly crafted bow case and quiver that was hanging on the wall and asking to see the weapons when Ćaske reentered the lodge and said, "Grandpa Ćetaŋiyotaŋka is coming!"

Wayuhi rushed outside to greet his grandfather. He could see him walking his horse in the light of the waxing moon and called out to him, "Grandfather! It's me! Wayuhi!"

As Ćetaŋiyotaŋka got closer, he said "Wah! Grandson!"

"It's good to see you again, grandfather!"

"Wayuhi! I just had a dream about you and here you are!"

"Let me take your horse," as he took the horsehair rope in one hand and shook his grandfather's hand with the other.

"Look out for her. She's still a free horse. Her herd is still around here somewhere."

"How long have you had her?"

"I can't say I've ever really had her. She kind of has me. She comes and goes as she pleases."

"Where did you find her?"

"She came to me in a dream. Then one day I came across a herd of Spanish Mustangs up on the Coteau de Prairies and we recognized each other."

Wayuhi could see she was a beautiful black roan mare with a black face and black stockings above her knees and large black eyes with an intelligent light glowing in both of them and appeared awesome in the night as she stood over 14 hands high. The moonlight on her roan colored body and long mane and tail gave her a bluish ghostly glow befitting the name Śuŋkawakaŋ—Spirit Dog, given to horses by the Lakota. He noticed that grandpa had a hand tied breakaway rope halter on her and rode her bareback, guiding her with knee pressure like a buffalo runner.

"Do you have a name for her?"

"I call her Ićamnawiyakpa. When I saw her in my dream, it was raining and there was thunder and lightning but still the sun was shining. The raindrops were sparkling in the sunlight like stars in the night sky so I named her Sparkling Storm."

"She looks like a Spirit of the Moon," Wayuhi said as he removed the poles from the corral gate.

"What are you doing here, grandson? We thought you were up at Matotidaŋ on the Sheyenne Oju."

Wayuhi removed the mare's rope halter and Ićamnawiyakpa eagerly entered the corral to be with Wayuhi's mare and foal. "I came to see you grandfather. I had a strong Vision Quest and then, a couple of days ago, my Medicine Spirit appeared in the midst of a buffalo hunt and said to come here. Something bad is going to happen in this valley!"

Ćetaŋiyotaŋka looked very seriously at Wayuhi for a moment then said, "Lets go inside and smoke. You must tell me everything as it happened."

Wayuhi replaced the gate poles knowing that if Ićamnawiyakpa wanted to leave she could easily jump the fence and followed Ćetaŋiyotaŋka into the lodge.

Inside the lodge, Ćaske had swept the earthen floor clean, placed fresh wood on the fire, and was busy shaping the glowing coals with the fire stick as Wayuhi followed his grandfather in through the back door, Ćetaŋiyotaŋka ducking his head in the doorway because of his height and an upright eagle feather and a deer hair roach worn in his turban.

"Kuŋśi and my mother have gone to the Green Corn Dance and the boys went to get some more grass for the mares," said Ćaske.

Ćetaŋiyotaŋka removed the light blanket he was wearing over his bare shoulders and had retrieved his long pipe stem and sat down facing east on one of the deer hides as Ćaske continued to shape the hot coals. He gestured to Wayuhi to sit down on one of the deer hide covered seating platforms to his right as he removed an intricately carved red pipestone bowl from his pipe bag and attached it to the pipe stem. He began filling the pipe bowl with kinnikinnick from the bag as he quietly prayed to the Great Mystery and the Seven Directions.

Wayuhi sat down cross-legged and began thinking about how his grandfather's imposing warrior's presence has always belied his spiritual gentleness. In the light of the fire he appeared dark and sinister with dancing shadows emphasizing the deep lines of his weathered face, his hooded eyes, and the high raptorial arc of his nose while the deep rhythmic resonance of his prayer was soothing and compassionate. In his turban he wore a notched eagle feather attesting to recent brave deeds in desperate battles with the Ojibway while his bare muscular chest bore scars from the sacred Sun Dance. Only his name, Ćetaŋiyotaŋka—Sitting Hawk, seemed revealing of his contemplative nature yet warning of the predatory potential of hunting hawks.

When he finished loading the pipe, he plugged the bowl opening with fresh sage and placed the pipe in a wooden rack that held it in an upright position with the mouthpiece pointed up toward the Great Mystery. Ćaske paused to sprinkle dry cedar grains on the hot coals and Ćetaŋiyotaŋka retrieved two small stones, one painted red and the other painted blue, and passed them through the purifying smoke and placed them directly in front of him on the west point of the perimeter of the coals to represent the guardians of the Thunderhawk. He then made the sign to Wayuhi to talk.

"Grandfather, it's good to see you this way again. When I was little, you always took the time to talk to me about this Waȟpetoŋwaŋ Fireplace to tell me about the Sacred Circle and our Dakota traditions and I have always respected you for that. I have done my best to follow our ceremonial ways that you said would lead me from darkness to light, from ignorance to knowledge, and from sickness to health. I have been ready to suffer any kind of pain if it meant that the Sacred Circle would be made strong and our people would live. You have educated me in the ways of my mother's people where I have gained knowledge of the earth, the rivers, and the Seven Fireplaces. I have also been educated in the ways of my father's Northern Sissetoŋwaŋ people and learned the ways of the horse, the buffalo, and of the Isaŋti warrior.

"When we were growing up around here you always said the Great Spirit has mysterious ways. He is our Grandfather, you said, and He would never let anything bad happen to His relations His grandchildren without first warning us of danger..."

While Wayuhi spoke, Ćaske completed fashioning an image of his grandfather's medicine spirit in the coals—a Thunderhawk with outspread wings. As the hot crimson coals shimmered in the dim firelight, the bird seemed to be alive and inhaling Wayuhi's words while exhaling fire and smoke into the darkness of the lodge. As the burnt firewood began to collapse, Ćaske restacked the burning remains in their original v-shape and went outside to return with four long pieces of split wood that he carefully placed on the live fire. With a small broom he tidied up the ashes around the image in the coals.

As the fresh wood ignited and the fire grew higher, the drum and the singing from the village seemed to grow in intensity as more villagers began to participate in celebration of the waxing Harvest Moon—the time to harvest green corn, the time for journeys to the northern lakes for the harvest of wild rice, and the time to harvest new ideas. Ćaske again sprinkled the holy evergreen on the coals and fanned himself off in its fragrant smoke with his eagle feather and sat across the fire from Wayuhi who continued to talk.

"During the Moon of the Red Strawberries our Amdowapuśkiya Band of Tataŋkanaẑiŋ's Otter Tail Village had moved to Matotidaŋ—Bear Lodge, and took our place in the great circle of tipis for the summer buffalo hunt. Early one morning, I had taken my horses down to the river to water them. I was standing watching the horses when I heard someone come up behind me. When I turned to see who it was, I saw it was a Ćaŋotidaŋ. I had heard the old people talk about the Little People but it was the first time I had ever seen one. He asked me in our language if I could help him get across the river, which still flooded the valley from the late thaw. I told him that we hadn't made any buffalo hide boats yet since we'd only been there for three days and that the high water current was still too strong to swim across. He thanked me and walked on downriver.

"When I mentioned to my dad what had happened, he was very concerned and said it was bad luck to see one of the 'Little People Who Live In Trees' because that could bring grave misfortune to a hunt. But to look a Ćaŋotidaŋ in the eye and talk to one was very dangerous since it could result in your death. My dad said I should have a ceremony to acquire power to overcome the evil wakaŋ of the Ćaŋotidaŋ. The only one he knew of that performed ceremonies in buffalo country was a Holy Man named Wahaćaŋkato—Blue Shield, who lived near Mniwakaŋ Ćaŋte two to three days ride to the north."

"I know of him," said Ćetaŋiyotaŋka. "He is a direct descendant of Ćotaŋka, a great Dakota Holy Man who learned from the Ancient Ones and lived in that mysterious land near a great lake we call Mniwakaŋ—Sacred Water. The Waśićuŋ—White people, call it 'Devil's Lake' for some reason known only to them."

"My dad had no trouble getting the Soldiers' Lodge to let us go to the Mniwakaŋ since my encounter had already threatened the hunt. The following day at sunrise we began our journey to Mniwakaŋ Ćaŋte—the Heart of the Sacred Water. I rode my stallion and brought a string of three halter-broken mares to give-away to Wahaćaŋkato.

"On the second night, we camped at Horse Buttes and saw a great herd of buffalo moving south toward Matotidaŋ. The sound of the bulls bellowing and grunting and wolves howling and hunting throughout the night stirred our passions and even Tataŋkayamni could sense the excitement of a good fast hunt. But hunting wasn't why we were out and the next morning we crossed the Sheyenne Oju and rode north into that mysterious land. We could soon see Mniwakaŋ Ćaŋte in the distance, a huge hill that looked like a giant buffalo's heart turned upside down. Near a small lake called Bdećaŋ—Wood Lake, just south of the Ćaŋte, we found the camp of Wahaćaŋkato."

Ćaske rose to restack the burning wood and began to spread out the fresh coals onto the image of the medicine spirit as Wayuhi continued.

"A Red Soldier rode out from the camp to meet us and said that the game scouts had seen us coming the day before and they were concerned that the herd we saw might catch our scent and cause them to stampede before their hunt. So most of the hunters had left before sunrise for the James River Herd and wouldn't be back until the full moon. He showed us where to camp and to find good grass near the lake for our horses.

"Toward evening Wahaćaŋkato returned to camp and invited us to join him under an arbor near the Soldiers' Lodge, which was a painted tipi placed in the center of the large circle of about thirty tipis. I told him of my encounter with the Ćaŋotidaŋ and that we had traveled there in hopes he would guide me in a Vision Quest to obtain medicine to overcome evil wakaŋ and to protect me in hunting and war. He accepted the responsibility and I passed my pipe to him, which we both smoked. He said the ceremony would take four days, without food or water, and we began by joining him in a Sweat Lodge that evening.

"Before sunrise at the new moon, when he said was the time to awaken spirits to help generate new life, I rode with Wahaćaŋkato the short distance to Mniwakaŋ Ćaŋte. After giving me instructions, the Holy Man returned to camp where he said he and my father would pray for my safe return in four days. At that time he said he would take me back to camp to interpret my visions. He said I had to empty my mind of thoughts, to stop the inner noise, so I could hear the voices of the spirits.

"When I climbed to the top of the butte, I found he had already prepared the site for my ordeal. A pit had been dug large enough for me to sit comfortably on a bed of sage with the opening covered with branches and a space left to crawl in or out. Around the pit were poles buried into the earth at the four directions with a different colored flag-like cloth atop each representing the Four Winds and each connected by a string of tobacco ties at ground level.

"Nothing happened during the first two days. I came out of the pit only before dawn of each day to go to each of the directional flags and pray to the Morning Star. On the second night, in the darkness of the new moon and a strong west wind, I could hear the voice of a woman calling my name and asking me to come out. She said she was a young White Buffalo Woman and wanted to mate with me. Toward morning her pleading turned to singing then gradually faded as it began to get light.

"On the third night, I could hear the screams of people and wild beasts and the sound of a soldier's bugle in the distance. Then soon after a herd of charging horses shook the ground and the cover of the pit so hard that leaves from the branches fell down on me. I firmly held on to my pipe since Wahaćaŋkato had said that nothing would harm me if I did so since many things may come to visit and test my strength and bravery.

"Everything had quieted down by the time the Morning Star rose in the east. And when I went out to pray in the silence of that holy hour, a beautiful Northern Goshawk was circling above. When she landed with her wings spread, she was all white underneath with black striped wing and tail feathers. The top of her body and wings were dark and she had a dark colored mask over her eyes like a raccoon. From her perch atop the northern pole, she told me stories of the mysterious land of Mniwakaŋ and of Ćotaŋka who she said was buried under the very ground where I stood on the Great Mound of the Ancient Ones and whose spirit was coming to visit me."

With the sound of the collapsing firewood, Ćaske again restacked the burning remains and refurbished the fire with fresh wood from outside. Ćetaŋiyotaŋka sat with his eyes closed yet attentively listened as the fireman began spreading the new coals over the glowing image while Wayuhi continued.

"On the fourth night in the darkness of the pit, I could hear beautiful flute music that seemed to come from the Four Winds when suddenly something began to take shape before my eyes. I could soon see that it was a white eagle yet it seemed luminous like a ghost. Overcome by the power of its presence, I clutched my pipe and began to cry to the Eagle Spirit to pity my helplessness. The Spirit spoke to me in words I could somehow feel with my body as well as understand and said not to fear him since he was my protector and would come to warn me of any danger. He said he had broken the evil wakaŋ of the Ćaŋotidaŋ. He said to make a flute in a certain way and to catch the songs of Ćotaŋka I had heard during the night. Finally, he said when I need his protection for hunting or for war; I should play those four songs on my flute. Then it got dark once again and the flutes gradually faded until dawn.

"I prayed to the Morning Star at each of the four directional poles for the last time when Wahaćaŋkato returned. He helped me down the steep butte since I was exhausted from my ordeal yet I felt an inner strength I had never before experienced. We returned to his camp where he had a Sweat Lodge set up to complete my ceremony.

"I entered the Lodge with my father, Wahaćaŋkato, and two of his helpers. The Holy Man reminded me that I had raised my pipe to the Great Spirit and that it was now sacred and knows all things. He reminded me that I had brought back to them the pipe I had offered and that I should tell nothing but the truth. He said if I lied, the great Thunderbird of the west would punish me.

"When it came time for me to speak, I told them of all I had experienced during my four days. When I had finished, Wahaćaŋkato said it was good I had listened carefully to all that came since they may have had messages from the Great Spirit who makes his wishes known through a vision or through a Holy Man.

"He said the white buffalo woman appeared to test my strength or discipline to ignore the temptations of this world. He said any man who is attached to the things of this world is one who lives in ignorance and will be consumed by his own passions. By not submitting to her, the spirits knew you were a strong warrior worthy of their attention.

"He said the sounds of war with the bugles, screams, and charging horses of the third night were from the bad Black Road. He said Mniwakaŋ Ćaŋte was a 'holy place' since it is where the good Red Road which runs north to south crosses the bad Black Road which runs east to west. He said the Ihaŋktoŋwaŋna Nakota call it the 'Heart of the Sacred Water' because it represents the center of our Sacred Circle and he who travels the Red Road lives for the happiness of his people who always face south, the source of life. The Waśićuŋ—who travel from east to west, call it 'Devil's Heart' because to them it represents the center of their path of evil and destruction and he who travels on the Black Road lives for himself and not for his people. In either description it is the same hill, but two different worlds or ways of life cross it.

"He said the messengers from his ancestor Ćotaŋka were very important since I now had his guardian spirit that he called Wanaġiwaŋmdiska—White Eagle Ghost. He said I must fashion the flute as instructed in my vision as soon as possible. He then gave me this white center-tail eagle feather that belonged to Ćotaŋka. He said I should always wear it when I go on a journey especially for hunting or war since it will help protect me as it represents my medicine.

"I rested for one day, then we prepared for our journey south to Matotidaŋ. Before we left, I presented the three mustangs—a dun roan mare and two bay roan mares, to Wahaćaŋkato who was very pleased. He said I had established a relationship with the Great Spirit and through this relationship, I would bring strength to my people."

"Good! Very good, Grandson!" Ćetaŋiyotaŋka said. "Our Lakota cousins call that ceremony Haŋblećeya—Crying for a Vision. It is good that you cried and humbled yourself in the presence of White Eagle Ghost. If you are always sincere, and truly humble yourself before all things, you will surely be aided. The Great Spirit always helps those who cry to Him with a pure heart. But what you told us happened two moons ago. Something must have happened more recently to bring you home like this."

"It did, grandfather. We arrived back at Matotidaŋ on the New Moon of the Ripe Chokecherries. The whole camp was making ready for the hunt since we had been in sight of that huge James River Herd since we left Mniwakaŋ Ćaŋtay. Each year at Matotidaŋ, we would usually run the buffalo on a flat prairie between the James River and the Sheyenne Oju as they traveled south toward the Sand Hills. During that moon, hunting was good and we made much buffalo meat and many robes. I found a long piece of white elm and carved a flute exactly as told by White Eagle Ghost. Each morning before a hunt, I would walk out onto the prairie and play the four flute songs of my vision and wear my white eagle feather for protection.

"We followed that herd as far as the Sand Hills and then let them go since it is difficult and dangerous for our horses to run in that sandy, marshy soil. During the Full Moon of the Ripe Chokecherries my father took our family to join our Ihaŋktoŋwaŋna Nakota relatives who were camped at Punished Woman Lake. They were hunting small herds of buffalo and elk around the headwaters of the Big Sioux River on the Coteau de Prairies.

"Then, during the New Harvest Moon, as we were running a small herd of buffalo near Lake Kampeska, a prairie fire suddenly engulfed us. I dismounted and tied a piece of wet buckskin over the eyes of Tataŋkayamni and began to lead him through the fire. We broke through the heat and smoke into a large round area twenty paces across with tall prairie grass untouched by the blowing fire. Hoka! It seemed to be a holy place as it became very silent with a ring of fire and smoke encircling us. Then I began to hear the music of flutes from all around us. Tataŋkayamni, who was still blindfolded, began to toss his head and whinny. I removed the buckskin from over his eyes and he began to settle down as White Eagle Ghost appeared before us.

"Then my medicine spirit spoke to me. *Wayuhi, your people are in great danger. The valley of the Wakpa Minisota is going to erupt into an evil war. Go to Yellow Medicine. Take your people to the Center of the World where they will be safe. Go now and I will provide for you.* At my day camp I loaded what little I had on my horses and came here."

Ćaske, totally fixated on Wayuhi's story, was startled as the burning firewood collapsed. He rose and began attending to the fire as his grandfather spoke.

"Grandson Wayuhi. Several nights ago I had a dream that you were standing in the middle of a great crucible of fire. I thought that something bad happened and you had passed into the Spirit World. Then a voice said that you were coming home. I knew then that our long kinship with the Waśićuŋ had ended and as we would soon be walking the Black Road, I feared for our people.

"You have established a relationship with the Great Spirit who has spoken to you through White Eagle Ghost to warn us of grave danger. Let us now smoke the pipe and ask the Great Spirit to guide us in our journey to the Center of the World."

After the prayers were completed and all had retired for the night, Wayuhi walked out into the darkness knowing that this was the last night that his people would sleep in peace in the valley of the Yellow Medicine. The drumming had stopped and all was quiet. He looked into the corral and saw that Ićamnawiyakpa had jumped the fence and was gone forever.

Pistolero

Captain Wolfgang Luckenbach completed his breakfast of steak, eggs, and tortillas, refilled his tin saddle mug with hot coffee and climbed the narrow flight of stairs to his quarters. *Fort Snelling sure nuff has the best damn quarters that I've had in my seventeen years in the army with my own kitchen and cook down there and all,* he thought. His billet had a home like appeal to it even though it smelled of boot polish and gun oil. He could feel the warm morning blustery wind flowing through his bedroom window inviting him outside as he opened the door to the back veranda of the Officer's Barracks. As he stepped out onto the deck, he was surprised to see that no one was out enjoying the warm Sunday morning sunshine.

Lured by laughter and the honking of disturbed Trumpeter Swans he could hear coming up from the river, he ambled over to the deck railing. He saw two Indian canoes that appeared to be coming from Mendota or maybe from Kaposia farther down the Mississippi and heading up the Minnesota River. He wondered how far they were going and wished he were going with them. He knew from the Nicollet map on his wall that if they paddled far enough, they would find the prairie. And he yearned for the freedom of the prairie the way a wolf yearns for the freedom of the night.

As he sipped his hot coffee he remembered that his quarters for a large portion of his army career consisted of living like a wolf—sitting and sleeping on the ground in the darkness with no campfires, out on the windswept prairies of south central Texas and along the Rio Bravo hunting with the 2nd Cavalry. But in this case they weren't a pack of hungry wolves hunting buffalo but a pack of vengeful soldiers hunting Comanches.

"Is that you, Luke?" asked Major John Sadbery, one of the post physicians, as he came out on the deck from his quarters.

"Hey good mornin Doc! Y'all surprised me. Didn't think anyone else was about."

"I just came over from the hospital doing my morning rounds. I suppose that most everyone is over at the schoolhouse or in town attending church services."

"I was going to attend myself til I found that it's a Catholic Mass they're ahavin over yonder."

"I would guess that most of the troopers here are Catholics since they're mostly Irishmen from back east. They been volunteering for infantry or cavalry training by the droves since it's about the only way they can eat around here."

"Don't seem that most of em have ever been oun a horse before in their life but once and that was here."

"Unfortunately for several of them that was once too often since I have a bunch of boys in the hospital next door with busted butts from being bucked off on their first day of horse drill."

"I seen it! It was like a damn Texas wild horse rodeo—horses ajumpin ever which way, feet aflyin in the air. Damn funniest thing I ever seen!"

"Well you got your work cut out for you Luke if you're going to make horse soldiers out of those boys."

"Actually I was brought up here just to train a banda of young Sioux mestizos comin over here this week. Even brought my own horse with me oun the boat since I'll only be here a few months."

"What kind of special training are they getting?"

"I'm sposed to make rangers out of em and they already call emselves the 'Renville Rangers'. They say these machotes have grown up round horses and guns and such so I'm kinda looking forward to testin their cajones."

"Are you going to train them here by yourself?"

"Heck no. They'll go through regular basic trainin here then I'm to provide advanced cavalry trainin since they can already ride and shoot. Those that got the cajones will go oun into ranger trainin. And I brung a couple of old boys to help me with all that."

"Isn't that kind of a diversion from the way the Army has been doing things? I mean since the war began, we've been sending boys into battle who've never ridden a horse or fired a weapon! Why only a month after the 1st Minnesota completed training here they were dodging bullets at Bull Run and got whipped."

"We all gotta do somethin. Shiloh and now Johnny Reb's kickin our butt in Virginia."

"You're absolutely right! We lost at Bull Run, McClellan got stopped at the Peninsula, and now I see our 3rd Minnesota has surrendered to the Rebels in Tennessee."

"Jeb Stuart's out there ausin ranger tactics that we all developed back in the '50s fightin Comanches in Texas."

"Did you know Stuart down there?"

"Heard of him after he transferred to the 1st Cavalry in '55. I was in the 2nd Dragoons when he up and married our CO's daughter. It wasn't until I transferred to the 2nd Cavalry Regiment that I got to know him better."

"You were in the Dragoons?"

"Well hell yes, Doc! I grew up in Blanco River country around San Marcos in the old Lone Star Republic. I joined up as a boot with the 2nd Dragoons in October '45 when I was seventeen."

"My god Luke, I didn't think you were that old. I wondered why you wear that Dragoons belt buckle."

"You might say I earned this here belt plate! I paid my blood dues in the Mexican War in Company 'D' under Captain Charlie May and Old Paddy Starr."

Luckenbach sloshed the remaining coffee in his cup in the grounds settled at the bottom and dumped the remains over the railing to the ground below. He thought about how the 2nd Dragoons found themselves in every fray from the opening salvos of the Mexican War to the Battle of Chapultepec in September of '47. He set his cup on the railing and reached into his shirt pocket for his pack of Bull Durham.

"You said that the boys are going to get cavalry training and then ranger training. What's the difference?"

Luckenbach finished rolling a cigarette then struck a match on his boot bottom and lit it. He inhaled deeply as he leaned against a vertical support post of the railing and exhaled slowly while he put the spent matchstick back into his shirt pocket. He wished he had some of that dark, rich tobacco he used to get in Mexico back in '46.

"Well, in cavalry trainin y'all get equitación and target practice then lots of mounted and dismounted sabre drill. Tactics taught aint much different from Napoleon's 'Maxims of War'—front line sabre assaults of enemy positions and such followed by infantry. A ranger, oun the other hand, is someone who operates pretty much behind the enemy lines."

"What kind of training did the Mexican Cavalry get?"

"People from the Royal Cavalry School in France trained Mexican Cavalry in Napoleon's tactics; specially those damn Tulancingo Cuirassiers and Jalisco Lancers."

"You know most physicians who have been in battlefield hospitals have said they've treated very few sabre wounds. Most of the trauma was caused by gunshot and, to a lesser extent, artillery. Do rangers still use sabres?"

"Rangers, least-wise the way I train em, have done away with the sabre. Don't even own one of the damn things myself. Aint had one since the Mexican War."

"Today you see most of our Generals walking around carrying sabres. Does that mean they still advocate their use?"

"Most of our generals these days are infantrymen and don't know beans bout cavalry. Their swords are just ornaments, like their cavalry. Use em mostly as pickets or messengers."

"Was the Mexican cavalry effective?"

"We all probably feared their lancers more than anyone else, but our modern weaponry finally outdated em and blew em to hell and gone."

"When was that?"

"It was at the Battle of Cerro Gordo in '47 that I first seen Colonel Hayes and his Texas Rangers in action with those new Walker Colts. Boy howdy! Those Colt hand-cannons blew right through those Cuirassier's armor, picked em up offen their horses and slammed em oun the ground yonder! Soundin like so much stove pipe hittin the ground!"

"How did they fare against those Lancers that you mentioned?"

"Once they all were in range of those Colts, there was no way those Lancers could even get close nuff to skewer anybody."

"You know, as a physician, I don't think that the Mexican Army was as effective against us in Mexico as Mother Nature was. More men died of disease down there than were killed in action. The biggest killer was yellow fever around Vera Cruz."

"I know. I had a touch of it there my own self."

"It sounds like the Mexicans may have developed a lot of respect for the Texas Rangers."

"I know they developed mucho respeto for the way they used those Walker Colts. That was the reason Mexicans called em 'Los Diablos Tejanos!'—Those Texian Devils!"

"Do you use Colts yourself?"

"I been carryin at least two Colts ever since."

"At least two? How do you carry more than two?"

"Ah, usually I carry two of those new 1860 Army Colts in holsters oun my belt. And when I'm in the field, I usually carry two more in a double pommel holster over my saddle horn givin me a bunch of .44 calibre one-way tickets to hell to deliver."

"Sounds like you like them well enough."

"Probably the best damn weapon since the Roman short sword!"

"Have you done away with rifles too?"

"Not quite yet. I always arm a company of troopers with '59 Sharps Cavalry Carbines that they carry oun slings in addition to a brace of pistols. Allows us a good loung-range how-do-you-do before we come aknockin."

"I've always wondered why they hang their rifles from shoulder slings. You'd think that they would use scabbards attached to the saddle."

"The carbine clipped to a sling will keep y'all from alosin it in battle. But, mainly, the added weight of a rifle oun one side of a horse oun loung hard trips is a great cause of saddle galls, something we strictly guard against oun a loung campaign."

"So that's how you train rangers?"

"That's how I train rangers. To be pistoleros."

"So tell me how ranger tactics are going to help us in Virginia. I saw in yesterday's 'Pioneer and Democrat' that a Colonel Starr of the 9th Virginia and eighty of his men were surprised and captured in Summerville, Virginia last month. It said that 300 rebel cavalry rode into town at full gallop and found all of the 9th asleep!"

"That be James Ewell Brown Stuart no doubt. He's been in Virginia ever since his ride around McClellan at the Peninsula last June."

"Then in the same issue was another article about guerrilla raids. It said that the town of Independence, Missouri surrendered after a complete rout of our troops by Quantrel and over 500 of his guerillas. And that's not far from here!"

"Well, as you can see, the idea is to group cavalry into full brigades and send em off oun destructive raids into enemy territory. The objective is to weaken the will of the enemy's population to fight, and to destroy their agricultural and manufacturin capabilities."

"Have we actually used those kind of tactics anywhere?"

"That's just what the 2nd Cavalry tried to do and the Texas Rangers did to the Comanches. In '55 I transferred from the Dragoons to the newly formed 2nd Cavalry at Jefferson Barracks with a commission. By '56 we all were back in Texas."

"Back to protect the settlers?"

"Yeah. To do that we had an HQ at Fort Mason and set up an outpost oun the Brazos near old Fort Belknap; our orders were to patrol, pursue, and punish any hostile Indans found in the State. I led patrols that traveled as much as six hundred miles and remained in the field for thirty days. By '57 our patrols had pretty much cleared the Texas frontier of hostiles between the Red River and the Rio Grande."

"So you were effective."

"You might say so but the 2nd only patrolled the frontier country. We didn't pursue the Indans into their home country north of the Red River or into the unmapped Llano Estacado. So you might say that we were only half effective."

Luckenbach took one last drag on his cigarette and field stripped it dropping the remains into his empty coffee cup where he'd flicked the ashes. He noticed two more Indian canoes coming upriver toward the opening of the Minnesota. The Trumpeter Swans again voicing their concern with their honking echoing across the misty bottomlands along Zebulon Pike's Island. *Now there's a twist,* he thought. *When we saw Indans amovin back home we all were the ones that got upset.*

"Where did the Texas Rangers come in?"

"Well when Floyd took over the War Office, he ordered the 2nd Cavalry to Utah Territory for the Mormon Expedition. That just flung the gates back wide open and within weeks the Comanche Moon rose again."

"How's that?"

"Ah 'Comanche Moon' meanin the September full moon. That's when Comanches and Kiowas camped up along the Canadian would be amakin medicine to begin their winter raids into Texas and down the Comanche Traces through the Big Bend country into Mexico."

"How long has that been going on?"

"Been doin it thataway for a hundred years or more I reckon. Loung as there's been Texians and Mexicans. That's a very fearsome time that strikes terror into the hearts of my people back home. They don't say things like 'Beware of the Comanche Moon!' just to hear emselves atalkin."

"I've heard that said and always wondered what it meant."

"Anyway, the State took things into their own hands and old Rip Ford was appointed Captain of the Rangers.

"Rip?"

"Rip stands for 'Rest In Peace.' I reckon they called him that cause of all the vermin he sent to their maker—hostile Indans, outlaws, banditos and such."

"Did he have any mandate from the Governor?"

"Ford was given a free hand and told to take immediate drastic action. I reckon those was the bloodiest times in Texas history since the Alamo years. Bout the spring of '58 old Rip let-er-rip.

"What kind of tactics did 'Rest In Peace' use?"

"He fought Indan style—surprise the enemy and kill em in their tents, that simple. His motto was 'Attack, kill, strike fear, and dominate!'"

"Did it work?"

"Boy howdy! In a fight against old Iron Jacket, he took the war right to their big camp along the Canadian, right smack in Indan Territory. Rangers tore into that camp with those Colts ablazin and killed Iron Jacket and seventy-six of his warriors and captured over three hundred horses and totally demoralized those Comanches by breakin their medicine."

"He must have taken a lot of causalities."

"Lost two of his own men. But in the process you might say Ford wrote an important Anti-Guerrilla Chapter in our Ranger Manual—ifn we had one."

"How was that?"

"He showed that guerrillas could be chased, found, and killed by Rangers anywhere in the frontier. He had penetrated where even the Spanish dared not tread and where our American military were reluctant to campaign."

"Say Luke, I've certainly enjoyed talking to you here this morning. I think I'll go down and see if I can rustle up some breakfast. Good luck with those boys from Renville County?"

"Adios Doc!"

Still leaning on the railing in the morning sunlight, Luckenbach stretched and took in a deep breath of fresh air. He could see the bright green leaves of the oak trees near the river shimmering in the breeze against the turquoise blue morning sky. He could feel the day beginning to heat up as he looked back down on the river. He couldn't see the flock of Trumpeter Swans but could hear them occasionally from their nesting area on Pike's Island. Then he heard a large fish jump and splash back into the river. When he turned to look, he saw a circle of ripples about where he had seen the canoes earlier. He wondered what Tribe those Indians could have been.

Damn! I got that old uneasy Indan feelin again. I thought the Sioux had all been moved out west with the Treaty of 1851, least-wise that's what I was told.

When Luckenbach returned to his quarters, he went down into the galley for the metal pitcher filled with fresh, hot water that his cook always left on the wood stove knowing the captain would be going out for his Sunday morning ride. He carried the hot ewer back up the stairs, quickly poured the water into his washbasin, washed-up, and pushed his light brown hair back over his head with his wet hands. Then he shaved and trimmed his moustache, as it was getting uncomfortably long. He put on a white cotton shirt tucked into his blue denim pants with the red stripes of the 2nd Dragoons down the sides and flared over his boots. He left the six additional buttons on the lower legs unbuttoned to allow a little more air circulation.

As he clipped on his dragoon belt with one of his holstered Army Colts, he was glad it was Sunday and he didn't have to wear those regulation wool clothes since it felt like it was going to be another hot, humid day. He put on his eagle head spurs, grabbed his slouch hat, and went out the front door of his quarters. As he was crossing the mess room to the front door of the barracks, he noticed two young officers sitting at a large round table reading the morning newspaper. They both saw him and smiled as one of them waved.

"Captain Luckenbach, could we see you for a minute, sir?" asked 2nd Lt. Frank Chapman.

Luckenbach walked over and pulled up a chair threw his hat on the table and sat down. "Say I didn't know y'all shave tails were old nuff to read."

"Well that's why we called you over here sir. To draw on your wisdom, you being our elder and all," 2nd Lt. Howel Brown said jokingly.

"Alright gentlemen, but make it quick cause I got an important horse awaitin."

"Sir, it says here in this morning's Saint Paul 'Pioneer and Democrat' that the President has created an Army of Virginia to be under the command of a Major General Pope. Do you know anything about him?" asked Chapman.

"Yeah. Seems like he had some limited success in Mississippi. He was also born in Kentucky and moved to Illinois at a young age—just like Lincoln. And, most important, he's related to the President by marriage! How's that grab y'all?"

"Oh my God!" Chapman said as he threw his paper down on the table.

"Sir, it says that he's going to be in command of three Major Generals—Sigel, Banks, and McDowell. Have you heard anything about them?" asked Brown.

"I don't think that any one of those old boys has any more sense than a nose bag full of horse feed. They're probably just a step above being incompetent."

"Sir we can't understand how people like that get into those positions of authority," said Chapman.

"Well y'all just come out of West Point which means y'all been detached from the real world for aspell. Y'all need to understand that, in these days of war, a lot of former civilians now wear leaves, gold eagles or stars on their shoulders due to their political and influential appointments. Most of em don't belong in their authority, but General Pope's stuck with em."

"Sounds to me like he's one of them sir. How do you think he'll fare against someone like General Lee or Stonewall Jackson in Virginia?" asked Brown.

"I believe there are two things Pope can do. First, he needs to organize his horse soldiers into brigades, all capable of offensive action cause we been only ausin cavalry for pickets and messenger boys. Second, he needs to put John Buford in the field with his cavalry. Buford's one of the best damn soldiers that ever set astride a Morgan!"

"Where do you know him from sir?" asked Brown.

"He was a Lieutenant in the 2nd Dragoons when I served in that outfit bout ten years ago in Texas."

"That means he knows something about cavalry tactics," said Brown as he took a deep breath and nodded approvingly toward Chapman.

"He learned bout cavalry the hard way—survivin winters in the saddle, coordinating troops of men, and the value of a good horse and what it took to keep em thataway."

"We're sure happy to hear that sir," said Chapman. "Since we've completed our training here with you, we'll be shipping out tomorrow to join up with our 1st Michigan Volunteers in Washington D.C. It's our understanding that we'll be one of four Regiments under the command of none other than Brigadier General John Buford!"

"Well boys I wish y'all luck and good huntin. Y'all be under very capable leadership with General Buford, believe me. Just remember that, in spite of the way I been atalkin here this mornin, we're soldiers. And a soldier's solemn duty is to follow orders, not to question em."

"I want to thank you for everything sir," said Brown. "It's been a great month here!"

Luckenbach got up and shook hands with the young officers, grabbed his hat, and exited the barracks onto the Fort Snelling parade grounds.

Walking across the field toward the gatehouse, Luckenbach could see a standing room only crowd around the schoolhouse for Catholic Mass. The windows were all the way up and the doors were open allowing the soldiers outside to participate in the services. He looked toward the Sutler's Store and could see it wasn't open yet. He was expecting an order of Bull Durham that might have been on the riverboat shipment that arrived the previous night. With southern tobacco being hard to get these days and in big demand, the Sutler had finally found a dealer in Chicago who still had a supply and had promised to send what he had as part of his patriotic duty. Walking out through the gatehouse, Luckenbach returned the salutes of the sentries who respectfully saluted the un-uniformed Captain as he began the hundred-yard trek to the stables.

When he arrived at the barn, Luckenbach stopped again to read the brass plaque attached to the cornerstone, which read:

Built by the United States
1st Regiment of Dragoons

D Company
1849

He remembered when he joined the Dragoons as a youth for the promise of adventure. Instead of enjoying the privileges and comforts promised him, he found he was no different than a common foot soldier. He spent his time performing drill, fatigues, guard and military functions, in addition to building their own quarters and stables, and raising some of their own food. All this came after tending to his mount and tack, additional duties that weren't required of the infantryman. But then, he thought, at least people who use the stables built them.

Typical of Dragoon style, he thought as he entered from the west doorway, were the building's large double doors on each end of its east-west axis, which were usually left open during the warm summer months and provided a nice cooling breezeway through the building. There were ten officer horse stalls on the east half and an open bay for enlisted men's horses on the west half on each side of a passageway that was about five paces wide and connected both doors. Adjacent to each officer's stall was a narrow walk-in room with a padlocked door, for the individual storage of tack, grooming materials, a saddletree and other personal stable use items. And adjacent to the building was the signature of a Dragoon horse barn—a huge partially wooded pasture of over a thousand acres.

As he walked down the passageway, he was surprised at how rapidly the improvements had been made in the maintenance of the stables. He remembered his father always saying that the guiding principle for good horse management was 'cleanliness is next to Godliness'. And being an old Dragoon, Luckenbach was as concerned for the condition of his horses as he was of his troopers.

When he had arrived from Fort Riley, Kansas in July, he found the mounts in such poor condition, un-groomed, under-nourished, and living in such crowded conditions, that he fired off a letter to the Adjutant requesting change. Within days, recruits were detailed to stable duty on a daily basis. Simply replacing the straw beds in the stalls daily and scrubbing the stall, passageway floors, and drainage tiles weekly resulted in a very familiar and pleasant stable odor, summoning childhood memories of his father's stables, compared to the stench of about a month ago.

He arrived at his assigned stall and unlocked the door to his tack closet and retrieved his saddle, saddle blanket, and bridle and carried the gear out the east doors of the stables. Once outside, he swung his saddle up on a horizontal pole of the corral around the farrier's shed, near the pasture gate, as he did with the saddle blanket and bridle.

"Say Captain suh, that's a mighty fine looking saddle y'all got there," said Corporal Moses Griffin, the stables farrier who was in the corral busily tidying up the rim of a Morgan's hoof with a rasp.

"Ah thankew, Corporal," Luckenbach said taking a lot of personal pride in the fact that enlisted men talked freely to him. Having been an enlisted man himself, he was well aware of the social stratification in the military that had been a carry over from 18th Century European Armies. Unlike most Union Officers who considered the soldier to be expendable and of no more value than cannon fodder, he considered the social division between officers and enlisted men not only distasteful but also inappropriate in a democracy, a democracy his father had discovered in the writings of Rousseau and realized in moving to America.

"Sho nuff aint no regulation McClellan Saddle suh," he said as he dropped the finished horse's hoof and stood brushing hoof shavings off of his well-worn leather apron.

"With due respect to General McClellan, who aint never been in the cavalry, I don't think he's ever set for any spell oun one of those damn contraptions of his."

"Don't like em suh?"

"Like ridin oun a damn wooden rockin horse!"

"Suh what kinda saddle is that y'all got there?"

"It's a 1850 Texas Saddle. Been developed in Texas by Texas Rangers and workin cowboys who actually use em."

"Sho fine looking," said Moses as he threw his rasp onto the workbench in his shed.

"Got a five inch cantle, a rawhide covered saddle horn, and the stirrups are made of wide steam-bent wood. And its got wider fenders but weighs bout the same as the McClellan."

"Ah see that it's double rigged too. That front cinch and rear padded flank strap sho nuff make it a mite easier on the ole horse."

"Yeah that single rigged McClelland puts a bunch of stress oun a horse when ropin wild horses in the field."

Moses walked the Morgan toward the corral fence and tied its halter rope to the ring on the hitching post. As he walked back he stroked the Morgan a couple of times on the left quarters as Luckenbach smiled at the gentle action of a man who understands horses. "While ah got y'all here suh, I been ameanin to ask bout this here new shoe'n roster we all got on the wall up yonda."

"Yeah?"

"It's part of y'alls new maintenance program suh. We done set up a schedule where each horse gits shoe'n every fo weeks an we been anoticin that y'alls name aint on the list."

"That's right Mose cause I intend to keep him barefooted."

"Barefooted suh?" Moses said as he unbuckled his leather apron and tossed it on the workbench.

"That's right. Healthiest feet I ever seen oun a horse were unshod barefoot Comanche ponies."

"The manual say that shoe'n protects the hoof from bein worn away faster than it grow."

"Hell them Comanche ponies run all day loung over rugged ground and still have stronger, healthier feet without shoes than our shod remounts ever will."

"Y'all seem to know lot about Comanche horses suh."

"I should. Spent nuff time in the saddle achasin em."

"How do Comanches treat horses any different than we all do?"

"Well y'all be alookin all day loung to find a farrier's shed or a horse-barn in a Comanche camp," said Luckenbach enjoying the image of the tall, lanky, big-eyed Negro leaning his head around the tipis of a hostile Comanche camp with young proud warriors sitting there looking at him like he'd lost his mind.

"They just let them horses run wild suh?"

"That's right. A free-roamin pony is amovin all the time, covers 15 to 20 mile a day. Oun top of that he's with a herd, and horses like nothing more than bein together."

"How bout they all's diet?"

"Hell a horse like that eats what he needs and when he needs it. Oun top of that he eats and drinks in a natural, head lowered position. Then he puts his feet in water each day as he drinks from rivers and the like to get a balance of moisture in his feet."

"The manual say that a horse cain't be kept fit lessin he be stabled and its grass eatin kept down."

"Corporal, that manual don't say or know beans bout the frontier. I doubt if there's anything bout a natural wild horse in it let alone one with a natural wild Indan oun it. And where in the hell did y'all learn to read?"

"Ah taught myself suh."

"Well I'll be damned!"

"Suh seems like y'all do everythin just the opposite of what it say in that manual."

"Two things I won't do with any of my horses, Corporal. First of all, I flat won't put shoes oun em, especially oun a mount that's expected to run over rough country for any length of time; ain't nuthin worse than a horse throwin a shoe in the heat of battle. Second, I won't keep em in a stall."

"In the short time y'all been here suh, ah cain't recollect eva seein a horse in y'alls stall."

"Won't neither."

"Say that dun stripe stallion acomin out yonda must belong to y'all," said Moses looking out across the pasture.

"That's him alright."

"That Mustang's the one aleavin unshod tracks out there. When I first saw them tracks, I figured that the Sioux been ascoutin our herd."

"How'd y'all know it's a Mustang," asked Luckenbach testing the corporal's horse knowledge as he nodded toward his horse that now stood near the pasture gate anxiously bobbing its head and snorting.

"Sho nuff got a Mustang's confomation—couplin is smooth, chest is narra but deep, with the front legs ajoinin the chest in an 'A' shape an all. Got the dorsal stripe and the chestnuts are…"

"All right! Y'all seem to know a bit bout horse flesh," said Luckenbach approvingly as he began to roll a cigarette.

"Yes suh Captain. Ah was a stable slave on the Allan Plantation near Memphis where they all breed fine Tennessee Walkin Horses."

"Well I'll be damned again!" Luckenbach said smiling as he struck a match on his boot bottom and lit his cigarette."

"Yes suh. Ah been round stables aworkin as a farria and alistenin to horse talk as long as ah kin rememba."

"I reckon a farrier is kept pretty busy with em Walkers."

"That's right suh. Shoe'n is critical to the big lick Walker's special pace."

"How's that?"

"Well suh, very long hooves assist the natural action of they alls famous runnin walk. The hind shoe plates got to have extended heels to give em that glidin gait."

"Seems like a lot of good breedin went into those Tennessee Walkers."

"Yes suh. The foundation sire was Standardbred Black Allan, right off'n the Allan Plantation, who came from a line a trotters out ova Morgan mare."

"My daddy often talked bout infusion of Tennessee Walker blood into his Spanish Mustang strain but he didn't like what he thought was abusive shoe'n and sore'n to get movement."

"Captain suh? I just knowed that y'all come from a horse family care'n the way you do bout horses an all," Moses said with a big toothy grin.

"That's right. I grew up on a ranch in Texas. My daddy's been abreedin Texas Longhorn bulls and Spanish Mustangs there for bout 25 years now."

"Where'd he ever git aholt of that Spanish strain?"

"He looked for wild horses that had the conformation of pure Spanish blood. Two full brothers, Hernando and Francisco, were his foundation stallions, sired by a buckskin stallion named Buckshot and out of Comanche blood oun the dam's side. Pretty soon we had us a manada."

"Y'alls name don't sound Spanish."

"It's German. My folks were from Bavaria and immigrated to America where they all called us Dutch stead of Deutsch."

"Y'all born in Texas?"

"Naw. Born in Berks County in southeastern Pennsylvania. My folks decided to move to the new Republic of Texas in '37 just a year after the Alamo when I was but nine year old."

"How'd they keep the Spanish bloodlines, ah mean all them feral horses arunnin round an all?"

"He got a list of criadoras at several big Mexican estancias. We used to take mares to the Hacienda De Andas north of Monterrey where they all have maintained a selective breed of Andalusian Barbs for over a hundred years."

"Sho got a nice confomation," said Moses appraising the horse as he started toward the pasture gate.

"Well the Mustang aint a big horse as y'all can see. But he's a compact, muscular horse, and he's astandin oun strong legs," Luckenbach said while stuffing his cigarette into the coals of the farrier's furnace, then walking over and grabbing the bridle off the fence.

"Appears that he kinda looks like y'all Captain," Moses said laughing while sliding the wire hoop up off the two vertical posts that held the gate secure and allowing it to swing open.

"I reckon that's right. I don't weigh but 170 pounds soakin wet with my boots oun and dun colored hair and all."

The young stallion reared up as the gate opened and began a high stepping prance for the twenty feet or so toward Luckenbach while nodding its head up and down as if greeting an old friend. Luckenbach presented the bridle and the horse immediately lowered its head. The captain slid the snaffle bit into its mouth with the noseband over its muzzle and lashed the headstall up over its ears. He dropped the ends of the braided rawhide reins to the ground as a signal to the horse to stand still. Then he gently stroked its muzzle as he quietly said "Que pasa Amarillo?"

Mose closed the gate and was walking around the horse looking at the mustang's feet as he said softly to himself, "Got nice feathered fetlocks." Then he squatted down for a closer look and again said softly, "Got short heels with a sloped hairline formin that triangle foot that ah seen on wild horses."

"Y'all mind ifn ah look at the underside?" he asked loudly.

"Go oun ahead, Mose."

Mose picked up the horse's left front hoof with his left hand in expert farrier fashion as he began to examine the bottom of the foot. "Why that's rightly amazin suh! Looks like the bottom of the coffin bone sits nearly level to the ground. Our manual say to trim hooves so that the bottom edge of the coffin bone is not level with the ground. It also say that the hairline should be nearly horizontal."

"Y'all been a slave too loung, Mose. Part of bein free means that y'all can think for yourself. That manual aint no better than the man that wrote it."

"Well suh, y'all kin keep a mule chained to a post all its life. Then one day y'all comes along and cuts the chain and that mule still gonna stand by that post."

"Mose, what y'all are aseein there is a free natural foot," said Luckenbach smiling. "Aint never been a shoe oun it or a nail in it!" he added as he walked toward the corral fence to get the saddle and blanket.

"Ah kin see that suh, frog bein wide with the heels and bulbs wide apart an all. And the bars are straight givin a strong heel strucha. Best ah eva seen!" as he dropped the horse's foot back to the ground.

"Mose, I think y'alls mulo is astartin to move!"

"Captain, y'all are a rebel ifn y'all know what ah mean, not sayin that y'all are in the wrong army now ya understan!" he said laughing.

Luckenbach placed the saddle blanket on the stallion as he thought of his father as the true rebel. In the spirit of Rousseau and the natural man he taught his children to rely on impulses and intuitions, trusting emotions rather than thoughts, the heart rather than the mind. At the dinner table he often quoted from Rousseau's "Social Contract" that he said became the textbook of the French Revolution or recited parts of his favorite poems like the one from Wordsworth…

> *Sweet is the lore which Nature brings;*
> *Our meddling intellect*
> *Mis-shapes the beauteous forms of things:—*
> *We murder to dissect.*

The saddle blanket was an example of *the lore which nature brings* as he remembered trading an army slouch hat for the blanket from an Indian youth in Utah a couple of years earlier. The thick textured blanket was the color of natural sheep's wool with nature's dyes used to color wide black borders inset with a row of white triangular stars with turquoise colored diamonds in the middle and red tassels hanging from each corner, looking typical of the Navajo style made in Arizona Territory somewhere. He placed his saddle over the doubled blanket and reached under the stallion for the girth strap and cinched it firmly to the front ring. He repeated the activity with the flank strap to the back ring only leaving it a little loose for comfort.

"Got a name for y'alls horse, Captain?"

"Yeah, his name's Lobo Amarıllo."

"What's that mean?"

"It means Yella Wolf. I knew a young Comanche War Chief with that name. He would paint his face yella with that loung black hair of his ablowin in the wind. That's who this horse reminded me of with that dun colorin and that loung black mane and tail, somethin wild, natural, and free."

"Captain suh, y'all are one hell of an unusual Yankee Offica!"

"And y'all are one hell of an unusual farrier. Ifn I ever need one, which I seriously doubt, I'll know where to come."

"Thank ya suh. Reckon ah gots to git to cleanin up ma furnace. Expectin the Colonel at high noon to git his Morgan, him orderin me to come in on the Sabbath an all."

Luckenbach swung the reins around Amarillo's neck and mounted to the sound of creaking leather as he said smiling, "Keep y'alls mule amovin, Corporal," and put his mount south toward the Minnesota River.

Picking up the Shakopee Road south of the fort, Luckenbach could feel Amarillo loosening up and beginning to flow into his paso gait. *Now that's what my daddy's horse breedin is all about,* he thought, *a gait naturally born into a horse and not forced in any meddlin way.* Within a mile or so down the trail, he began to slow the horse as he approached the remnants of an old trading post.

The decaying log structure had a collapsed roof but the four walls and the porch remained intact. Above the porch was an old weather beaten sign with the peeling outer layer of paint exposing the barely legible words "Columbia Fur Company" underneath. The Sutler at Fort Snelling had told him of how shrewd capitalists of competing fur companies in the region after the War of 1812 had exploited the Indians and completely depleted the region of fur bearing animals.

As a result the starving Sioux Indians were forced to sign over vast areas of land in southern Minnesota and accept strips of reservation land farther to the west along the Minnesota River as well as the promise of annuity payments from the American Government as compensation.

After years of fighting Kiowas, Comanches, and Apaches in the southwest, Luckenbach was drawn to Indians who fought to preserve their homeland. As a warrior himself with a military code of ethics, to fight for home and family was honorable, so he admired a warlike spirit. Soldiers respected the traits they most revered in their own ranks. Moreover, their self-esteem could be raised if they saw the enemy as brave, determined, and intelligent. Luckenbach was puzzled by the paradox of a great Tribe of warriors accepting the humiliation of exploitation, starvation, and deportation by the Americans without bloodshed. Texians, he knew, paid dearly for every blood-soaked acre of land wrought from the proud Comanches.

Continuing south along the old Indian trail, Amarillo resumed his comfortable gait. Crossing over high windy bluffs above the Minnesota River, Luckenbach could see that the thick woodlands continued to follow the course of the river but elsewhere the forests were thinning and beginning a transition to a tallgrass prairie. He began to pass fields of big bluestem as high as his horse's back with leaves beginning to turn from bluish in color to a reddish purple. Mixed in with the bluestem was thickspike gayfeather creating a carpet of purple and russet that covered an entire valley.

He passed a high outcropping of Sioux quartz of reddish and fairly smooth slabs. High on one of the slabs was what appeared to be a petroglyph of a Thunderbird with outspread wings similar to what he had seen on rocky cliffs along the Rio Bravo in Texas. Luckenbach knew the symbol was sacred to many Tribes and represented a powerful spirit that flashes lightning from its beak and whose flapping wings create thunder. He also knew that the rock probably served as an ancient sentinel to a sacred ceremonial place of power.

He followed a narrow branch of the road that descended the bluff onto a large flat wooded shelf above the flood plain of the river. He found well-worn paths and the packed earth of open communal spaces, with pole frameworks of many structures still standing, and with even a nearby creek, which had been dammed creating a small pond about twenty yards across and twice as long, spilling over the wooden barrier into its original course and rushing toward the Minnesota. Luckenbach could see that the place had been occupied for many generations. As the day was heating up and having found an interesting place to spend some time, he dismounted and removed the tack from Amarillo, allowing him to drink and cool off in a shaded area of the nearby creek.

Leaving his hat on the saddle horn, Luckenbach walked over to the sandy shore of the creek upstream from his horse, took a drink of cold fresh water in the cup of his hands, splashed water on his face, and pushed his hair back with his wet hands. Feeling refreshed, he walked over and sat on a log in the shade of a huge ancient oak tree and began to roll a cigarette. He was aware of a very strange feeling that had overcome him; as if he were being watched by a predator or again in the ominous force field of Pennsylvania Dutch hexenmeisters as often happened in his youth back in Berks County. He could no longer hear the crows cawing or the sound of the waterfall, almost like time itself had stopped. He struck a match on the log and lit his cigarette and leaned back against the tree facing the distant Minnesota River, clearing his mind and consciously relaxing all the muscles of his body while maintaining a high-level awareness of his surroundings—a tested warrior readying himself for battle.

Amarillo climbed up out of the creek and hurriedly crossed the open space to a large patch of grass, standing alert and snorting with his ears erect and focusing on the old village area. Luckenbach stood up and discarded his cigarette and drew his revolver from its flapped holster, cocked it and held it upright, as he turned toward the abandoned village. There, sitting in a circle in the communal space near several now intact lodges of the village, as it must have appeared a hundred or a thousand years before, were seven Indian men with very startled expressions looking at him. A few of the men had turned around completely from their cross-legged seated positions on the ground to see him. The men shifted their gaze to the stallion in equally wondrous amazement as Amarillo reared and whinnied.

A man with red face and body paint and long white braided hair and wearing only a breechcloth and moccasins stood and took several steps toward Luckenbach and stopped. The Indian looked deeply into his eyes then turned his head toward the pond as Luckenbach followed his gaze. There, in the center of the pond, was a pole standing about six feet out of the water and tied to it was what appeared to be the huge fossilized skull of an elephant with long curved ivory tusks dripping water as if it had just emerged from the depths. Luckenbach shifted his attention back to the white haired man who was clutching a long stemmed red-stone pipe in both hands, as he appeared to be handing it toward Luckenbach. Sensing that he was not in danger, Luckenbach returned his Colt to its holster to accept the pipe and as suddenly as the vision had appeared, it disappeared.

The astonished Luckenbach was standing with his hands out in total disbelief of what he had just witnessed as he could once again hear the crows and the sound of the waterfall with the village restored to its deserted, weed-infested condition. The pond was clear and still with not even a ripple attesting to what he had seen.

It reminded him of the witchery of Comanches on the prairies of south Texas. At times while being pursued, the Indians with black painted faces would simply disappear like the wind, as if they had become ghost riders and in so doing usually spooked horses and troopers alike in his command. He looked toward Amarillo who, with the perceived danger gone, was now peacefully grazing on the patch of green grass as if nothing had happened. As he put his hat back on he looked at the deserted village with a new apprehension, then saddled and bridled the young stallion and began the nine-mile ride back to Fort Snelling.

As Luckenbach approached the horse barn, he noticed that several young recruits were in the passageway grooming their horses after their afternoon at target range practice. Some were busily cleaning leather gear, while others were standing in groups engaged in boisterous, youthful conversation. He rode up to the west entrance and, as he dismounted, a group of recruits standing near the doors came to attention and saluted. He returned their salute and entered the stables leading Amarillo.

"Stables! Atten-hut!" yelled one of the recruits as he saw the Captain.

"At ease," said Luckenbach embarrassed by the continued respect given him when he was out of uniform. The recruits, however, knew the veteran was one of the best equestrians and shootists in the Union Army. He had become a living legend among the young recruits as a Dragoon, Indian fighter, and pistoleer, primarily from his mounted demonstrations of rapid, deadly marksmanship on the target range.

"And that be a fine stallion you have there Captain, sir," said one of the recruits in a strong Gaelic accent as Luckenbach wound his way through the passageway to the officer's side of the stables while several of the horses were stomping their hooves and whinnying in the presence of the young stallion.

"Thankew Private," he answered as he stopped in front of his stall and opened the door to his tack room. He always felt guilty having his own personal stall since the enlisted men's stables consisted of open bays with the horses sharing a common food and water trough. But then he thought his father would have said that the open bay is better because horses like to be together where they can see, touch, and smell each other.

Luckenbach returned the tack to his storage room, brushed the stallion down, and checked under his hooves for any rocks he might have picked up, then walked out of the stables toward the pasture gate as Amarillo followed him. When he opened the gate, the stallion rushed into the open field seemingly anxious for the freedom of the huge pasture and to be with his waiting new herd again.

Magic of Odin

Astrid Arntsdatter Mundahl woke up to the rooster's heralding of sunrise to collect eggs, milk cows, and complete other chores before breakfast as she did every morning. Astrid had taken service on the Bruner Farm near Beaver Creek in the Beaver Falls Township of Renville County. She lived in the large new barn built of hand-hewn oak beams skillfully fitted together with German mortise and tenon joinery where a harness room had been converted to living quarters. It had a small cot with a straw filled mattress, an emigrant chest for a table, a wood stove for cooking and heat, a wooden chair, and a small window. The frugality of her lifestyle was consistent with the simple and rudimentary life of her earlier youth in Arendahl, Minnesota.

Astrid walked out into the barn to the smells of the new wooden structure and of straw mixed with fresh cow droppings; the sounds of nesting hens cooing, and the fluttering wings of two startled Barn Swallows as they darted out through the open double doors; and the rhythmic displays of cows swishing their tails at flies as if anxiously awaiting their morning ritual.

After collecting a basket full of eggs in the hay loft and dropping hay down to the cows below, she carefully descended the stairs and entered one of the stalls placing a small dairy stool and a tin of water with a clean rag on the right side of her favorite cow—Annfred. Then as she playfully patted the bovine's tail head, she could see particles of dust rise in the morning rays of sunlight streaming through spotless windowpanes while Annfred instinctively moved her rear right leg back. Glancing through the open doors she saw an Indian woman and a young girl walking up the cornfield path from the southwest toward the river road below the farm. "They must have yust come from crossing the river," she said to Annfred.

She went out of the barn and called to them, "Hallooo! Would you like some cold water and some fresh eggs?"

The woman and child stopped, said something to each other, then crossed the road, unhitched the gate and ascended the sloping farmyard toward Astrid. The woman was young with the tall, thin body typical of Dakota women with long black shiny hair in a single braid down the back and was very striking with her reddish copper skin drawn tightly across her high cheekbones. She wore a black calico blouse and wrap-around skirt with red and blue ribbons sewn along the hemline over beautifully quilled moccasins resulting in a very sibylline air about her. The girl, appearing about eight years old, was similarly dressed and carried a large tanned buckskin bag that was also embroidered with floral porcupine quill-work and looked as if it were empty.

As they approached Astrid, she handed them a pail of cold well water with a ladle. The woman took the pail and set it down in front of them. She took out a ladle full of water and handed it to the girl who began to drink. The woman gazed at Astrid for a moment then said, "I see that you are a very kind woman."

"Well our lot is very difficult at times and the least I can do is share what little I have to help another woman," said Astrid surprised that the Indian woman spoke such good English.

The girl finished drinking, re-filled the ladle, and handed it to her mother, which seemed obvious from their physical resemblance. The woman took a long drink holding a hand under the dripping cup-shaped bowl. She set the dipper back into the pail and wiped her face with the cool water collected in the cusp of her left hand.

"Would you like to have some fresh eggs?"

"That would be good," said the woman.

Astrid went into the barn and returned with her egg basket and said, "Take as many as you want."

The two visitors each took one egg. The mother cracked her egg on the pail rim and raised her face to the sky as she allowed the contents of the raw egg to slide into her mouth. The girl awkwardly but successfully followed her mother's featly actions and they handed the broken eggshells back to Astrid.

"Is that all you want?" asked Astrid.

"They would just break in the bag," answered the young girl.

"I see that you will soon have a baby. And I see that it will be a strong healthy son. The Great Spirit will watch over you since you have a good heart," said the woman.

"Well thank you."

"Big thank you for your sharing. I will see you again."

Astrid could feel her strong spiritual charisma as she said, "Who are you? What is your name?"

"My name is Howaśtewiŋ or Good Voice Woman in English."

"My name is Astrid. Please come back again," Astrid pleaded.

Howaśtewiŋ and her daughter returned to the road and began walking south-east, stepping across the stoney Beaver Creek ford and on down the river road.

It was the first time that Astrid had ever spoken to or even been near Dakota people. Since her and Johannes had moved to Camp Township in Renville County last year, she had occasionally seen them at a distance across the river.

She had always thought it odd that the farmers didn't make an effort to be on good terms with the Indians since they were such close neighbors. Max Bruner had said that the men were lazy and refused to work. He said they would often come around begging for food or stealing chickens. He said that he has had to run them off of his property on several occasions. *Strange*, she thought. *It seems as though we're on their property.*

Finding the milk pail she had meticulously cleaned the night before, she slowly sat down and washed the cow's bag and teats and began milking. As usual the udders were full of milk from the rich grass of the Minnesota River bottom-land. The melodious rhythm of the streams of milk hitting the pail always had a mesmerizing effect on her as she began to think of her parents and growing up in their musical Haugean Church community. Still feeling the spirit, she began to sing a church hymn to the milk-pail rhythm knowing that the dairy cows enjoyed the morning concert, as they would often moo contentedly.

> *O at eg høvde tusing munde*
> *Og tusing tunger i høer mund,*
> *O at eg etter oske kunde*
> *Udaff mit hjertes dyse grund*
> *Red prise Gud, som det sig bor,*
> *For alt det gode, han mig gjord.*

With three cows mooing in the background, Astrid remembered her mother, Marie Hovin, saying that their church founder, Hans Nielsen Hauge himself, urged his followers to sing the songs of faith not only in church but also during the conduct of their daily lives. *Music is the pathway to the soul,* he would shout in Norwegian as he developed the salmemesse or liturgy of hymns to be sung by all—a more democratic pattern popular among Norwegian Americans, rather than music meant to be sung by a choir and heard by the congregation.

Astrid finished milking Annfred and poured the contents of the pail into a large metal milk canister and began to get settled around the next cow, Ingafred. Before starting to milk, however, she removed several cockleburs from her tail.

"Nothing is more awakening than a heavenly deliverance in the face of a cow's tail with a load of cockleburs imbedded in the end," she laughingly said aloud to the cow.

Awakening, she thought. *My mother had an awakening in her youth and now my parents have the power of the kingdom in them, which has shone forth in the conduct of their daily lives.*

Since Ingafred had somewhat of a mean streak in her and often kicked the milk bucket over, Astrid was trying to think of another song to soothe the savage beast when suddenly she felt her baby kick, quickly followed by another abrupt movement in the other side of her womb.

"Uff da!" She cried out as she heard the running footsteps of someone coming into the barn.

"Hallo Astrid!" sang out Greta, the Bruner's six-year-old daughter.

"Guten morgen, Greta!"

"Wie geht es dir?"

"Ausgezeichnet! I yust felt my baby move!"

"Wie heißt sie?"

"Sprechen sie Englisch, Greta?" asked the surprised Astrid.

"Ja!"

"Well then, my baby is going to be a boy," she said. "I know it now and I can tell by the strength of his kick and I will name him after my father."

"Vas is his name, dann?"

His name will be 'Arnt Yohannesen Mundahl' because the same name does the same good."

"Ich verstehe nicht! Tschüs," Greta said as she grabbed the basket of eggs and carefully walked out of the barn and back to the house where her mother would soon be preparing breakfast for their large family.

Astrid finished milking Ingafred and again poured the contents of the pail into the milk can. As she began to prepare Winnifred for milking, the cow stubbornly resisted moving her rear right leg back to expose her udder. A hard push on her right flank solved that problem and she washed the cow's bag and teats and began milking.

Astrid hoped her husband, Johannes, would approve of her having named their firstborn son after her father when he returned from the war. She knew that Johannes's family were fiskers from Mundal, a fishing village on the Sognefjorden in Norway, who may be more flexible when it came to Norwegian tradition since they had never been landowners. According to naming custom, the firstborn son, who probably would inherit the farm, was named after his father's father. When the wife had inherited the farm, the boy was named after his mother's father.

Her father, Arnt Hovin, was a Haugean—a pietistic Christian, who wanted to leave Norway partly because of religious persecution there and the promise of religious freedom in the new land. Also he was tired of what he referred to as *ukyndighend*—ignorance, and *vedhaengen ved gamle nedarvedåe skikke*—adherence to old, handed down customs. But the final conclusive decision was made when he received a letter from his brother Thor in America who wrote, "Every poor person who will come here and work diligently and faithfully can become a well-to-do man in a short time."

A few days later the Hovins left the Bakklandet church district of Trondheim, Norway with a group of Haugeans—farmers, craftsmen, and other merchants, and arrived in New York in July 1844 and finally settled near Norway Grove, Wisconsin a few months later. The rolling woodlands and prairies of Wisconsin stood in stark contrast to the steep mountains and blue-green waters of Trondheimsfjorden.

Most of the immigrants in Arnt Hovins group were wanting to settle in established Norwegian communities in the new world where they hoped to enjoy both the material wealth of America and a reestablishment of old Norwegian values. But Arnt would remind them that they had to shed their old world norms like a snake sheds its skin and adjust to the new American environment.

As was common in America after a locality was settled, young people, especially young married couples, would move on to new districts where there was either free or cheap land giving rise to Norwegian colonies across mid-western America like stepping stones across a river. *Not unlike our Viking ancestors*, her father once said, *who established stepping-stones across the North Atlantic from Norway to Vinland—the Faroes, Iceland, Greenland, and, finally, Leifsbudir in Vinland.*

Seven years after arriving in the new land, the young Arnt and Marie Hovin with their three children including the six-year-old Astrid, joined a party of ten families consisting of 50 men, women, and children, their wagons, oxen, horses, 100 head of cattle, some hogs and sheep, and migrated to Fillmore County around Arendahl, Minnesota, on land made available by the Treaty of Traverse des Sioux in 1851. *Hallelujah!* her father had cried upon finding their new home. *He has shown his people the power of his works in giving them the lands of the nations.*

The lucky ones found good land on the rolling prairie above the Root River and, if they were industrious and sensible, reaped a good life for themselves. The others who were more urbanized and so inclined founded independent businesses, as was the case with Arnt Hovin and his brother Thor.

Astrid finished milking Winnifred and emptied the pail of milk into the five-gallon metal receptacle. The container was near full and was much heavier than she thought she should attempt to carry given that she was nine months pregnant. As she was done with her chores and decided to wait for the Bruner boys to carry the milk to the house for their morning breakfast, she returned to her room to wash up and change into clean clothes.

As Astrid sat brushing her long blonde hair, she was looking at her daguerreotype of Johannes, taken last November in a studio after finishing his training at Fort Snelling, standing proudly in his uniform of the new 3rd Regiment Minnesota Infantry, D Company, United States Volunteers.

Yohannes, she thought. *You are my courageous young warrior, my Viking knight in Union blue. I love you for who you are; your determination to be a soldier fighting in a civil war for the new land that you dearly love and for frigjørelse—liberation, of the African people; and your mysterious ways of believing in the world of Odin and your revering of Tor, the powerful thunder God of our Norsk ancestors, even though it has estranged you from the Christian piety of your parents and mine who say that your beliefs are nothing more than a rebellious outcropping of your old heathen Viking blood. To die, you said, like your ancestors with a sword in your hand and to be chosen by the Valkyrje to enter the great hall of the slain—Valhalla, is a fantasy of your youth.*

Her father often spoke of Norway, where the bones of her ancestors lay in Trøndelag—the rich land of the north with high slopes heavy with grass for the fattening of cattle and sheep. And of the jagged coast to the southwest, where the bones of Johannes's ancestors lay in Sogn and Hordaland—the land of dark fjords and bare pastures where generations of hardy men grew sinewy and bitter with poverty. This was the land of the Viking settlements of old, where the black water and grey rock fjords launched shallow-draught, clinker-built, dragon-shaped langskips with their twenty benches loaded with violent freebooters to spread their potion of seawater and blood throughout the uncharted world—lands to the south and west that looked very rich to hungry eyes peering over their iron-rimmed wooden shields.

Whatever the forces driving the young Vikings into their kjølfugls to seek the freedom of the open seas to wrench plunder and land from incredulous victims, so it was driving the young men of Sogn into emigrant sloops to seek the freedom of the new world to find riches and land that, they were told, was their manifest destiny. As the old world of Vinland was frigjørelse to the Viking, the new world of America was New Canaan to the men of Sogn. They were among God's chosen people who after eight hundred years were once again headed for the Promised Land.

"Astrid!" called out Christian, the Bruner's thirteen-year-old son as he entered the barn with his younger brother.

"I'll be right out," answered Astrid from her room as she strode toward the door.

"Ve have kommen for die Milch, ah I mean the milk," said Christian as he picked up the milk vessel with the help of Emil. "And das Frühstuck, ah I mean breakfast, vill be ready soon."

"Guten morgen Christian, and you too, Emil! Tell your mother that I will be there in yust a few minutes. And thank you for helping me with the milk."

"Okay," said Christian.

"And your English is getting better, Christian."

"Ja. Ah yes, thank you, Astrid."

"Bis später!" yelled Emil laughing as they swung the heavy two-handled milk can out through the open barn doors.

Returning to her room, Astrid opened her emigrant chest and laid her hairbrush in the upper tray. Having put on her gingham maternity dress with a violet and white-checkered pattern, she thought that the brooch given to her by Johannes would look very nice on this Sabbath morning as she opened her small jewelry box and retrieved the pin.

It was a very old medallion of Viking origin the size of a circle formed by her thumb and index finger, which had probably served as an agraffe on a sword scabbard. Cast in silver with twisting colubrine shapes and tendrils forming open knots and loops, it exuded the energy of sea serpents reminiscent of the Vikings themselves. Set in the center of the modified clasp was a multifaceted gemstone of pale violet crystalline quartz—amethyst.

Johannes had given it to her before he left for the war and he said the piece had been in his family for many generations. He said the coming times would be hard for her and she needed courage to implement change or transformation that would be imparted by the stone and confidence to trust in his belief in the protective spirit of Odin to bring him safely home that would be imparted by the silver artifact. Astrid pinned the brooch onto the front of her dress, wrapped her light woolen lavender colored shawl around her shoulders, and headed for the Bruner house.

As Astrid approached the house, she thought about the events leading to her coming to the Bruner's last spring. Johannes had wanted her to return home to Arendahl where there were women who would care for her in the delivery of her baby. Breaking the patriarchal traditions of Norway, she was determined that this beautiful land on the Minnesota River was their new home and this was where their baby would be born. She had prayed to God to be merciful and grant her wish. Now it was not up to her to find help but up to God to work his mercy.

How quickly God had responded in all His goodness, she thought as she remembered her chance meeting with the Bruner's last April. She was walking down the muddy river road looking for one of her horses during an early thaw, when she saw a wagon rapidly approaching in her direction with the horses kicking up mud and the wagon wheels splashing water from the melting snow filled ruts in the road. She hurriedly stepped across the road to get out of the way when she slipped on ice and slid down into a shallow, grassy ditch. Having seen her, the team handler pulled the huge horses to a stop, wrapped the reins around the vertical brake handle, jumped from the wagon and ran over to her.

"Kann ich Ihnen helfen, Fräulein?" he asked.

"Nein, danke," she answered as she stood up brushing muddied grass off of her pant legs and bottom.

"Es war meine Schuld," apologized the man.

"Sprechen Sie bitte etwas langsamer," asked Astrid. "Ich bin Norsk."

"Wird sie sich wieder erholen, Max?" asked the woman sitting on the wagon seat.

"Ich weiß nicht," he answered.

The woman climbed down from the wagon and hurried over to Astrid and looking at her asked, "Are you going to haf a baby, Fräulein?"

"Yes."

"Are you on your vay home?"

"No, I was yust looking for my horse. I was following her tracks, but now I lost them."

"Ja ja, der Indianers stole it no doubt. Those heidnisch Indianers steal from us venever they get a chance!" retorted Max.

"Blödsinn, Max! You shouldn't be valking around here like this in your condition, Fräulein! It's dangerous for you und der baby!"

"You are right. It is danyerous and my mare probably was stolen."

"Help her up on der vagon, Max. Ve are going to take her to her home."

Max Bruner turned his team around and headed north toward Camp Township. When they arrived at the Boyum home where Astrid was staying, Olga was aghast at the living conditions there—the Boyums, who were only teenagers themselves, with two small children and Astrid living in a small one-room Soddy, a small potato patch and corn field that couldn't possibly yield enough produce to feed everyone, un-corralled livestock leaving piles of dung everywhere, and still without chopped wood put up for the coming winter.

"Fräulein, you must come home mit us for your baby's sake. I am a Hebamme, ah mid-vife, und can take care of you und der baby und ve haf a good place vhere you can stay."

God had indeed answered her prayers! Within a few minutes, she had her belongings loaded on the wagon and was on her way to Beaver Creek and the Bruner homestead. *Hallelujah! He makes his marvelous works to be remembered,* she thought. *Her baby would be born on this new land of the Minnesota River!*

Astrid entered the house from the back kitchen door. Olga and Gretchen, their twelve year old daughter, were busy preparing a breakfast of Bauernfrüh-stuck, Pfannkuchen, Mehlspeise, Rühreier, and Kaffee with plenty of Milch for her family.

"Guten morgen Olga and you too Gretchen!"

"Ja, guten morgen, Astrid. Sit at der table, Fräulein. I haf something here for you," Olga said as Gretchen began taking plates of hot food from the stovetop out to the dining room.

Astrid carefully sat at the table as Olga took a steaming tin cup off the stove then set it on the table next to her as she sat down.

"Now then, Astrid. I haf told you over und over das a healthy pregnancy should be 'gentle, natural, and herbal.' Ja?"

"Yes."

"Ve haf pretty much talked about us mid-vifes being 'gentle' mit a pregnant voman. Out of respect for der voman, ve try to keep everything clean und alvays vash our hands before touching her. Und ve helped you to learn to understand und trust your 'natural' God given body since you haf been mit us. But now das you are in your ninth month, ve need to talk about 'herbal' things."

"Is that what is in the cup? Herbal things?"

"Ja wohl, Astrid, an herbal tea. I get der herbs from Good Voice Voman. Der same voman you vere talking to this morning."

"She seems very nice. What does she do?"

"She is the youngest daughter of Parent Hawk, a Medicine Man who has taught me many things, und she is learning to be a mid-vife among her people across der river. The Indianers haf der healthiest pregnancies und babies das I haf ever seen. Und the reason is das their mid-vifes practice 'gentle, natural, und herbal' birthing practice und they haf been doing das for hundreds of years."

"But how on earth does she get across the river?"

"Das is a mystery das I cannot answer. Her und her daughter's clothes are alvays dry ven they come to der house und ve haf never seen a canoe or boat along der shore."

"What is in the tea then?"

"There are red raspberries in there das vill help you mit morning sickness und help avoid ah Fehlgeburt, ah how you say…"

"Miscarriage?"

"Ja, miscarriage. Und nettles haf good nutrients und vill help mit night leg cramps. Dann raspberry leaves vill help you haf a safe und comfortable childbirth und a very happy baby!"

"So I yust drink this now?"

"Ja wohl. Und you vill haf a cup of hot tea every morning until your baby is born. Dann ve need to start you on herbs to help you make good breast Milch," Olga said as Astrid drank the tea.

Astrid set the empty cup down and with a big smile said, "That was very good!"

"Help me carry der rest of these dishes into der other room und ve vill haf a good Deutsch Frühstuck dann. Ja?"

Astrid carefully carried the large serving dish of German pancakes through the swinging kitchen door and into the dining room. She set the dish on the large dining table where three of the younger Bruner children were sitting impatiently waiting for breakfast, as they looked wide-eyed at the plate of hot Pfannkuchen. Max was sitting at his customary head of the table smoking his carved ebony and ivory crested Bavarian pipe.

"Frühstuck es fertig!" said Olga loudly as their three older boys began coming in from the front room.

As the youngsters wrestled their way onto a bench along the table to see who could sit next to Astrid, Max was busily tapping the ashes out of his pipe as he said, "Astrid, you haf been mit us now since last spring. I vant to tell you how much ve value your being mit us und Olga und me feel das you are vun of our own. Ve haf not a church built yet here. Der nearest Lutheran Church ve haf ist in New Ulm, vich is a long vays for us to travel. I vant to thank you at this time for spending time mit our children to read to them der Holy Scriptures from der New Testament und to teach to them der beautiful Christian songs in your language das ve hear you singing out in der barn."

"Danke, Herr Bruner," said Astrid blushing as some of the younger children giggled at the image of Astrid singing to the cows and chickens out in the barn.

"Also, Fräulein, I haf been to Arendahl und I know das your Haugean Norwegian relatives are hard vorking and God fearing people. I saw two Lutheran Churches there und ve haf none. I know too das in your church, vomen preach der Gospel in public, read Scripture, und serve as Elders. So at this time, I ask of you to say a small prayer to God Almighty before ve eat our morning meal."

"Danke, Herr Bruner. I rejoice in the presence of the Holy Spirit in this wonderful home!" Astrid said in Haugean formality as she bowed her head and clasped her hands in an attitude of prayer.

"Oh God. Thank you this morning for this wonderful Christian home here on this earth of thy Devine creation. Thank you this morning for the blessing of this kind family that you have brought here to enyoy the fruits of thy making. I ask that you bless their children with long life, happiness, and good health. And please, oh God, provide them thy love and grace to convert them to thy Holy Kingdom.

"Oh God. Convert us all and allow us to see the light of thy Kingdom shining on our path of life so that we may be saved. Please send thy Anyels of Mercy, oh God, to protect my young husband Yohannes who is fighting in a terrible war in the east and bring him home safely to see his new son who, with thy Devine blessing, will be born strong and healthy. Bless this food, oh Heavenly Father, as we take of thy great abundance on this day of Sabbath, and may every day be God's day as it is in this home.

"Oh God. I ask that you be my rod and staff both in sickness and in health. Deliver me from evil and prepare my soul for a blessed death. And when I walk through the darkness in the valley of death, send an Anyel of Mercy to accompany me. I pray this for all who have accepted your son Yesus, to whom you have given power to become the children of God. I den Hellige navn Gud Fader, Son og den Hellig Ånds! Amen."

"Ah ha! Danke schon, Fräulein!" said Max almost shouting.

"Ich hatte gern Pfannkuchen, bitte!" cried out Greta impatiently wanting to start eating.

The food was passed around and consumed to the happy sounds of edacious young people laughing and talking youthful nonsense in German and broken English. After the hearty breakfast was completed, the brood excused themselves and retreated outdoors, while Astrid sat chatting and drinking Kaffee with Max and Olga.

"Astrid. I hear you speak of conversion. Vat does das mean?" asked Max.

"Our Church teaches that the membership of our congregation be held only by those who by the conduct of their life show that they are living in fellowship with Yesus Christ."

"But how does der conduct of their life show das they are converted?"

"You look at how a person's faith expresses itself in daily life. I try to avoid the wrath of God by being faithful in my work, by reading the New Testament, and by praying partly in my own words and partly through prayers learned by heart."

"You talk about der conversion of children. Does not baptism forgive der infant of Man's original sin, vich vould allow them to enter into der Kingdom of Heaven?"

"My parents believe in infant baptism, but seem not to accept the Bible's teaching of original sin. They say the Holy Spirit is able to create faith in any heart open to Him. What heart is more open than the heart of an infant?"

"Our church teaches das every human being ist born sinful. No human heart, not eben an infant's, ist by nature open to God, but opposed to God und resists Him."

"My parents have said that after infant baptism, the Haugeans look for a conversion experience of conscious acceptance of the grace of God and surrender of life to Him."

"Haf you had a conversion experience dann?" asked Olga.

"No. It is not up to me to be saved, but up to God who works His mercy."

"Fräulein, I think das God ist now vorking His mercy. Ist not your husband in der 3rd Minnesota Regiment?" Asked Max.

"Ya!" said Astrid in a concerned Norwegian fashion, the word inhaled with a short implosive breath of air.

"Ven vas der last time das you heard from him?"

"I have not received a letter from him for over a month now and I am very worried."

"I vas in New Ulm vhere I got this old copy of der 'Minnesota Deutsche Zeitung' und it ist dated August 1, 1862. It says das der 3rd Minnesota surrendered to der Rebel Cavalry under General Forrest on July 13th in Murfreesboro, Tennessee."

"Vi prise Gud!" exclaimed Astrid as she reached for her broach that Johannes had given her.

"There vere two differing reports. Der first by Dr. Butler, a Surgeon of der 3rd Minnesota, said das Colonel Lester, Commander of der 3rd, vas an utterly incompetent leader. He said das Col. Lester vas stupefied und utterly paralyzed mit fear, und so der regiment of fine stalwart men gave up to a parcel of rebel cavalry, numbering about 1000 armed mit shotguns.

"Der other report by Mr. Hathaway, Company I, 3rd Minnesota, said das der enemy numbered about 2000, consisting of 700 of der celebrated Texas Rangers armed mit pistols, two Georgia Regiments of 500 each, und Kentucky troops. He said das der 3rd vas less than 500 strong at der time of der surrender, und their artillery vas low of ammunition. He said das Colonel Lester called a council of var before surrendering. Five officers voted for surrender, und three against."

"Were any of the Minnesota soldiers injured?"

"It says das two vere killed. Corporal Greene, of Company I, und Private Woodburn, of Company C, und six vere vounded, but your husband's name vas not among them."

"Oh thank God! I pray for Yohannes's sake that their surrender was not a cowardly act. He is a proud courageous warrior and he would never live it down."

"Astrid, it matters not vether Colonel Lester's decision vas a cowardly act or a heroic vun. It is simply a matter of your point of view. Ja? Vhen they voted as they did, those men chose life over senseless slaughter. Deep in their heart, der families of der men of der 3rd Minnesota who haf der husbands and sons come home alive vill always see Colonel Lester as a great hero."

"He is right liebsten. It is alvays der vomen and children vho suffer der longest in vars."

"God has vorked His mercy, Astrid. Johannes is alive und vill be coming home to be mit you und his new Säugling!"

With the joyous thought of her husband still being alive, Astrid's heart was lifted up to Heaven so that even her baby was kicking with joy. She reached again for her Viking brooch attached to the front of her dress and could feel a strange warmness emanating from the silver agraffe. As she tilted the brooch up, she could see a pinkish burst of light breaching like a whale from the stygian depths of the amethyst gemstone.

"Odin has also worked his magic for Yohannes," she whispered.

Day of the Warrior

Nous levons avant le soleil! he remembered his grandfather shouting to awaken him before sunrise as he stepped out of his new house and saw the twilight of a new day beginning to light up the sky over the hills beyond the Minnesota River.

His grandfather was both a Voyageur—a French-Canadian who traveled these rivers in a birch-bark canoe from the Great Lakes to the interior of western Canada, and a Coureur de Bois—a man who was familiar with frontier life, spoke an Indian language, and was strong enough to survive like a mountain man in this wild country. It was his grandfather, Jean-Jacques Charbonneau, that he thought of again as he removed his birch canoe from its storage scaffold near his brick house.

Veux-tu faire un voyage avec moi? he would ask the wide-eyed little Matohota inviting him on yet another voyage to explore the enchanted river and the shallow crystal-clear little creeks that feed into it that were always alive with turtles, frogs, muskrats, and an abundance of fish—smallmouth bass, walleye, northern, catfish, and bullheads, where he could see the sandy bottom strewn with rocks and mussel shells from the bow of his magical canoe.

Matohota easily hoisted the heavy birch bark canoe up on his shoulders and balanced it on the cherry wood portage yoke, contoured to fit comfortably over his shoulders that he built into the gunwales of the canoe. Using his hornbeam paddle as a walking stick, he began his trek down to the river.

Of Franco-Dakota decent, he had the dark skin and the countenance of his Dakota grandmother while inheriting the brown hair and the powerful musculature of his French Canadian grandfather. Since his brute strength was apparent as a very young boy combined with his dark reddish brown coloring, and as she was aware of his spiritual gift, his grandmother named him Matohota—Grizzly Bear, as is Dakota custom while maintaining his surname of Charbonneau, as is French custom.

The Ojibway had killed his father, Antoine Charbonneau, or so he was told when Matohota was very young. His mother, Winona, told him stories of how his father often traveled alone by canoe for many weeks to hunt, trap, and raid upriver into Ojibway country. He would return with his canoe filled with goods and loot—tanned moose robes, beaver and otter pelts, eagle feathers, wool trade blankets, iron pipe tomahawks, flintlock rifles, kegs of black powder, bars of lead, cast iron cooking utensils, and as usual, several ripe Ojibway scalps. Not one to keep anything for himself, he would always distribute the cargo to his forever indebted Mdewakaŋtoŋwaŋ kinsmen.

He never came home from one of his solo expeditions. Later, a Dakota raiding party returning from the upper Mississippi River said that they had found his canoe, but no sign of him. For years after people would whisper around campfires that he had taken an Ojibway wife and disappeared into the far north woods, as was not at all uncommon for his hot-blooded voyager breed. They said that was true because there was not an Ojibway alive who could have killed the powerful hunter-trapper-warrior Antoine Charbonneau, a man who the Isaŋti Dakota respectfully named Pahayużataŋka—Great Scalp Taker.

After several months, when it became painfully evident that Antoine would not be coming home, Jean-Jacques took responsibility for the rearing of young Matohota. In those days the Charbonneau family lived in the Piniśa Village of the Mdewakaŋtoŋ Dakota on the north shore of the Minnesota River near the mouth of Nine Mile Creek so called because it was nine miles from Fort Snelling. Among the Dakota it was their custom that brothers of the late husband would take responsibility for support of the widow and the training of an orphaned boy. Since Antoine had no living brothers, both having been killed by the Ojibway and resulting in the bloody vendetta waged by the younger Antoine, it was the wish of his mother, Okadawiŋ, that Jean-Jacques raise their grandson to continue his schooling for the knowledge and abilities required to survive in the coming world, knowing the world as they knew it would soon be gone forever.

Among the Dakota the training of young boys was extremely important since their very existence—present and future, depended upon the skill and bravery of their young men. But for a boy of Franco–Dakota blood to stand strongly on two legs with a foot in both worlds, the task was to assimilate the spiritual world of the Dakota and the material world of the Waśićuŋ.

Matohota carried his canoe across the rim of the prairie. Before descending down through the treed river valley, the path wound past his cornfield as well as several others in the Indian Agency's grid work of individual farms of Maŋkato's Village, adjacent to and south of the Redwood Agency. He set his canoe down with the bow propped over the split rail fence he built around his two-acre field. He knew the fence wouldn't keep out deer, rabbits, and blackbirds, but it did seem to deter roaming horses and especially human raiders since his field was the only one of many untouched by malevolent ravagers in the night.

Although people could easily cross the fence and damage his corn, they knew there would be holy hell to pay if Matohota caught them in his field. Not unlike his powerful grizzly bear namesake, identifying itself with five deep parallel slashes in tree trunks high above the ground with deadly gaff like claws, Matohota identified himself with similar markings chopped with an axe high on vertical poles placed at each of the four corners of the field serving as an ominous warning to all who would maliciously enter there.

Looking at his crop of green corn with ears laden with beadworks of dew sparkling in the morning sun, he contemplated the ranks of long, orderly rows standing like tall green uniformed soldiers with glinting bayonets ready for action. *Strange,* he thought, *how the Waśićuŋ has to separate and line everything up.* He had seen the Iaśića farmers and how they separate all their crops and then plant them between orderly furrows—the corn here, the potatoes there; the soldiers at Fort Ridgley and how they separate the men by rank and then march them around in orderly columns—the captains here, the corporals there; and the Agency school and how they separate their children and set them at desks nailed to the floor in orderly little rows—the first grade here, the second grade there. To understand the Waśićuŋ, you have to first understand how to segregate things and people and place them in straight orderly lines and then hoard everything for yourself.

To understand the Dakota, you have to first understand the chaotic order found in the natural world like the horns of a bull elk with the uniqueness of its irregularities and imperfections, where there are no straight lines. You have to understand how everything is related and fitted together in an amazing variety of plants, birds, insects, fish, reptiles, animals, and people. And you have to be willing to share your harvest with all these relations who then share their bounty with you, thus completing the essential Sacred Circle, the Hoop of the Dakota Nation.

His grandmother, Okadawiŋ, had told him that this was Wasutoŋwi—the Harvest Moon, the third period of the summer cycle, the time of his birth. The time of the year when the sun's power is diminishing and the days are growing shorter with autumn approaching. It is the time for reaping the gifts of Mother Earth from the plants laboriously sown in the spring and nurtured during the summer and celebrating with great feasts and sharing with all our relations. *It is the time of the Turtle,* she said, *to proceed with patience to ensure the stability of our people and our capacity for persistence.*

Matohota turned toward his propped-up canoe when he noticed two people coming up the Agency Road from the southeast. Being Sunday morning, he thought they were probably on their way to the Christian church at the nearby Redwood Agency. But as they approached he recognized two young Wahpekute men he knew to be from Red Legs's Village farther downstream, men whose church was the forest and the very ground they stood on. Dakota men who steadfastly refused to give up the old ways of the chase and could neither understand nor accept the Wašićuŋ policy of confinement on the reservation from the Treaties of 1851 and 1858—the Dakota here, the Wašićuŋ there. Like his father Antoine, they were free hunter-trapper-warriors and would not participate in government acculturation programs, which struck at the very heart of Dakota village life.

"Wah! Brother-in-law, I didn't recognize you with your hair cut and those farmer clothes on. I thought you were an Iašića scarecrow standing out there, innit!" Wasuduta said in Dakota knowing that Matohota was fluent in their language as well as French and English.

"Didn't recognize you either, standing up and walking sober like that. I only see you when you're staggering around or passed-out someplace," Matohota retorted jokingly, as is Dakota custom to badger your brothers-in-law.

"Matohota, I heard you were bootlegging whiskey for those traders and staggering around drunk yourself like those other breeds!" said Hepi coming to the aid of his older brother.

"Heard about you too, Hepi. They said you were passed out in that Iašića brewery in New Ulm with your feet sticking out from under a table! Said they recognized your moccasins, dirty with big holes in them," Matohota snickered, always getting in the last word. Since what these sober Dakotapi detested most in life, next to the Iašića, were Dakotapi who hung around the trading posts and towns like New Ulm in drunken stupors, Matohota knew that the best way to get their goat was to accuse them of getting drunk on American whiskey, or even worse, Iašića—German, beer.

Both Wasuduta and Hepi laughed and shook hands with the smiling Matohota as Wasuduta said, "Good to see you again in your usual good spirits, innit!"

"Where you going hunting?" Matohota asked seeing that they were leaning on flintlock trade rifles with bandolier bags and powder horns hanging on opposite hips while dressed for the chase with leggings, breechclouts, and moccasins. Both were shirtless with bandannas wrapped around their heads with their long hair in braids.

"We're on our way to Redwood River country," said Hepi.

"The Iašića have killed all the deer around the Big Cottonwood, innit," said Wasuduta.

"Then they sold all the hides to the traders without even sharing with us," added Hepi.

"Now those Iašića are stealing land near our village and they keep pushing us farther up this way," said Wasuduta.

"Then they get drunk and take target practice at our children and abuse our women!" admonished Hepi angrily.

"Hate's getting pretty strong around here; just waiting for something really bad to happen," said Matohota with a look of despair.

"Matohota, the Soldier's Lodge has been saying bad things about our relatives who have taken up Iašića farming, cut their hair, and wear pantaloons, like you," said Hepi.

"I know. That's why many of our people around here have had crops damaged or their fields burned. I have a big family to feed; if I catch anybody trying to destroy my crops, I'll stop them!" said Matohota assuredly as his blood began to heat up.

"Matohota, I believe you, innit. You are a powerful grizzly bear and a fierce warrior like your father, Pahayužataŋka. You protect your home and your family like that and our Isaŋti Wahpekute people have great respect for you—our relative, and your ways."

"We're not going to starve again like last winter. Even if I walk the Wašićuŋ Road, I'm still a Dakota and that's why I can talk like that!" said Matohota.

"That's true, you live like an Iašića with your plowed field and your brick house, but at the same time you are a hunter and share with your relatives like the Dakota you are," added Hepi.

"He takes the best from both worlds, innit!" added Wasuduta.

"The problem is jealousy. Lot of our people around here don't like it that we get special favors from the government agent for taking up Wašićuŋ ways, but I don't care what they like!" scowled Matohota as he crouched under his canoe and began to lift it.

"And where are you going?" asked Hepi.

"Up Birch Coulee Creek."

"What's up there?"

"Purple coneflowers."

"Wah! Flowers?" exclaimed Hepi as if trying to envision the vicious grizzly bear of a minute ago that was ripping apart field raiders now picking flowers.

"Kuŋśi Okadawiŋ wants me to get some medicine roots for my little boy's swollen throat," answered Matohota balancing his craft and reaching for his paddle.

As Matohota started down into the wooded valley of the Minnesota River, Wasuduta tapped on the canoe with the barrel of his rifle and said, "Brother-in law! Again, I will see you, innit."

The path to the river was steep and slippery, covered with a canopy of leaves, smelled of damp decaying wood and ivy undergrowth, resonated with the sounds of insects, and its muggy air was alive with swarming mosquitoes. As Matohota finally reached the river at the ferryboat landing below, he was reeling from the exertion and felt he had been eaten alive. He set his load down on the south dock and carefully rolled it over onto the water.

After wiping the sweat from his eyes, he could see the ferry still moored to the loading dock on the other side of the Minnesota since it was still early with no travelers about. Anyone wanting to cross could ring one of the cast iron bells hanging from a framework on pilings securing a system of pulleys and rope on either side of the river. The ferryboat operator, Hugh Miller, living in a house a short distance away on the north side, would come out and transport you the fifty yards or so across the river, for a small fee of course.

He rocked the canoe sideways several times to allow water to begin to moisten the dried birch covering up to the outwales of his five thwart vessel. He climbed into the stern, found a comfortable position sitting on his heels on the cedar planking, sprinkled tobacco onto the water, pushed-off from the dock, and began paddling the short distance upriver toward the mouth of Birch Coulee Creek.

Au début de nos voyages, on commençait par jeter du tabac a l'eau pour montrer notre respect au pouvoir de la nature, he could hear his grandfather reminding him to always offer tobacco to the waters when going on a voyage, out of respect for the powers of nature.

Respect, he thought. *That is what being a Dakota is all about. Respect for the Great Mystery, the sacred ceremonies, the relationship of all creation as part of our Sacred Circle, and for the powers of nature like grand-père Jean-Jacques talked about.* His grandpa learned these things when he took an Indian wife and entered into a kinship relationship with Dakota people. He learned to share what little he had—game, weapons, tools, and harvest, and even his very life if need be, with his relatives who in turn shared theirs with him. *These are our ways; this circle of sharing that is held sacred by my people and is the center of the Sacred Circle of our world, the sacred hoop of our Dakota Nation.*

His grandpa talked about his French people who came into this country beginning in the days of his grandfather's grandfathers. Voyageurs and Coureurs de Bois from Quebec, Trois Rivières, and from France itself who took Dakota or Ojibway wives and brought blankets, cooking utensils, weapons, trinkets, and brandy to the Dakota who in turn showered them with valuable furs and a secure comfortable life. And from these marriages was created a whole new Tribe of people—the Métis.

The morning sun was now over the prairie horizon bordering the river valley cut deeply through it by torrents of ancient glacial runoff. The sunshine and the cool breeze provided welcome relief from his trek through the steaming gauntlet of ravenous mosquitoes. Paddling against the moderate current was easy as Matohota headed upstream listening to the water slapping against the birch side panels of his craft and dripping from his silent paddle while smelling the purifying scent of cedar from the wooden framework and floorboards of his canoe.

He thought again about grandpa Charbonneau who talked about the Americans who later came into this country in the days of his youth after the War of 1812 and built a great fort and opened trading posts where Dakota people could get blankets, cooking utensils, weapons, trinkets, and whiskey, but now on credit, for precious furs. The Americans, who brought their own wives, acknowledged kinship with the Dakota by calling them the children of the Great White Father who they could trust because, in the Dakota world, a father would never abandon his children. But what the Americans also brought with them was the black pestilence of greed because soon the little furred animals were gone and the Dakota were left with nothing but their land. Soon that too would be gone.

He thought about his relatives—Wasuduta and Hepi and the terribly sobering things said about the Iašića. *The Iašića*, he thought, *the bad talkers as we call them in our Dakota language because of their guttural sounding speech, the Germans. The Iašića have taken our land, run off all the game, and refuse to share their harvest. They shame our women and frighten our children. They are outsiders no different than the hated Ojibway!* He sang an appropriate warrior's song taught him by one of his Lakota relatives:

> *Tehaŋtaŋ naŋtaŋ pelo*
> *Tehaŋtaŋ naŋtaŋ pelo*
> *Tehaŋtaŋ naŋtaŋ pelo*
> *Tehaŋtaŋ naŋtaŋ pelo*
> *Tehaŋtaŋ naŋtaŋ pelo*

Iašíća ki nake ćeya pelo
Hey hey ho.

Matohota arrived at the outlet of Birch Coulee Creek and was pleased to see that the water level was still high enough to navigate his long canoe. The foliage was thick along the edges of the creek and filled with song sparrows and common yellowthroats. He paddled up the creek against a fairly strong current and occasionally ducking under fallen logs or sliding over sand bars with disturbed wood ducks exploding from backwaters. Reaching his destination, he pulled the stern of his canoe up into the thick underbrush of the creek and, taking his hornbeam paddle, climbed up the steep bank to the prairie above.

He carefully looked out across the prairie before exposing himself since he knew that the Iašíća were now living on this side of the river and there was always the possibility of a vengeful roving Ojibway war party in the region. Seeing that all was clear, he followed a deer path through the tall big bluestem across the prairie hills to where he knew was a field of perennial purple coneflower.

He remembered coming to this prairie as a little boy with his kuŋši Okadawiŋ. *Who is that woman?* He had asked as he pointed to what he saw as a beautiful young Indian woman standing in a glowing purplish pink light with red face paint wearing a long fringed white buckskin dress embellished with red, purple, and blue floral quillwork.

Okadawiŋ looked to where he was pointing. *What you are seeing may be a Medicine Spirit! Let's go closer to see if any plants live there,* she said. What they found was a field of daisy-like prairie flowers she called *Ićahpehu*—purple coneflower.

Grandson, she said with solemn emotion in her voice, *you have the gift of the Medicine Bear! My grandfather was a healer, a Medicine Man, named Šiyaka. He said that the bear was one of the most powerful of all animals and their spirit could convey knowledge to a healer. So those with Bear Medicine were considered the most powerful of all Medicine Men!*

Although the bear is fierce and quick-tempered in many ways, she continued, *he pays attention to plants that no other animal even notices. The bear can see the healing spirits of these plants and digs them for his own use since no other animal has such good claws for digging roots! You must nurture your gift by listening to the voice of the Medicine Bear who will bring you healing power through…*

Matohota's thoughts were interrupted as he stopped to examine the tracks of two people who had crossed the deer path and hurriedly continued across the grassy field. He examined the crushed grass and could see that the juice that had exuded was still very fresh. *Iaśića,* he concluded because men wearing heavy boots made the tracks. *Probably out hunting deer. And they're still around here somewhere!*

Matohota proceeded with extreme caution lest he be mistaken for a deer. As he soon arrived at the prairie flowered hillside adorned with flowering spurge, red milkweed, rigid goldenrod, and the magical purple coneflower, he did not see the beautiful buckskin clad woman again, but he had a strong sense of her presence. The prairie garden had attracted dozens of Monarch Butterflies and was of such regal brilliance that he experienced a strong sense of spiritual humility and began to pray aloud in Dakota.

"O Tuŋkaŋśidaŋ Wakaŋtaŋka, Tate Topa, Peżuta Mato, omaśika ka omakiya namagu he! O de peżuta wan uŋ omayakihe uŋ oyate owićakiye do. Ka he waŋna hokśidaŋ mitawa kiŋ he uŋ owa kiya waćiŋ. He uŋ ećeda yedo mitakuye un nipta yedo. Mitakuye owasu!"

Matohota walked over to the nearest plant and pushed the pointed end of his hardwood paddle deep into the soil clockwise at each of the four directions around the plant then lifted the flower with the leaves, stem, and roots intact from the earth. He repeated the process with three more plants and tied them into a bundle and shook the dirt from the roots.

As he placed the coneflowers into a bandoleer bag slung across his chest, he heard a rifle report from over the hill and immediately thought the Iaśića hunters had seen a deer. Then he heard a woman screaming followed by another shot. He reached for his paddle; his only weapon besides a small Green River trade knife sheathed on his belt and ran in the direction of the shooting. He stopped in heavy undergrowth on the other side of the hill and crouched behind a bush when he saw a young Indian girl screaming in terror and running in his direction although she had not seen him. Following her by about ten paces and gaining fast was a tall, bearded white man carrying his spent rifle in one hand and brandishing a large bowie knife in the other. He could see the second man about fifteen yards away with his back to him standing over the bloodied body of a woman and busy reloading his rifle.

Mon Dieu! he thought. *He shot her!*

As the girl ran past she stumbled as she saw him out of the corner of her eye. The enraged Matohota stood and with both hands swung his hardwood paddle at the running man and hit him with a powerful blow on the left side of his neck almost decapitating him as blood spewed out like a pulsating red geyser as the fatally wounded man fell to the ground with his life pumping out of him.

As the other man turned to see what was happening, Matohota, like a charging grizzly bear, had already covered half the distance between the two. As the startled white man raised his rifle and pulled the trigger with the ramrod still in the barrel, he shouted "Schießt!"

Matohota reached him in full stride and plunged the sharpened point of his paddle through the man's chest with the tremendous force of his momentum slamming him to the ground and killing him instantly. He yanked the paddle out of the German with one foot on his belly as he drew his knife and sliced the scalp off the man's head. He held the blood-dripping scalp up to the clouds as he let out a cry of victory that seemed to explode across the prairie, like the detonation of a time bomb releasing all of his pent up rage. The rage built up by many years of painful humiliation of his Isaŋti Mdewakaŋtoŋwaŋ people by the Americans and, lately, the disrespectful and abusive behavior of the Iaśiĉa, the Germans.

He stuffed the scalp under his belt and knelt to examine the fallen woman. He could see that she had died instantly with a large caliber rifle ball in her back as they were probably running from her sotted assailants. He ran back to find the young girl. She was sitting near where she had stumbled and seemed to be in shock as she trembled and stared wide-eyed into space. He picked her up and she began whimpering for her mother as he carried her back to Birch Coulee Creek. He sat her into the bow of his craft and could see she wasn't injured and couldn't be more than eight years old.

As he rinsed the blood and grime from his paddle and placed it in the canoe, he whispered to her "Inina yankapi iĉanna wagikta," knowing Dakota children are trained to be very silent when the enemy is about.

Returning to the scene of the bloodshed, he went to the body of the woman. He turned her over and recognized her as a young woman from the village of Taoyateduta, on Crow Creek a few miles north of his village. Near her was a bag full of tipsina—turnips, which explained what they were doing on this side of the river. With his knife he quickly dug a shallow grave in the soft earth and placed her in it and covered her.

He picked up the dead man's rifle with the ramrod still in the barrel. *No wonder the rifle didn't fire,* he thought as he pulled the ramrod out of the barrel and slid it into the thimbles. *Crazy drunk forgot to put a percussion cap on the nipple!* Seeing that it was a fine well-oiled half-stock plains rifle of about .45-calibre with an octagonal barrel and a shoulder strap, he slung it over his shoulder as well as the white man's accoutrements bag and returned to the body of the first fallen man. He quickly relieved him of his scalp and placed it under his belt with his companion's. Since the dead man would no longer need his large stag-handled bowie knife, he also slid the sheathed knife under his belt, picked up the second rifle noting that it was identical to the other half-stock and made his way back to the creek.

The swift current at the mouth of the Birch Coulee Creek had propelled him well out into the mainstream of the Minnesota where he was able to glide downstream in its current to the ferry boat landing with little effort. The girl had curled up on the floorboards and fallen asleep from the exhaustion of her horrifying experience.

He looked at his paddle with a newfound sense of pride since it had served him admirably as a cane, oar, shovel, and deadly weapon in a morning that seemed to have happened in a heartbeat. He felt the solid heft of the finely grained reddish-brown hornbeam hardwood called caŋmaza—ironwood, by the Dakota and probably considered too heavy as a paddle for a lesser man. His grandfather had modeled it after canoe paddles he had seen used by the Tlingit Indians in western Canada. Their skill in using them as weapons, and often their only weapons, was highly respected by hostile and friendly neighbors alike.

The paddle came up to his armpit while standing and was as wide as his hand with outstretched fingers was long at its widest point. Jean-Jacques had told him to keep it pointed with somewhat of an edge on it at all times for emergencies not unlike what he had just survived.

Chacun d'entre nous avait sa rame recouverte de dessins sculptes, he remembered his grandpa telling him how each Voyageur had his own paddle covered in hand carved designs.

On one side of the elaborately carved paddle was the worn but legible phrase,

Nous créons de nouveaux sentiers dans ces contrées sauvages
qui mènent partout dans cette nouvelle terre,
Le Canada

On the other side was the inscription,

Jean-Jacques Charbonneau
Trois Rivières, Nouvelle-France
1838

1838, he thought. *On my tenth birthday, grand-père Jean-Jacques gave me the paddle to tell me something good about his life.*

"Merci, grand-père," he said aloud since on the river he could feel his grandfather's presence. "Your 'rame' has served me well today!"

Matoȟota reached the still deserted south ferryboat landing and pulled his canoe up onto the shore. He unloaded his cargo and helped the girl step onto the dry ground. She appeared reasonably calm but still seemed unable to walk. He pulled his craft into the underbrush until it was well hidden from view and turned it over leaving his paddle on the thwarts. He cut some branches and laid them on the exposed white birch bottom as an added precaution. He shouldered one of the rifles and the bandoleer bag of accoutrements, picked up the young girl with one powerful arm and with the second rifle cradled in the other for use as a walking staff, began the quarter-mile climb back up the steep river trail.

As he neared home his Isaŋti Waȟpekute wife, Waȟćaziwiŋ, saw him carrying the young girl and came running down the road to help him.

"Kuŋśi Okadawiŋ ekta aya," he said.

As she took the girl from the exhausted Matoȟota, he stood with perspiration running down his mosquito bitten body and soaking his blood stained clothes. He wiped the sweat from his brow, slung the second rifle over his shoulder, and trudged unsteadily behind her to the house.

Waȟćaziwiŋ had taken the child to Okadawiŋ, an herb woman who lived in a traditional bark lodge built for her behind their brick home. Seeming to know immediately that the child was in shock and suffering from mild dehydration, Okadawiŋ laid her down on a bed, removed her clothes, and began to wash her with a cool, damp cloth. As soon as the girl had cooled off somewhat, Okadawiŋ found her supply of hokśi ćekpawaȟća—pasque flower, and prepared her a cup of tea boiled with the crushed herb. In a very short order, the soothing effect of the herb took hold and the girl calmed down and fell asleep.

Seeing that the young girl was doing well and feeling recovered from his exertion, Matoȟota entered his house and saw his two wide-eyed young boys staring at him from the table. He gave his oldest boy his bandoleer bag containing the purple coneflowers and told him to take it and his little brother to see kuŋśi Okadawiŋ. "She's going to take care of his sore throat," he said in Dakota as he walked the boys to the door.

The two-story brick house was built during late spring as a gift from the Indian Agent Galbraith, or Galbraith wanted it to seem like a gift since he knew that, to the Dakota, a gift was a means of initiating a kinship obligation. Then Matoȟota and his family would be obligated to reciprocate by listening to him and doing as he said. But Matohota knew it was owed him by the government for becoming a farmer Indian—cutting his hair, wearing store-bought clothes, farming his own plot of land, and hoarding his own food in his new basement.

He knew it was the communal kinship life of the Dakota the Americans objected to since it was the very essence of their culture. Destroy their system of communal hunts, gardens, and of sharing and you've dealt a fatal blow to the heart of Dakota culture. He had no obligation to Galbraith or any Wašiću, nor would he allow that to happen. He was doing these things for food to help insure the survival of his family and of all his relations because without food, they die.

He leaned the two rifles in a corner, placed the bowie knife and the bag of accoutrements on the table, and laid the two fresh scalps in a painted parfleche container used for that purpose. He hung the scalp case from a nail over the outside doorsill, like a painted shield designating the lodge of a warrior for all to see.

He removed his shoes and soggy clothing, poured cold water into the washbasin, and wiped himself down with a soaked towel. Since the soiled garments were the only set of store-bought clothes he owned or had conceded to buy on credit from the greedy traders, he put on his lighter and more appropriate breechcloth and moccasins—appropriate, that is, for the Isaŋti Mdewakaŋtoŋ warrior he had become.

He sat in a chair with his legs stretched out and his feet on another chair, wrapped a long damp trade cloth around his head turban fashion, and, with the cool refreshing breeze flowing in from the wide-open windows, finally began to breathe easily and think about the morning's tragic events. He could hear the church bell ring from the nearby Episcopal Church—still in construction and with no roof, as he again sang his warrior's song to the rhythm of the bell:

> *Dakota hokšidaŋ*
> *Tehaŋtaŋ naŋtaŋ pelo*
> *Tehaŋtaŋ naŋtaŋ pelo*
> *Tehaŋtaŋ naŋtaŋ pelo*
> *Tehaŋtaŋ naŋtaŋ pelo*
> *Iašića ki nake ćeya pelo*
> *Hey hey ho.*

MONDAY, AUGUST 18, 1862

Mita Makoće!

It was dark and silent in the tipi except for the sound of burning wood. He was lying on his back with his head on the woman's lap. She was wearing a black dress and shawl with her long black hair tied above her head and spilling loosely over her shoulders. When the mysterious woman looked down at him, he was startled to see the left half of her oval Ojibway face painted black while the other half was emblazoned with black and white vertical stripes. He was totally mesmerized by her falconine beauty as the fire rhythmically lit her face and cast an ominous shadow on the conical wall behind her. Emerging out of the eerie blackness was her white painted hand with a long extended talon-like finger slowly reaching toward him. As she touched his solar plexus a clap of thunder exploded in his ears and the simultaneous shock of a lightning bolt flashed through his body.

"Wah!" he shouted as he sat up in bed. He looked around and, to his relief, recognized the sanctuary of his grandparent's lodge. He breathed easier as he could see the propitious light of a new day entering through the chinks in the bark siding of the east wall. He noticed that grandpa had a small fire in the middle of the lodge that was smoldering with coals glowing in the semi-darkness like red, orange and yellow fire opals. He put on his moccasins and strode over to the waning fire—pushing back the hot coals, restacking the wood, and blowing on the radiant embers. As the flames burst and grew larger, he could see that his grandparents were already out of bed and, knowing them, hard at work outside.

Wayuhi wrapped a blanket over his bare shoulders, picked up his flute and grabbed his two halters on the way out into the morning cooled by a recent thunderstorm as the sun was rising into a crimson-red sky over the Minnesota River Valley on that ill-fated day. Kuŋśi was building her cooking fire as he walked over to her.

"Kuŋśi. Do you need any help?"

"No, grandson. Go ahead and see to your horses."

"Where's grandpa?"

"He went to council with Iŋyaŋgmani. They're going to talk about the warning you brought to us."

"When will he be back?"

"I don't know. I'll have some hot food ready soon so don't go far."

Wayuhi walked past the corral that held his mare and colt to the back pasture west of the lodge. He noticed that someone had rounded up three horses out of the pasture and had them haltered and tied to the pasture fence. He blew a high-pitched note on his eagle bone whistle carried around his neck and saw

Tataŋkayamni emerge from a stand of choke cherry trees across the pasture and come trotting toward him as he opened the pasture gate.

After haltering the stallion, he did the same with the mare and led them back through the village toward to the Yellow Medicine for fresh water with the colt eagerly prancing behind them. As he passed near Iŋyaŋgmani's house, he could see several horses grazing nearby belonging to men who were attending the meeting of the Soldier's Lodge. The path dropped down to the flood plain, through the Three Sisters Gardens, and down again to the river.

He released the horses leaving them free to stand with their feet in the shallows of the Yellow Medicine as they drank. The sun had risen well above the horizon and was filling the deep gorge with its vitalizing warmth. Since his grandfather had told him that in the life of a Dakota there was only one inevitable responsibility—the daily recognition of the Great Mystery, Wayuhi made his way to a deep pool upstream from the horses, removed his blanket, breechcloth, and moccasins, and plunged into the clear, cool water. With his purification bath completed, he dressed and stood facing the sun to offer a prayer that his people would live.

He sat on a large flat rock in the sunlight and began playing the four songs of Ćotaŋka on his flute as he could hear thunder rolling in from the south. The songs filled him with a strange feeling of personal power and self-confidence as the music mixed with the distant thunder echoed through the high-walled ravine. Even the mustangs seemed in a sanguine disposition as they climbed up out of the rock-strewn riverbed to graze on the succulent bottom grass.

When Wayuhi arrived back at his grandparent's lodge, Ćetaŋiyotaŋka had returned from the meeting and was sitting at kuŋśi's fire. "Grandson," he said. "Iŋyaŋgmani and the other men of the Soldier's Lodge believe in the power of your White Eagle Ghost medicine. We are going to prepare for war but we know not who we fight!"

"Could it be the Big Knives?" Asked Wayuhi using the Dakota word to describe the Americans because of their omnipresent swords.

"No, the Big Knives are fighting their own war against each other. The traders say that the northern Big Knives are losing that war. We believe will be attacked by the Iaśića. They want our land and will not hesitate to kill us since they have no respect for us."

"What will we do now?"

"We have sent a warning to the Mdewakaŋtoŋ and the Waȟpekute at Red-wood Agency since the Iaśića are their neighbors. Then we need to take our people to the Center of the World."

"Where do you believe that is?"

"The Isaŋti believed that, a long time ago, it was at a place we called Mdote—a place where the great rivers flow as one, that the Waśićuŋ now call Mendota near Fort Snelling. But today it is the center of the Waśićuŋ world where whiskey now flows from a place of evil called Pig's Eye. It is there that they make the whiskey that is poisoning our people!"

"Our Northern Sissetoŋwaŋ relations have said that the Center of the World is at the Otter Tail Village of Tataŋkanażiŋ," said Wayuhi.

"I have heard them speak of that."

"They say that Earth Mother gives birth to great rivers at that place. From the Center of the World, the Minnesota River flows southeast, the Red River flows north, and, not too far from there, she gives birth to the Big Sioux River which flows south."

"They said that that was a holy place of the Ancient Ones."

"That is true. On a bluff high above Otter Tail Village is the big earth mound of the Ancient Ones. From the top of that mound, like from the top of the world, you can see Big Stone Lake far to the southeast that empties into the Minnesota and then flows to the Mississippi; and then you can see Otter Tail Lake, called Lac Travers by the French, that empties into the Red River of the North and flows to the Grandmother Land—Canada. Those rivers are like ancient roads to the world. Hoka! It is a place of great power!"

"I remember the French Voyageurs coming through here in great canoes when I was a young boy. They were always traveling north during the spring thaw when the Red River was moving fast and straight to trade for winter pelts from the northern Tribes and they always had gifts for the children of our village."

As they spoke, kuŋśi brought a pail of fresh drinking water with a buffalo horn dipper. Then, after giving them wooden bowls filled with hot venison and corn stew, she said "Grandson, your ina Wamnuwiŋ is living near the Redwood Agency. Her husband goes crazy on the white man's whiskey and treats her bad. Sometimes he is gone for many days and does not take care of his family. I go down there during each new moon and bring food for them. Otherwise, they would starve. If there is to be a war there, I fear for our daughter and little grandchildren with no one there to look after them."

"Which village does she live in?" asked Wayuhi.

"They moved to the Village of Red Middle Voice at Rice Creek."

"The whiskey drinking is very bad in the villages down there, grandson," said Ćetaŋiyotaŋka. "Since we are expecting an annuity payment from the Indian Agent Galbraith at any time now, the traders have been bringing in whiskey from Pig's Eye by canoe and giving it to the Indians there and putting marks in their big books. Then when the payment finally comes, the traders will bring out their big books and take all of their money again."

"The whiskey feeds a bad spirit in their body that drives them crazy, it makes them fight among themselves and even kill each other," said kuŋśi. "And after they've sold everything they have, they steal from their own relatives for that devil spirit in them. It makes them sick until they can buy more whiskey from those black-hearted traders. And now almost every Iaśića house is a whiskey store!"

"Grandson," said Ćetaŋiyotaŋka. "Today we are going to harvest our corn, squash, and what beans we can get since they are not yet ripe. We want you and Ćaske to go to Rice Creek to ask your ina Wamnuwiŋ to come back here with you. She must understand that it is not safe there for her children."

"What if her husband is there?"

"Hepaŋ is our relative. Try to bring him here so we can help him to return to his center, return to our ceremonial ways that will lead him from witkopi ekta wiwićamdeza—drunkenness to sobriety."

"Where is Ćaske?"

"He is busy preparing for the trip. Those are his horses you saw haltered and tied to the back fence."

"What will happen when we return?"

"Then we will leave for the Center of the World—the Otter Tail Village of Tataŋkaźiŋ—Standing Buffalo!"

The morning was warming up rapidly as a humid easterly breeze spilled over the bluffs and coursed through the deep river valley. Dark clouds from a thunderstorm farther south that was moving east would occasionally obscure the sunlight providing some relief from the morning heat. The old Peźutazi—Yellow Medicine, Road passed above the village and followed the southeasterly course of the Minnesota River, above the flood plain, all the way to Redwood Agency and beyond. The wagon road was well traveled and therefore the ride through the shaded wooded areas and across several creeks was easy going.

Wayuhi sat comfortably astride the bareback Tataŋkayamni in the morning heat wearing only a breechcloth, leggings, and moccasins, with his otter skin bag secured to his belt. He wore his hair loosely with the white eagle feather of

Ćotaŋka attached to his hair and hanging down. And strapped across his back was his sheathed elk horn bow and quivered arrows.

Before beginning their short trip, they stopped briefly at the nearby village of grandpa Mazamani to pay their respects and to give him the smoke tanned robe of a large buffalo bull Wayuhi had brought him. Grandpa was overjoyed by the gift and shared his pipe with his young takożapi wica—grandsons, and prayed that their trip would be fruitful and that they would return home safely. Before they left, Mazamani gave Wayuhi a knife in a fully quilled white buckskin sheath to be worn around his neck as a symbol of his Isaŋti people. The handle of the knife was crafted from a fossilized tusk of Uŋktehi, while the sharp, double-edged dagger-like blade was made of flint knapped obsidian.

Hoka! Wayuhi thought as he held the old knife. So you are Uŋktehi, the Dreadful Ones, the Spirits of the Waters. Grandpa Mazamani said you are both an old man and an old woman who changed yourselves into a great animal. He said he has seen your bones but has never seen you walk on this earth and believes that you live in the water. He said you are at war with the great Thunderbird and are the cause behind great floods and drownings. Your spirits, he said, have long ago taken a liking to our Isaŋti—Knife Lodge, people and will watch over us as we travel the rivers.

Ćaske followed closely behind riding a roan stallion and leading two pinto mares. "Ahhh brother," he called out. "How long will we be down there?"

"Long enough to find ina Wamnuwiŋ and try to bring her back home," he answered sliding the knife back into its sheath tied around his neck.

"That's too bad. I have a sweetheart named Waśtena—honey, living down there in Shakopee's Village."

Wayuhi looked back and nodded his head.

"It's just a little ways from where we're going."

Wayuhi smiled and shook his head as if in disbelief of his younger brother who seems to find pretty young girls everywhere he goes.

"Waśtena has a very pretty sister."

"I've heard there are lots of pretty young girls among the Mdewakaŋtoŋwan."

"But those are mostly one or two-pony girls, brother. You would have to give six ponies for this one! Aaaa!"

"Never have I seen a six-pony girl."

"Then you have to see this one, brother!"

Wayuhi suddenly pulled-up his horse and motioned for Ćaske to also stop. In the stillness, they heard a distant gunshot that echoed through the valley quickly followed by another. Wayuhi slid off his horse and quietly sauntered over to the edge of the road where he had a clear view of the river.

"Rifle shots. They seemed to be coming from over there," Wayuhi said pointing across the river.

"The Iašića live over there now. They were probably shooting at a deer. They are pitiful hunters."

"Why is that?"

"We always find game that has been wounded and run until they bleed to death. They don't even try to chase them because they can't run in those heavy boots and wool clothes. And then they trip on their own beards! Aaaa!"

They paused for a while watching the other side of the river and, since all seemed quiet, remounted to continue their journey. Having crossed Echo Creek, they were now only a few miles from Rice Creek Village. After struggling with his mares in the creek, Ćaske finally caught up with Wayuhi.

"Brother," he called out, as he pulled on the ropes of the mares distracted by a nearby grassy field. "I was talking about ponies. In the old days, our people could tell if we were in for a bad winter by watching our ponies. If their coats got really thick, we knew we were in for a long, cold winter."

"We still do that back home."

"But these people around here, these Mdewakaŋtoŋ. They don't have many horses, so they watch the Iašića. If the Iašića put up a lot of wood during the Moon of the Falling Leaves, then they know they're in for a bad winter! Aaaa!"

"Ho, then they found a use for those 'pitiful hunters'!" Wayuhi said laughing.

As they approached a long steep upward incline, they dismounted and began walking their horses. As Wayuhi thought about what Ćaske had said about the Mdewakaŋtoŋ not having many horses, it didn't seem as funny.

"Ah little brother," said Wayuhi. "Last night kuŋši said that quite a few people down here have given up our traditional Dakota ways—they have cut their hair, wear pantaloons, given up hunting, and like that. They are trying to become like the Wašićuŋ!"

"That's true. But they are on the Wašićuŋ Road because they have no choice," answered Ćaske.

"For me there is no choice either; only to walk the good Red Road of my Isaŋti Dakota people. It's like I said, the Great Mystery has made us different from the Wašićuŋ; if we were to walk his road, the Spirits would be offended and kill us!"

"If they leave the reservation to go hunting, Galbraith will cut off their rations and they will starve and die anyway since the Iašića have killed off all the game around here. Last winter the people here at Rice Creek ate their horses rather than take orders or provisions from that Galbraith!"

"Hoka! Then they are good, proud Ikćeoyate—natural people!" exclaimed Wayuhi. "I too would kill my horse, my great buffalo runner, before I took orders from a Waśićuŋ!"

"Red Middle Voice says that we humiliate ourselves by taking handouts from the Waśićuŋ. He says that we have become like squealing little pigs in a pig pen suckled by the tits of the Agency."

"Ho!"

"He says our leaders did not have the right to make their marks and give away the sacred ground where lie the bones of our ancestors, where our grandfathers have walked. He says it was the whiskey that made their marks for them!"

"Ho! Standing Buffalo says that only by walking the Red Road will we remain a strong people and resist the evil temptations of the Waśićuŋ," said Wayuhi. "We do not take handouts from anyone. We follow the buffalo!"

"Red Middle Voice, who even though he is not so young himself, has attracted many young warriors to his village."

"Why is that?"

"You have seen how a pack wolf behaves in the presence of a wolf chief. With its ears laid back and head lowered, the pack wolf licks the wolf chief's face and tucks in its tail. By lying down and exposing its soft belly and throat, a wolf is showing its willingness to follow orders, to obey. If it didn't, it fears it would be killed. That is how our leaders behave in the presence of the Big Knives—the Americans, for all to see. They have lost the respect of the young warriors."

"But what does he tell them?"

"He knows the young warriors hate the authority of the Waśićuŋ and they want to challenge them since our own leaders have been castrated like geldings. So he speaks against those leaders who take away our pride, the agents who take our freedom, the traders who take our money, and the bootleggers who take our lives. He refuses to call the White Chief 'Great Father'. That tells the young warriors that we are not children, but good manly warriors, and better than any Waśićuŋ!"

"Why did uncle Hepaŋ come here? Kuŋśi said whiskey runs him."

"Red Middle Voice and these young people here are helping him move from witkopi ekta wiwićamdeza, helping him cleanse that evil spirit from his body. He is having a hard time, but even if kuŋśi doesn't think so, he is getting better since bootleggers are afraid to come around here any more. They know they will be killed!"

The Peżutazi Road rose to the tallgrass prairie above the thickly wooded river valley. The cooling breeze of the higher ridge seemed to whisper through the tall big bluestem as many Tribes of insects and birds filled the tall grasses with their songs of life.

"I heard grandpa say there's a lot of whiskey drinking in the villages down here. How did that happen?" asked Wayuhi.

"These people here—the Mdewakaŋtoŋ and the Waḣpekute, have only been around here since I was a little boy. Grandpa says they came from the Mississippi River country—Kaposia, Red Wing, Wabasha, and places like that, after the Big Knives cheated them out of their land. They've been around drunken soldiers, river men, and bootlegging traders as long as anyone can remember. Many have been drinking whiskey for a long time, so long that now they can't live without it and can brawl and cuss as good as any White man."

"So they die without it?"

"Some of them have the whiskey sickness where they get big stomachs, turn yellow, and die the slow death. It's painful, brother, to see how our people have been poisoned by that evil whiskey!"

"What does uncle Taoyateduta do to stop the whiskey and the loss of our ways?"

"Nothing! Kuŋśi said he is on the Waśićuŋ Road himself. The only traditional Mdewakaŋtoŋ left around here are at Rice Creek, but Red Middle Voice is having a hard time keeping whiskey out of his village. It's everywhere!"

"How about the Waḣpekute?"

"Iŋkpaduta—Red Point, and his people are somewhere out west with the Lakota after killing over thirty Waśićuŋ south of here in Iowa country about five winters ago. The Big Knives never could catch him. And the people in Red Legs's Village are living close to the Iaśića at New Ulm where they make whiskey and beer and keep taking more of our land, but they still manage to hold on to our old ways."

"Why did Iŋkpaduta kill all those people?" asked Wayuhi.

"Some crazy drunken Waśićuŋ murdered his brother Siŋtomniduta who was their Chief and several of their women and children with axes. After that, the killings continued back and forth for about two winters when the Waśićuŋ somehow took all their guns, even though it was during the Hard Moon and they needed to hunt."

"Hoka!"

"Then, during the following Moon of the Sore-eyes, Iŋkpaduta who was now a Chief came back with new guns and killed thirty of them at a place called Lake

Okoboji. After that they crossed into Minnesota at a place where they made whiskey and killed twelve more."

"The Waśićuŋ called that a massacre."

"It wasn't a massacre! It was a war! Those Waśićuŋ were well armed. And most of them were bad men—murderers, horse thieves, and bootleggers, who deserved to die. That is one of the reasons Iŋkpaduta is considered a great leader among the young warriors at Rice Creek."

"What are the other reasons?"

"He is strong in these ceremonial ways, follows the buffalo and not the Waśićuŋ, and lives a life of wiwićamdeza. But, most of all, he has shown the young warriors that we can stand up to the Waśićuŋ. We can have pride!"

"But what does he say?"

"He says that the Minnesota is our country. That it must be cleansed of the evil whiskey, including those who make it and those who sell it, since it alone is the reason for our loss of power. So now you hear these young warriors singing 'Wakpa Minisota! Mita Makoće!'—Minnesota River! My country!"

As they reached the rim of the prairie, they remounted and rode the short distance to the wooded arroyo of Rice Creek where it flowed down to the Minnesota. They could see the village of Red Middle Voice near the mouth of the creek about a mile distant. Also noticeable was a large plume of smoke billowing from across the river and about half a mile upstream from the village.

"Where's that smoke coming from?" asked Wayuhi.

"I don't know. An Iaśića family lives around there someplace. They're probably burning stumps since I see he cut down all those big old elm trees that used to be there."

They left the Peżutazi Road and followed a trail down through the wooded ravine along Rice Creek toward the village.

The Rice Creek Village of more than fifty lodges sat in a large meadow near the confluence of the waterways—east of Rice Creek and south of the Minnesota. Several barking dogs announced the arrival of the young riders, with some busy people waving to acknowledge them but immediately returning to their tasks.

"Where are the Red Soldiers, the camp guards?" Wayuhi asked aloud to himself as he stopped and surveyed the village.

Wayuhi noticed that most of the dwellings were the traditional Dakota summer lodges identical to the bark-covered home of his grandparents with several tipis located to the west along Rice Creek that were in the process of being dismantled. A large red-painted buffalo-hide tipi formed the heart of the village. About five paces in front of the tipi was a tall Medicine Pole with a red-painted skull of a buffalo bull tied to the top identifying it as the lodge of Hoćokaduta— Red Middle Voice. The lodge, with its doorway facing east, sat adjacent to a large circular communal area with its soil packed hard by frequent use.

As they rode past the red tipi, Wayuhi noticed the tracks of two shoed horses and a buggy that came into the village from the north, from across the river. "Waśićuŋ!" he said pointing down at the tracks.

"Maybe not. See. There are no boot tracks. This is where they tied up the buggy last night."

"You're right. They would have left deep boot marks where they got off. And the rain washed away any moccasin tracks."

To the immediate east of the village was a huge, old elm tree, wide as a horse is long and perched atop a high outcropping of granite with its roots wrapped around and through the craggy fractures until reaching soil, standing tall and straight like a venerable warrior who has proudly counted coup on hundreds of raging spring floods, scorching summer fires, and brutal winters of popping trees. The Isaŋti Dakota revered these grizzled veterans that still existed in the sacred, primeval forests on their reservation or southwest side of the river, but as the Germans settled across that potamic border after 1858, most of those venerated methuselahs were cut down for the clearing of farmland or lumber for buildings, which only served to throw fuel on the already fuming hatred between the two races.

In the center of the communal area were the smoldering cinereous remains of a tower of horizontally stacked charred wood and embers of a large ceremonial fire that had been extinguished by the morning rain.

"Lots of ashes," commented Ćaske.

"That fire had been burning all night," said Wayuhi, both still sitting their horses.

"It looks like they had a powwow here last night and forgot to invite me! Aaaa!"

"I thought maybe they had a harvest dance here but I didn't see any corn fields."

"This is a hunter's village, brother. Ina Wamnuwiŋ is the only one here who plants corn with her Three Sister's Garden back there."

"Where does she live?"

"Over this way," said Ćaske as he swung his horses north through the riverine village.

Finding the lodge of Hepaŋ and Wamnuwiŋ empty with no sign of their whereabouts, Wayuhi walked the horses toward the Minnesota through trees still dripping from the morning shower. A barrier of sorts formed by driftwood piled up by high spring water levels over the many years prevented easy access to the river. He followed the natural gray-wooded barricade of logs and branches until reaching the mouth of Rice Creek where he found a wide opening. From the sandy river bank, he could see that there was a bend in the Minnesota where it joined with Rice Creek and flowed due east for a short stretch across a wide sand bar created by the confluence, a shallow, natural fording of the ancient waterway.

While the horses were drinking, Wayuhi's attention was drawn to the shadows under the trees on the opposite shore where he had seen a flicker of movement. Not the movement of game, but something else. He had a strange premonition of danger; that something sinister and unholy lurked over there. He watched the shadows for a long moment when suddenly an agitated crow flew into view as if it were screaming a warning to be heard above the flowing sound of the river. Then, as the westerly breeze shifted south, he could see and smell the smoke he had noticed from the bluffs sifting through the trees on the other side and streaming across the river as if seeking him out bringing both the aroma of burning wood and the fetor of death.

Wayuhi quickly returned to the lodge with the horses and let them out to graze in a grassy field nearby.

Ćaske came running over to the lodge when he saw Wayuhi and said, "From all the tracks I've seen around here, many people went south in a hurry last night. Some young boys over there said they went to Crow Creek but didn't know why."

"I know why! Today a war has started with the Iaśića!"

"How do you know that, brother?"

"Because I believe those Iaśića living across the river have already been killed."

"Did you see something?"

"No. But my medicine tells me something bad has happened over there."

"Then we should go see for ourselves."

"No! We have been warned to stay away! We must find ina Wamnuwiŋ and her children and try to take them back to Yellow Medicine. There is not much time."

As they went for their horses, Ćaske noticed a woman leading a white horse coming toward them from around the granite outcropping east of the village.

"Ina," he called out and went running toward her.

"Little son," Wamnuwiŋ answered as she stopped and threw up her arms to embrace Ćaske as he approached her. As his not so little brother picked her up off her feet, Wayuhi could see two young children walking behind her. Ćaske then took the hands of both children and walked along with Wamnuwiŋ to the lodge.

"Ina, do you recognize him?"

"Wayuhi! The last time I saw you, you were no bigger than my little boy here!"

"Ina, it's good to see you again!" said Wayuhi as he got a big hug. He was amazed at the family resemblance of his mother and her two younger sisters, and all looked exactly like kuŋśi Makadutawiŋ.

"My boys, as you know by now, something terrible has happened around here. Come and sit in the shade and I will find some food," as she tied her horse to a post near the front of her lodge. Lashed to the packsaddle on the horse were four bushels full of wahuwapa—ears of green corn. Ćaske removed the cargo, packsaddle, and the halter from the mare and let it go out to be with the other horses.

Wamnuwiŋ had her little boy climb up onto the high drying platform in front of her lodge. He came back down with a good amount of pemmican as Wamnuwiŋ returned with a wooden bucket of cold clear water with a gourd ladle floating in it and placed it in front of her visitors and her twins.

"Ah, my sons," Wamnuwiŋ said as she sat down with her guests. "These are very bad times for our people."

"We saw the tracks of shod horses and a buggy that came into the camp," said Ćaske. "What happened?"

"Yesterday, four of our young men were walking back from hunting up north in the Big Woods. As they stopped for water at a farmhouse, several Iaśića were standing outside and yelled insults and waved them away and even threatened them with a gun."

"Were those Iaśića drunk?"

"I don't know if they were drunk, but it sounds like they were. That farm is a whiskey store. Anyway, they started fighting!"

"Did they kill any of the Iaśića?" asked Ćaske.

"They said they killed all of them. Then they hitched up a team and came back here last night."

"Then what happened?"

"I went with Hepaŋ up to the red tipi when we heard about it. Red Middle Voice said the Big Knives would be here demanding that we turn over the four young men who did this. He said he has never taken orders from the Waśićuŋ and will not start now. He said the time is right to take our country back and push the disrespectful Iašiċa out of here, to take back what is rightfully ours.

"Then last night we had a war dance and Red Middle Voice said we have been insulted and humiliated in our own country long enough! That the time is right to fight for our freedom! Then you could hear them singing 'Wakpa Minisota! Mita Makoċe!' as the warriors danced."

"Why did they leave for Crow Creek last night?"

"Red Middle Voice only had about a hundred young warriors here. They went south to get the support of the Mdewakaŋtoŋ Soldier's Lodge and the leadership of Taoyateduta. And Hepaŋ went with them."

"But what happened to those Iašiċa across the river?"

"A very strange thing happened this morning. A man named Ċetaŋhuŋka—Parent Hawk, came here with six armed warriors. He said drunken Iašiċa had murdered his daughter yesterday and tried to kill his granddaughter. He said his medicine told him to rid our country of whiskey stores and evil bootleggers from across the river.

"Shortly after that we heard shooting from the Schwandt farm where they make whiskey, and then we could see smoke from the burning buildings. Later, two young boys went over there to see what happened. When they came back, they were horrified and said that all eight in that family had been killed and their buildings set ablaze. Then Ċetaŋhuŋka and his warriors appeared to have gone downstream toward Beaver Creek."

"Ina, grandpa asked us to come down here to bring you back to Yellow Medicine. He said they fear for you and your children as he knew there was going to be a war," said Wayuhi.

"He knew there was going to be a war?"

"Yes," he said nodding his head with a concerned look.

"Before he left, my husband Hepaŋ told me that he too had a vision that he would not see his family again. He said our freedom is lost and our world would never again be as we have known it."

They tied a travois on the white mare and loaded the corn and Wamnuwiŋ's things and began the journey back to Yellow Medicine.

Whiskey River

Luckenbach sat his tin saddle mug full of hot coffee on the table in the middle of the makeshift classroom in the Officer's Barracks of Fort Snelling where he was in the process of demonstrating the loading of a percussion revolver. He walked over and opened the window to the back porch since the thunderstorm seemed to have passed over.

He strode over to the back door, opened it, and stepped out onto the veranda. With rainwater still pouring off the overhang of the porch's roof to the ground three stories below, he saw the huge black thundercloud off to the east flash a bolt of lightning. He immediately began counting to himself, *One thousand one, one thousand two, one thousand three, one thousand four*, when he heard a clap of thunder. *Damn*, he thought, *the storm's already four mile away.*

He walked back into his classroom and, liking the fresh smelling air after a thunderstorm, left the door open. When his students completed their exercise, he took a few sips of coffee, sat down and picked up the Colt revolver.

"Y'all need to assure that each lead ball is firmly seated oun its powder charge," he said as he pulled the loading lever of the revolver's ramrod assembly down into each of the six chambers of the cylinder.

"With that completed, gentlemen," the Captain said as he attached the loading lever back to its barrel latch, "y'all pack tallow into each chamber over the lead ball, like this, to seal the chamber and prevent any flashover," as he proceeded to do so.

"What's flashover, sir?" asked one of the student officers.

"Flashover is when y'all fire a round and all the loaded chambers go off at once. Damned embarrassin in a fracas!" Luckenbach said as he wiped the front of the cylinder clean with a rag.

"Do those paper cartridges come with tallow, sir?" asked another.

"Nope. And that's why I don't use em even though they're standard Army issue. Least-wise when given the choice."

"I don't understand, sir. How do we prevent flashover with paper cartridges?"

"Well, it's like with the old muzzle-loadin muskets—tear off the end of the paper cartridge, pour the powder into the chamber of the cylinder, and ram the bullet and paper down oun top of the powder. Hopefully, that paper wadin will prevent it, but y'all can still get flashover, lessin y'all do it my way," said Luckenbach.

"And your way is to get rid of our sword, carry two or more Colts, and grease the cylinders. But how about powder loads?" asked another officer.

Luckenbach thought about how he preferred to hand-load each chamber with the grains of blackpowder proper for his intended use. "Oun the target range I like a lighter load of powder, say 23 grains, for greater accuracy. In the field I could do with a heavier load, say 34 grains, for more stoppin power since y'all don't have time to aim no how."

"What load do ya get with issued paper cartridges, sir?"

"Y'all never know for sure; then, to make matters worse, the paper tends to fall apart in the carryin pouch."

"I see you use round balls instead of the issued conical bullets."

"Yeah, I like em .44 calibre round balls, which I mold myself to my own specifications. They seem to mostly go where I want em to."

"Captain sir. Most of us were trained with the '59 Sharps Carbine and sabres. Do you mind if we handle that revolver to kinda get the heft of it?"

"Go right oun ahead, gentlemen. Don't worry bout it goin off since I ain't fitted the percussion caps oun it yet."

"Army Holster Pistol, Model of 1860," said one of the student officers liking the feel of the fully loaded gun in his hand.

"It's a fine weapon, gentlemen. Weighs half of what em old Walker Colt's weigh and better for shootin from horseback. Sights ain't worth beans, but then it weren't designed to be no target pistol. It was made for one thing and one thing only—killin at close range, for which it does a commendable job I might add," Luckenbach said as each of the twelve young officers had his turn at hefting the loaded weapon.

With the students standing around the table, he carefully fitted the percussion caps to each of the six chamber nipples. With all the loading done, he firmly held the hammer with his thumb as he squeezed the trigger and slowly set the hammer down on one of the safety pins located between each chamber on the back face of the cylinder.

"I always feel like I'm settin a wolf trap when I do that," he said as he placed the weapon into its polished black leather holster, fastened the flap, and set it with his other gear and stood up.

"Gentlemen, the purpose of my presentation today, as I said earlier, is to present y'all with an overview of modern ranger warfare. As we speak General McClellan is formin a Regiment of 6th Pennsylvania Lancers that he intends to use against rebel forces. Forces that are armed with long range .58 calibre C.S. Richmond muskets and deadly Army Colt revolvers similar to these, which they seem to be appropriatin in great numbers from our recent defeats.

"General McClellan is still fightin an 18th Century war. His techniques are straight out of a cavalry school in France with trainin in Napoleon's tactics. Today, the only thing useful from that era is his name oun a cannon—the Model 1857 12-pounder Napoleon. Loaded with a can filled with half-pound cast-iron balls, it can devastate a cavalry sabre charge at 300 yards. Done made cavalry, as we've known it, anticuado. Obsolete, in other words! So therefore, gentlemen, the sabre is now obsolete. I expect y'all to leave em in your quarters for the rest of the day. Any questions?"

"We're ready to start shooting, sir."

"All right then, gentlemen. Y'all know what to do to draw y'alls weapons and accessories from the quartermaster. Shortly after y'all hear the bugler sound 'drill call,' I'll expect y'all out at the Pistol Range."

"Room! Atten-hut!" commanded the student leader.

"Dismissed, gentlemen," said the Captain as the young officers began leaving the training room in their usual boisterous demeanor.

Having a few hours before his next class, Luckenbach returned his gear to his quarters, put on his waistcoat and slouch hat and set out across the parade grounds to the Sutler's Store. As he entered the store he saw three Indian men with the sutler and could hear them speaking in their language. Since he was wearing his woolen regulation uniform, he was relieved to find that the back windows were wide open and a cool breeze was flowing nicely through the store and out the open front door and windows.

"Luke! I'll be with you in a minute," said the Sutler as he leaned around his customers to see who had come into the store.

"No hurry, Jim. I'll just mosey roun the store abit," said Luckenbach as he perused the shelves against the walls for any sign of his expected tobacco shipment from Chicago.

Luckenbach thought about how Jim Duncan had been a wealth of information about this area and its people. His grandfather, with even a lake that bore his name where he had built a cabin, had settled here after the 1805 Zebulon Pike Expedition. Jim was born and reared in this frontier and could speak its languages—Dakota, Ojibway, some French as well as his native English. He was the same age as Luckenbach and, after five years, was beginning to turn the Sutler Store into a profitable activity as his father had sent him east to study business.

"Luke, your shipment came in. Looks like he sent you a case with about fifty packs of genuine Bull Durham," said Duncan coming across the floor grappling with the package.

"Well, that's a bit of a surprise. I was expectin a few packs, not a whole case," said Luckenbach as he accepted the package. "Should keep me goin for a spell!" he added as he joggled the package up and down testing its weight.

"If I need any tobacco, I'll sure know where to look."

"How much I owe y'all for this?"

"The invoice here says that he paid for it all, forty-eight packs at five cents each plus a buck and two-bits for shipping. It's all yours, Luke."

"Say, ah Jim. I been ameanin to ask y'all a question bout these Indans round here, y'all bein from these parts and all."

"What's that, Luke?"

"Well, I know it sounds kinda harebrained, but how do elephants fit in with these Indans or do they?"

"Elephants?" said Jim as he raised his eyebrows and looked over his eyeglasses at Luckenbach. "Elephants, or at least their ancestors, were very important to the Santee Sioux. In fact, they called them Uŋktehi, the frightful ones, or something like that."

"How'd they all get elephants clear out here? I seen elephants at a circus in San Antone. I always thought they all came from Africa or India."

"The Santee's would sometimes stumble across the bones and skulls of prehistoric mammoths in the lower wetlands. Imagine their shock when they saw those great skulls with them long curved tusks!"

"I can well imagine that," said Luckenbach looking down and nodding his head.

"Since they always found its bones in the banks of rivers or lakes, and since they'd never seen one walking on the ground, they assumed that it lived underwater."

"Well I'll be damned!"

"They thought that floods were caused when these great animals submerged themselves into the rivers. And people drowned because they angered Uŋktehi for desecrating the waters."

"Desecratin the waters?"

"You know. Relieving yourself in a creek or something like that."

"Were they all considered to be bad spirits?"

"I don't think so. In fact, they were fearsome and demanded respect but yet they were repositories of ancient knowledge since they were believed to be the manifestation of an old man and an old woman."

"So they all used the skulls in ceremonies and such?"

"Exactly. I've never witnessed them, but my grandfather had often talked about them being associated with the Medicine Dance of the Mdewakaŋtoŋ Santee's. One of those skulls with tusks can weigh up to 200 pounds. Why do you ask, Luke?"

"Oh, I don't know. Heard somebody atalkin, I reckon," answered Luckenbach wanting to share his experience of the previous day but at the same time, not wanting to sound like he had lost his mind.

"Not many people around here know about that, so it's unusual for someone to ask. In fact, those ceremonies most likely haven't been done around here for over fifty years," Duncan stated as he walked over to the counter to wait on a customer.

"Something else was botherin me, Jim," said Luckenbach after Duncan's customer had left. "Yesterday mornin I seen a couple of Indan canoes headin up the Minnesota. I thought the Sioux was all moved out yonder?"

"That they were. What you saw were most likely Indians transporting firewater from Pig's Eye out to the Redwood Agency for one of the Trading Posts there."

"Bootleggin! Out in broad daylight?"

"Exactly. Big profit in selling firewater to Indians and everyone is in on the take."

"What kind of profit y'all talkin bout?"

"Well, as high as 600 percent or even more!"

"I thought we all had laws against sellin whiskey to Indans!"

"The law is against selling firewater in Indian country, not selling to Indians. The trick is in how you define 'Indian country'."

"I don't understand."

"There's an 1834 law that vaguely defines Indian country as actual reservation land not ceded to the federal government by treaty or legislative decree."

"So any land that's been ceded by a Tribe is not Indan country."

"Exactly," said Duncan as he removed his spectacles.

"So any farmer livin oun land ceded to the government by a treaty, meanin most of Minnesota, can make and sell whiskey to Indans?"

"Exactly. Most of the German settlers up the Minnesota River who grow corn make and sell firewater to the Santee Sioux, or they trade it for any thing of value the Indian may have or can steal."

"So an Indan can step off the reservation and buy all the whiskey he wants?"

"He doesn't even have to do that if he's got the money, which the Santee will soon have since they're waiting for their annual annuity payment," he said as he twirled his glasses by one of its temples.

"And that's where the traders make money. They buy the whiskey for a dollar a gallon and sell it oun the reservation for seven?"

"Exactly. And if they sell it on credit, they mark it up even higher than that since the Indian doesn't know what he writes in his ledger."

"Don't they all have to worry bout getting caught sellin it in Indan country?"

"Not at all. In fact bootleggers act freely on reservations since most Indian Traders are bootleggers and licensed on the recommendations of the Indian Agent who, in fact, is also on the take."

"Well that's not surprisin. Then Indan Agents call in soldiers to risk they alls lives policin em drunken Indans!"

"Since bootleggers have been getting scalped in Sioux country lately, soldiers will most likely be called in soon. Rice Creek Village Santee's have put bootleggers on notice that if they're caught in their country, they'll be killed. There it's a problem of policing sober Indians!"

"Imagine that! Ausin cavalry to protect damn bootleggers!"

"Well we already use them to protect land grabbing squatters and gold grabbing miners, why not money grabbing bootleggers?"

"Fightin Indans to line the pockets of a few pendaho gringos doesn't strike me as a proper use of army time, energy, or lives. We all are ready to risk our lives for the good of the country, but not for the profit of a few greedy Indan Agents."

"But the greed doesn't end there, Luke. In fact, it's part of a federal 'Indian Ring' that goes from the Indian Agent, to the Regional Superintendent, to the Secretary of Indian Affairs, and to the Secretary of the Interior!" he added twirling his glasses again.

"Where does President Lincoln stand with all that corruption?"

"Hell, he invented the 'Indian Ring'. In fact, he has never challenged the American consensus on the necessity for Indian removal to make way for white progress."

"My gawd, Jim! Those Indans don't stand the chance of a fart in a wind storm!"

Duncan guffawed and dropped his glasses. Reaching down to pick them up he said while trying to be serious, "I think there's a bigger chance for them than that, Luke. As long as leaders surface like over at Rice Creek Village to make a stand against the flood of firewater that's drowning their people." Duncan put on his glasses and laughingly repeated the phrase "...fart in a wind storm" as he shook his head and walked over to wait on customers.

"I reckon y'all are right, to fight firewater with fire that is. Thanks a bunch, Jim. I'll see y'all later," said Luckenbach as he picked up his package of Bull Durham and headed out the door.

Watchers of Enoch

Waking again to the sound of the crowing rooster, Astrid sat up in bed and realized that she didn't feel at all sick nor did she get leg cramps during the night. *Yental, herbal, and natural,* she thought. *The red raspberry herbal tea and the nettles must be working, yust as Olga said they would.*

"I pray Herr Bruner's statement is also true when he said that Yohannes is alive and will be coming home to be with us," Astrid said aloud while looking at her swollen womb and speaking to her yet unborn baby. She felt the baby kick as if he could hear and understand her words.

"Uff da! Little Arnt Yohannesen Mundahl agrees!"

As she thought about Johannes, she couldn't help but think about the many silly omens and beliefs from the Old Country that were still maintained in Arendahl, especially with regard to courtship and marriage. Or at least, she once thought they were silly. Courtship, it was believed, was most successful during the waxing of the moon, especially around Candelas—February 2. Wishing to know the name of her future husband, she went out to a crossroads the first time she saw the moon in February of 1860. There, true to the belief, she turned around three times and said, "Tell me the name of the man I shall get." She then returned to her home and, standing in the yard outside, could not move until an unmarried man's name was mentioned. He would be her husband.

How silly she had felt standing alone outside on a cold moonlit winter evening for over an hour when at last she heard a horse with a jingle bell harness pulling a sleigh and coming down the road. The delivery sleigh pulled up in front of the Arendahl General Store, adjacent to their house, where the delivery boy unloaded a large wooden crate near the front doors. He then walked over to the house, carefully climbed the icy stairs of the front porch, and, not seeing Astrid standing in the shadows, knocked on the door.

When her father, Arnt Hovin, answered the door, the strange young man said, "Good evening, Mr. Hovin. I have come from Peterson to deliver the forty pounds of frozen lutefisk that you ordered."

"Ya good," her father said. "Shouldn't be a problem leaving the crate there overnight since it's below freezing. Frozen lutefisk don't smell too bad," he laughed as he paid for the delivery.

"Thank you sir," said the young man as he turned and carefully descended the stairs.

"Tusen takk," answered her father. "By the way. What is your name?"

"I am Johannes Hanson Mundahl."

Oh, heaven be praised! thought Astrid as she heard his name voiced.

"My father is an owner of the Norway Fish Company," Johannes answered distractedly as he saw Astrid in the light of the open door.

"Hellooo," he said to Astrid. "I didn't see you standing there."

"Hello, I was yust looking for my sister," Astrid lied with a lump in her throat as she laid eyes for the first time on the boy who would be her husband.

"Well, I'm very pleased to meet you," Johannes said striding over to her while removing his glove and offering his hand.

"My name is Astrid Hovin. I'm pleased to meet you, Yohannes," said Astrid, almost unable to get the words out as she accepted his handshake. He was tall and lean looking, even with a triple layer of winter clothes on. He had removed his stocking cap and shocks of blonde hair glowed like a golden crown in the backlight from the house, a chiseled nose, and dark brown eyebrows arching over Nordic blue eyes giving him a princely air that Astrid immediately fell in love with.

"So, this is your home. I'll probably be coming here often since I am working for my father now that I've finished school. I live only six miles from here, so I hope to see you again," Johannes said as he turned and headed for his delivery sleigh.

"Ya! Ya, I'll be here," said Astrid as, even now, she could feel the warmth of his hand.

Never again, she thought, *will I call the traditions from the Old Country silly!*

Even so, she still felt that some of the omens from the Old Country were childish. She remembered her mother, Marie, admonishing her of the many taboos throughout pregnancy in order not to harm the fetus. *Do not look a hare in the mouth*, she said, *lest the child be a harelip; do not to take part in a slaughter, lest the blood that hit you be reflected in birth spots on the corresponding part of the baby.* She said that during a difficult birth in the Old Country, all knots in the house were loosened and the birthing woman's hair would be untied to ease the baby's exit from the womb. If the birth became extremely difficult, the husband would destroy a sled, plow, or other implement to assist in a safe delivery. *If all was lost, however,* her mother said, *one could always take solace in the fact that all who died in childbirth would be with the Lord in heaven.*

Having finished her morning chores, Astrid was getting ready to stroll over to the house for her herbal tea, a couple slices of toast with butter, and maybe a little conversation with Olga and the girls. She left her room and walked through the passageway between the empty stalls having let the three milk cows and the two horses into the back pasture after the milking was completed.

When she got to the open barn doors, she stopped to look southwest across the river road where she had first seen Good Voice Woman and her young daughter. Astrid had never met anyone with such a captivating presence and was hoping to see them again as she had a strange feeling of their nearness. As she gazed across the road, she saw six black turkey vultures on a small hillside adjacent to the Bruner's cornfield. They didn't seem to be feeding on anything or in their usual aggressive disorder, but simply sitting there crowded together looking sinister with those reddish naked heads staring in her direction like Watchers of Enoch as if patiently waiting for something or someone to die.

Like a specter of death, the sight of the evil looking scavengers watching her brought about a cold galvanic shiver through her body with her arms breaking out in goose pimples. It was then that she heard several distant gunshots with two of the buzzards jumping into the air and flapping their wings but immediately returning to their rapacious watchfulness. Astrid's first reaction was to reach for her protective amethyst brooch, which wasn't there. She turned and, walking as fast as she dared, returned to her room where she recalled leaving it on her emigrant chest.

She entered her room and picking up the pendant, felt its reassuring warmth. She began to pin it onto the front of her dress, when she heard someone knocking on her door that had somehow closed. She went to the door, opened it, and was stunned by who she saw standing there!

"Prise Gud! Good Voice Woman!"

"Astrid. I was afraid you would not be here!"

"What on earth is the matter?"

"You must come with me for your lives are endangered! They are killing the Iaśića!"

"The who?"

"The Germans!"

"Who is killing the Yermans?"

"My people! You must come! We don't have much time!" Howaśtewiŋ exclaimed as gunshots sounded outside the barn.

"But I must help the Bruners!" Astrid cried as they could hear screams mixed with whoops and gunfire coming from the barnyard.

"It is too late to help them now! You must come with me for your baby's sake!" Howaśtewiŋ insisted as she grabbed Astrid by the arm and pulled her into the passageway toward the open back doors of the barn.

Once behind the barn, Howaśtewiŋ cautiously looked around a corner of the structure making sure all was clear on the south side before exposing themselves. Then they walked across a small corral, carefully ducked under a pole fence, and into the cover of trees as they slowly made their way southeast toward Beaver Creek.

The sound of gunfire from the Bruner farm stopped and all was quiet except for the occasional yells of Indian men echoing through the forest. Astrid was sure that all the Bruners were now dead and was sobbing uncontrollably for the wonderful people who were like a family to her.

Once at Beaver Creek, they followed the waterway upstream for about a hundred yards through a densely wooded area to a bend in the creek where Howaśtewiŋ found a small hideout beneath a stack of fallen trees. She helped Astrid into the natural shelter onto a bed of dry leaves where she could lay down and attempted to calm her.

"Astrid, there is nothing you can do for those poor people. You must think about the safety of yourself and your baby."

"But the Bruners! They were so kind and never hurt anyone!"

"Astrid, you must control yourself. It is very dangerous around here. You must be very quiet," Howaśtewiŋ said in a whisper as Astrid began to settle down.

She took her large buckskin bag by its shoulder strap and gave it to Astrid as she whispered, "Here is some food—turnips and dried meat. And you have plenty of water with the creek right here."

"But where will you be?"

"You will not see me again, Astrid. But someone will be here for you tomorrow."

"But why on earth will I not see you again?"

"Remember. No matter what happens, you must be very still. Your baby's life may depend on it," said Howaśtewiŋ in a whisper as she receded into the shadows of the forest.

"Good Voice Woman!" Astrid called in a subdued voice. There was no answer as all she could hear was the flowing water of the creek. Then, feeling contractions in her stomach and sharp back pain, she laid down on the bed of leaves using her folded lavender shawl as a pillow. She reached for her amethyst Viking brooch but it too had disappeared.

Sign of the Medicine Bear

Matohota woke to the sound of thunder with rain pelting the roof and clattering against the windowpanes of his house. *Ah, a nice gully washer will cool it off for harvesting the corn this morning,* he thought. Careful not to awaken his wife, knowing that her and kuŋśi Okadawiŋ had taken the young girl to her home at Crow Creek and did not return until late at night, he dressed and walked out into the kitchen, slowly closing the door to the bedroom.

He looked up into the open loft where he could hear his two boys soundly sleeping. He knew they too were tired since he had kept them up late for a Sweat Lodge Ceremony. Their uncle, Wanaġiċikadaŋ—Little Ghost, a Waḣpekute who was a nephew of Iŋkpaduta, and his sons had taken care of the ceremony where they prayed for the little girl who was being returned that night to her family at nearby Crow Creek Village of Taoyateduta—His Red Nation, known as Little Crow by the White people.

He opened the fire bin of the kitchen stove, stuffed a couple pieces of wood and strips of dried bark into it, struck a match and lit the dried bark. When a small fire began crackling, he closed the door to the fire bin and opened the stovepipe chimney flue part way.

When he was satisfied with his fire, he picked up one of the rifles he had taken from the dead Iaśiċa and sat at the table. As he raised the half-stock plains rifle to his cheek, he could see the manufacturer's name—*Golcher & Simpson, Sᵗ Paul,* engraved on the octagon barrel and could feel its perfect balance. He laid it on the table and admired the splendid .45-calibre muzzleloader with its platinum and silver fittings and highly polished partially checkered walnut stock adorned with the initials of its unfortunate owner, or someone the Iaśiċa had stolen it from no doubt, in nickel silver.

What is this power of the White man to make such fine things? Grand-père had always said that you could judge a man by his rifle. What kind of man could own such guns? he thought.

He retrieved the second rifle from the corner and noted that it was identical to the first in every detail. Even the initials on the nickel silver honorary plaque were identical confirming his suspicion that the weapons were stolen. *How else would pitiful drunken murderers like those get such fine rifles?* he wondered and then frowned as he reminded himself of how he had acquired them. *But then,* he thought, *the powers move in mysterious ways. Providing you with things like this for some reason!*

By pushing a ramrod down the barrel of each rifle, Matohota identified the rifle that the inebriated assailant had loaded, but had forgotten the percussion cap. Opening the accoutrements bag that was laying on the table, he found a leather pouch, opened it, and removed a small metal percussion cap. He brought the hammer of the rifle back to half-cock position and carefully fitted the essential fulminate cap to the ignition nipple.

Mon Dieu! He thought. *Something as little and simple as that had saved my life!*

Not wanting to leave the dangerous loaded weapon lying around the house, he decided to take it outside and clear the round. He opened his front door and, stepping out onto the wet porch, heard a distant popping sound. Realizing it was gunfire coming from the north he jumped down the stairs and ran to the road in front of his house where he could see several plumes of smoke coming from the vicinity of the Redwood Agency about a mile distant as the sporadic shooting continued.

His first thought was that Ojibway were attacking them and that he needed to protect his family. He returned to the house and went to the bedroom to awaken Wahćaziwiŋ, who was up and getting dressed.

"What is happening out dare?" she asked in English.

"Something at the Agency. I think we're being attacked by the Ojibway!" he answered as he returned to the kitchen and carefully leaned the loaded rifle in a corner.

"What should we do den?" asked his wife.

Since their two boys were awake and peering down from the sleeping loft to see what all the commotion was about, Matohota said, "Go get kuŋśi Okadawiŋ and bring her over here! And bring grand-pères rifle and bandolier bag!"

As Wahćaziwiŋ went out the back door, he called the boys down from the loft and grabbed the unloaded rifle that was lying on the table. Holding the weapon upright and pulling the ramrod from its guide, he emptied the accoutrements bag onto the table hoping he had the supplies to load it.

"Go out by the road and watch for anybody coming this way," he said to his 16-year-old son Antoine as he tipped a brass-bodied powder flask for a measure of powder into the charge spout.

"What's going on?" asked Antoine, who was taller than his father and looked exactly like his namesake.

"I'm not sure, but looks like someone is attacking the Agency," he answered as he poured the 50-gram charge of powder into the upright barrel of the rifle.

"Who?"

"Ojibway! Don't know who else it would be. Our own people wouldn't be raiding the agency for food since our fields are ready for harvest," he said as he rammed the patched lead roundball down the barrel and firmly atop the powder charge. He wondered about his cornfield but felt it was safe from fire since it was still wet from the morning thunderstorm.

"Do we get a gun?" asked his brawny 14-year-old son, Waćiŋća—Cub, looking wide-eyed at the magnificent muzzleloader. At a time like this, he was glad he had taught his boys about firearms. By their sixth birthday, grand-père Jean-Jacques had insisted that they become familiar with weapons. *By the time they are full-grown men, using weapons should be second nature to them. That's the way I raised your father and that's the way I raised you!*

"Come here once," he said to Waćiŋća. He felt of his son's throat as he said, "Feels like the swellings has all gone down."

"Kuŋśi gave me some medicine last night and it's alright now."

"Good! Now go pull those shutters over each window and make sure they're barred from inside." Grand-père had told him to build a strong house with heavy wooden shutters and doors with gun ports that can be barred from the inside. To make sure there are no trees near the house that can obstruct you field of fire, and always make sure you have plenty of water, food, and powder in the house.

Matohota pressed the percussion cap onto the nipple, slid the ramrod back into the silver thimble-guides, and leaned the loaded Golcher & Simpson into the corner with its charged twin. He then returned the rifle accoutrements to the canvas bag and laid the bag near the rifles.

Wahćaziwiŋ entered from the back door behind Okadawiŋ. "Grandson," said Okadawiŋ in Dakota. "Those are not Ojibway that are attacking the Agency! It is not their way to make war like that."

"What do you mean?"

"The Ojibway would attack our villages or seek out an individual family for a blood feud."

"But who would it be then?"

"It is our own people!"

"Why? We are not starving!"

"The patience of our people has long been worn thin by the Americans and has finally broken!"

"Dat is true, husband," said Wahćaziwiŋ as she laid grand-pères rifle and bandolier bag on the table. "Last night we took dat little girl back to her family at Crow Creek. After she told her people how doze drunken Iaśića had killed her mudder, and after she told dem dat dey would have killed her too if you had not come along, doze people went into a rage!"

"They wanted to have a Scalp Dance to honor you and the great deed you had done. They said you are a great warrior like your father Pahayużataŋka. But since you weren't there, they had a War Dance and here that young girl's grandfather, whose name is Ćetaŋhuŋka, vowed to burn all the whiskey stores and kill all the Iaśića bootleggers from across the river! He said it is the White man's whiskey that is killing our people!" added Okadawiŋ.

"And den late at night, after moonrise, Red Middle Voice and Shakopee came into da village wid about a hundred young warriors from Rice Creek. Dey were all armed, wore red headbands, breechclots and leggings, with dere faces painted for war."

While they were talking, Matohota picked up the Kentucky rifle from the table and emptied the contents of the bandoleer bag onto the table. He laid out the powder horn and a small buckskin bag containing about half a dozen .50-calibre lead balls, opened the brass patch box that was built into the stock of the rifle and removed a patch. "What were they doing there?" he asked.

"Dey had come down to counsel wit Taoyateduta. Dey said dat some young men had killed several Iaśića near da Big Woods and said dat dey needed his leadership since da Big Knives would be demanding blood," said Wahćaziwiŋ as her husband pulled the ramrod from its guides.

"We didn't believe they would make war against the Americans since we supposed that Taoyateduta would advise them against it. He has been to the lodge of the Great White Father and seen his great armies with more soldiers than leaves on the trees. And he himself has cut his hair and become a farmer Indian as he knew it was senseless to resist the White man any more since the old days are gone forever."

As Okadawiŋ spoke, Matohota poured an estimated measure of black powder into the upright barrel of the rifle from the powder horn. "And that's why you didn't wake me up and tell me about it when you came home late last night? You didn't feel that anything was going to happen?"

"Yes! I mean no! We didn't believe anything was going to happen."

Matohota rammed a patched ball down the barrel and seated it firmly over the powder charge. He removed the ramrod from the barrel and inserted it into its thimble seats then pulled the hammer with the flint attached to half cock and laid the deadly Kentucky weapon on the table.

"By attacking the Agency and trading posts, our people have started a war against the Americans," said Matohota.

"This is the chance that the Americans have been waiting for," said the exasperated Okadawiŋ.

"Soon the Big Knives will be here from Fort Ridgley with cannons to push us off this land!" said Matohota.

"What will we do now?" asked Waȟćaziwiŋ.

"I have to go up to the Agency to see for myself what is going on. It might be just a few drunken fools who are shooting things up. I can't believe that the Mdewakaŋtoŋ Soldiers' Lodge is behind this!"

Matohota went to the door and called Antoine back into the house. He picked up the huge sheathed Bowie knife he had taken from the dead Iaśića and thrust it into his belt. He placed grand-pères bandolier bag across one shoulder and the powder horn across the other. He picked up the flintlock Kentucky rifle and headed for the door as Antoine entered.

"Now you boys stay in the house! You have those rifles so don't let anyone near the door! And even if you know them, tell them to keep their distance! Since we are breeds and farmers, they don't consider us any different than the hated Iaśića. I'll be back shortly."

As Matohota made his way up the road toward the Agency, he thought of his kuŋśi Okadawiŋ. She said this was Wasutoŋwi—the Harvest Moon. *It is the time of the Turtle,* she said, *to proceed with patience to ensure the stability of our people…*And yet today she said that *the patience of our people has long been worn thin by the Americans and has finally broken!*

I have learned patience, he thought. *I have learned the new ways of the White man. I have plowed my field, planted corn, and taken care of the young plants by weeding in the hot summer sun and keeping away rabbits and crows. I have defended my field against raiders—our own people who hate us and would destroy all we have built because we have left the village and they think we have given up the old Mdewakaŋtoŋ ways forsaking our people and becoming like White people.*

Matohota passed through the Indian Agency's grid work of individual farms of people from Maŋkato's Village and was pleased to see that his field was intact and well soaked from the morning cloud burst.

But I haven't given up the old traditions, he thought. *I am still a Dakota and share all I have with our relations. I take part in our ceremonial ways, speak our language, and raise my boys in that way. I pray to the Great Spirit and the Seven Direc-*

tions but at the same time I know of the Good Book and the Jesus Road. I live like I was told by grand-père Jean-Jacques Charbonneau, standing with one foot in the old world of the Dakota and the other in the new world of the White man but, for some reason, I don't feel welcome in either world.

*What happens to our people if we lose our patience with…*Matohota's thoughts were interrupted when he rounded the bend in the Agency Road. He heard screams and shooting and saw that several buildings in the Agency compound were on fire with even the Episcopal Church, in the process of being built and yet without a roof, in flames. Further up the road he could see that the stone warehouse was intact but was being looted by several people. After recognizing two of the men who were loading goods into a wagon, Matohota approached them to find out what was going on.

"Grizzly, which way are you going?" asked one of the men in Dakota with the acidulous odor of whiskey on his breath.

"What do you mean?" answered Matohota in their language.

"I mean we are finally at war against the White man. Which side are you going to fight for?" he said with a smile being sober enough not to antagonize the parlous Grizzly Bear, armed or not.

"Who is at war with the White man?"

"The Mdewakaŋtoŋ Soldiers' Lodge is being led by Taoyateduta and have killed all the bad traders!"

"Mon Dieu!" he said. His first thought was for François La Bath, a trader whose father, Michel La Bath, was an old fur-trading friend of his grandfather Jean-Jacques and was married to one of his Wahpekute wife's aunties, Hapisti-ŋna. He immediately turned and began running the easy quarter of a mile up the road to the La Bath Trading Post.

As he neared the Post, he was relieved that the log building had not been put to the torch. He thought that, since his mother was a Dakota related to Wabaśa and he had a Dakota wife and children, La Bath's life might have been spared. A short distance to the north, he could see that the three other trading posts were engulfed in flames with people drinking jarred whiskey and shooting wildly into the air as loot was being carried away.

Matohota stopped within twenty yards of the trading post when he noticed unfurled bolts of cloth and empty whiskey jars scattered around the front of the building and the door wide open with some of the windows broken out. He unslung the Kentucky rifle and poured a bit of powder into the priming pan and cocked the hammer back. Walking slowly toward the doorway with his powerful rifle at the ready, he could see the body of François La Bath lying face down on the wooden floor in a pool of blood.

He carefully stepped into the ransacked store, making sure none of the killers were still lurking about. He saw La Bath's big book, the ledger with the names of Dakota people and the amounts owed him, strewn on the floor with the pages ripped out, absolving all debt to him in one brutal act. Then he saw the fully feathered skin of a crow that had been dropped on the body of La Bath. It was the sign that Little Crow himself had killed him.

He stepped out the back door and quickly walked to the tipi where La Bath and his wife, Hapistiŋna, lived with their five children. The tipi was empty with dying embers smoldering in the fire pit. Matohota found signs that she had survived and fled to safety as it looked as if she had hurriedly left with what little she and her children could carry on horseback.

He returned to the log store and, laying his rifle on the counter top while not spilling the powder in the priming pan, turned over the body of La Bath who had been shot in the chest at close range and scalped. Thinking someone would yet set the building on fire; he grabbed him by the armpits and easily pulled the heavy body out of the store and the short distance to the tipi. He placed him on the west side of the lodge—a place of honor opposite the doorway, with his head to the north.

François La Bath, he thought. *You called my wife Miċuŋkśi—your daughter, and called me Mitakoś—your son-in-law, since your wife was a sister to Waḣċaziwiŋ's mother. You always helped us and treated us fairly when it came to doing business with you, and you gave me good prices for pelts when I was trapping. But you were very stern with others and you were accused of being dishonest since many people owed you money. You also bootlegged whiskey to a lot of people around here who always resented you by blaming you for their drunkenness after they sobered up. So I can see why somebody might shoot you if given the chance.*

He faced east and respectfully prayed in Dakota. "Grandfather Great Spirit, Four Winds, Medicine Bear, hear my prayer! Seven Directions, look upon me! Pity and help all of our people in our time of need. Help this good relative, François La Bath, along the Ghost Road by sending the Man Carriers to take his Spirit on his homeward journey to the Land Beyond where his father and grandfathers now dwell. I ask you these things so our people will live." Not having cedar grains to burn, he picked up a handful of earth and sprinkled the symbol of Wiċahuŋkake—our Ancestors, over the body and concluded his prayer with, "All my Relations!"

He covered La Bath with a trade blanket left in the tipi hoping that someone might provide him a proper Ghost Keeping Ceremony and burial. As he began to leave the tipi, he stopped shortly as he saw two armed Indian men approaching rapidly from the north. Not knowing their intentions or state of sobriety, he sprinted the short distance to the log cabin where he had left his rifle.

He picked up the loaded big-bore flintlock and pulled the hammer back to full-cock position as he stepped out the front door to confront the possible danger. Stopping as soon as they saw Matohota, one of the men raised a hand to block the morning sun from his eyes and then raised his rifle in the air as a sign of recognition with the other. Matohota was relieved and even happy when he saw that the men were none other than Wasuduta and Hepi—his Wahpekute relatives.

"Brother-in-law," said Wasuduta in Dakota. "Good to see you here today, innit!"

"Good to see you too," he answered in their language.

"We are worried about our auntie Hapistiŋna and our uncle François and their children, innit. We heard about the war and came as fast as we could hoping to help our relations. Are they safe?"

"François has been killed," said Matohota who could also have referred to La Bath as uncle since his father Antoine had taken him for a brother in a Dakota ceremony when he lost his own blood brothers to the Ojibway. In the Dakota way, he could also have referred to him as father, but he preferred neither since then he would have had to call his own wife cousin or, even worse, sister.

"I laid his body in the tipi in a good way."

"What about our auntie?" asked Hepi.

"I think she left with the children on horseback. I don't know where she could have gone. There is no sign that anyone else was killed here," answered Matohota as he placed his rifle hammer to half cock, set the rifle butt on the ground and leaned against the long barrel in one fluid motion with the brass tacks on its elaborately studded walnut stock glinting in the sunlight.

"She might have gone to the village of Taoyateduta at Crow Creek," said Hepi. "There were about two hundred lodges there when we came through just now."

Knowing she may well have seen Little Crow kill her husband, Matohota doubted that she had fled to his village at Crow Creek.

"It has become the War Village since that is where the Mdewakaŋtoŋ Soldiers' Lodge is camped," said Wasuduta. "You should take your family over there where they will be safe if you are going to join the fight, innit."

Where they'll be safe? thought Matohota.

"I have to get back home. Just came up here to see what was happening and my family is probably worried," said Matohota.

"We'll go with you, innit. We're going back home and it's on the way. There's nothing we can do here," said Wasuduta as they turned and started south down the Agency Road.

"Where did the warriors go after they killed the traders?" Matohota asked.

"Some went over to the Redwood Agency but most went to fight the Iaśića and clear them from our land," said Hepi.

"The Iaśića? Those are just pitiful farmers; they're not soldiers! You have to attack the Big Knives at Fort Ridgley first or they'll be coming after us with cannons!"

"We are not making war against the Americans, innit," said Wasuduta. "It is the bootlegger and the Iaśića who make and sell that devil water that is killing our people that we are going to drive from our country!"

Because the Iaśića spoke German, Matohota had long realized that many of his people thought they were a different Tribe from the Americans, who they believed all speak English. Different languages distinguish different Tribes; it has always been that way. Are not the Ojibway different from the Winnebago, and speak different languages, and both different yet from the Seven Fireplaces, made up of our Dakota, Nakota, and Lakota people, called Sioux by the White people, who are all related by our common language?

Even the French, were a different Tribe from the English. They speak different languages and fought each other in the French and Indian War to rule the Indian fur trade in the Mississippi North Country. Then the Big Knives or Americans, were a different Tribe from the English who spoke a similar language but wore different uniforms and fought each other in the War of 1812 to again see who would rule our country.

Finally came the Iaśića—the Bad Talkers or Germans, stealing our land, destroying our hunting grounds by clearing the stolen land, then refusing to share their bounty from that stolen land when our people were starving, even though we were patient and shared with them. But worst of all, most of the Iaśića farms were whiskey stores where they traded anything they could get from our people for their evil brew. It was then that our patience was broken as we saw our leaders give away our sacred ground and our people die because of that devil water.

"Brother-in-law," said Matohota. "The Germans and Americans are one Tribe. My grandfather Jean-Jacques often told us of Canada and America. Though they are nations of many tongues and different Fireplaces, different beliefs, they all try to sing one song. And that song is freedom since Americans are now fighting each other to free the Hasapa—Black man, from slavery."

"But what about our freedom, innit? Red Middle Voice has told us that we have been robbed of our country and penned up on this little strip of land to be treated like little children by the Americans."

"We must remember that we have allowed that to happen. When we were powerful, they made relations with us and we were obligated to share with them. But now they are powerful and only take from us."

"That is very puzzling to me," said Hepi. "I cannot understand how the Americans can be killing each other to give freedom to the Black Nation while they take away the freedom of the Red Nation."

"Then they tell us that it is uncivilized to take Ojibway scalps while they kill their brothers in great bloody wars," said Matohota shaking his head. "They are a strange people."

"I too am confused, innit," said Wasuduta. "You say we are at war with the Americans, but it is our own people who have killed our relative! I must paint my face black and sing my war song, but where do I seek vengeance?"

"François was the victim of the White man's sickness. Not from small pox or the whiskey sickness, but from the sickness of only caring about himself and his own profit at the expense of his people. His death is as pitiful as the death of our many relatives who have died of the whiskey sickness—turning yellow with big stomachs and suffering while singing their death songs. Where do you seek vengeance for them?"

"Ho, you speak the truth, innit. They have chosen to walk the Black Road, the White man's path of evil and destruction and to live for themselves and not for their people. They have tried to live like White men and have offended the Spirits; that is why they have been killed, innit!"

"Brother-in-law," said Matohota. "Our people have destroyed the hated trading posts first because they represented the evil world of the White man and his need for profit. Our people too are slaves but to a lust for the goods of the White man. For these goods we have had to provide furs, which the White man kept demanding more and more to satisfy his greed until all of the beaver and otter were gone.

"Since the Iaśića cleared the land and scared away all the game, we had to rely on those trading posts for food and provisions while they made marks in their big books. Then when we received our annuity payments for all the land our leaders have given to the Americans, the black-hearted traders would be sitting at the table with their big books smiling while grabbing all of our money."

"I see what you are saying, innit! They have broken the Sacred Circle, the Hoop of our Dakota Nation!" said Wasuduta angrily.

"So in that way, it's like you said, François chose to walk the Black Road that only led to his destruction. You can't blame our people for his death, brother-in-law. Like our people have had to pay the price for his goods, he has had to pay the price for his choice to walk that bad road," said Matohota again choosing not to tell his brothers-in law that it was Taoyateduta, the wily Chief Little Crow, who killed their uncle since surely they would have sought him out and killed him.

"Ah, brother-in-law," said Wasuduta. "They should have named you 'Eagle Bear', innit. You are strong and fierce like the grizzly bear but are way up there and see far and clear like the eagle."

"What I can see is that now we have to prepare to fight the Big Knives. They will say that our people have fired the first shot and American blood has been spilled. Where will the Big Knives seek their vengeance?"

"Our leaders have chosen to walk the Black Road of war and destruction, so they will all have to pay the price, innit?"

"We all will have to pay the price. Just like we all had to pay the price of losing our land after our leaders signed it away."

"But why would the Americans try to punish all of us and not just those who have spilled blood?" asked Hepi.

"The Americans badly want this land and they have been given the excuse they have been waiting for to push us out onto the prairie to a desolate country they already call Dakota Territory."

As they passed the Agency's stone warehouse, they could see the building was emptied with the doors left wide open. The shooting and the screams subsided from the smoking buildings of the Agency and they saw several armed warriors hurriedly heading toward the steep river road down to the ferry landing.

"The Big Knives are coming!" yelled one of the warriors.

"Where?" asked Matohota.

"They've been seen across the river marching from the fort!"

"It's like I said, relatives," said Matoȟota to his brothers-in-law shaking his head with a look of despair. "Now we have to make ready to fight the Americans!"

As Matoȟota approached his house, he could see that his boys were vigilant as one of them was watching him with his rifle through the gun port in the front door. He had more than a father's pride for his sons. They are learning to stand with a foot in both worlds by learning the ways of the Dakota and the White man. They speak fluent Dakota, pretty good English, which they can also read, and write, and some French. *Where will their roads take them in this crazy life?* he wondered.

"Grandson, is it like I said? Is it our people who are attacking the Agency?" asked Okadawiŋ as he entered the house.

"Yes! Taoyateduta is leading the Mdewakaŋtoŋ warriors and they have killed all the traders!"

"And François La Bath, is he dead?" Okadawiŋ asked.

"Yes."

"And auntie Hapistiŋna and the children?" asked Waȟćaziwiŋ.

"I think they are alive and fled to safety."

"Grandpa Jean-Jacques said this would happen after the Americans cheated us out of our homeland and forced us out here!" said Okadawiŋ.

"Husband, what should we do?"

"Whatever we do, we have to do it quick! American soldiers are marching toward the ferry crossing and many warriors have gone down to fight them."

"We should go to Little Crow's village," said Okadawiŋ.

"Kuŋśi, I found the sign of Little Crow near the body of François La Bath. I don't think that half-breeds or farmer Indians are welcome in his camp."

"Taoyateduta hate uncle François for a long time, ever since he would not give him more credit for food or whiskey," said Waȟćaziwiŋ.

"Then we must go to the Métis," said Okadawiŋ.

"The Métis? They are too far to the northwest," said Matoȟota shaking his head.

"Grandson, this is Wasutoŋwi—the Harvest Moon, the time when the Métis are at the lake country that our people have named Kaŋdiyohi—the Buffalo Fish Place," said Okadawiŋ.

"Why are they there?"

"They have been camping there during the Harvest Moon for many years to harvest wild rice and catch Buffalo Fish. They always stop there on their way from the prairie to sell their cartloads of buffalo hides in St. Paul where they fetch good prices," said Okadawiŋ.

"I remember now. Grand-père Jean-Jacques would go up there to be with those people he called 'Gens Libre'—Free Men, where he would eat skillet fried fish and potatoes, drink wine, sing songs, and talk about the old days in his French language."

"I heard they don't like the White man's ways, his laws or the hobbles of his so-called civilized life. They believe that all men are born to be free," said Antoine not only looking like his namesake but sounding like him.

"Then that's where we should go!" announced Waćiŋća brandishing his Golcher & Simpson in the air.

"Alright. But we must leave today," said Matohota.

"What about our corn crop?" asked Wahćaziwiŋ.

"I'll take the boys over and we'll bury as much as we can for later and bring some back to carry with us."

As evening was approaching, the Charbonneau family began their trek down to the ferryboat landing with only the few possessions they could carry on their back. Matohota was sad to be leaving his home place, the house and the field they had worked so hard to build, nurture and maintain. He thought about when they left Maŋkato's Village after nearly starving to death during the past winter. It was François who had saved them with food and blackpowder. Matohota had vowed to become a farmer to raise crops to pay him back, although François would probably not have accepted payment. When they left the village, they were called 'Cut Hairs' and scorned by people who they thought were their friends. *Maybe it is among the Métis that we will finally be made to feel welcome,* he thought.

It was sunset when they arrived at the bottom of the steep trail to the ferryboat landing. His wife and grandmother were still horrified by the destruction and killing they had seen at the Agency. Then, with the full moon rising like a huge blood red omen of death in the eastern sky, they could see several bodies of soldiers on the other side of the river who were attacked by Dakotas as they attempted to cross the Minnesota by ferryboat. Now Matohota knew the Americans would surely be back, and back for blood.

He found his canoe he had hidden the day before and was surprised that it was virtually unscathed in spite of the vicious firefight that had taken place. As darkness was setting in, he pulled the canoe to the waters edge, set it in the water, and retrieved his hornbeam paddle.

"We have to go to the mouth of Beaver Creek and it's about five miles upstream," said Matohota to his family as he offered tobacco to the waters—an offering to La Vielle asking for safe passage.

"We can't get everybody in the canoe." said Antoine.

"That's right. We have to make two trips."

"I don't want to stay back here with all those ghosts over there!" asserted Waćiŋća.

"Father, there's only room for four in the canoe. So you and Cub paddle with grandma and mother and I'll wait here for you with our stuff," said Antoine. "I'm not afraid of ghosts!"

"I brought the other paddle," said Waćiŋća.

As Matohota was making his second trip with Antoine paddling in the stern of the canoe, the Full Harvest Moon had risen and directly above him he could see the Wića Akiyuhapi made up of seven twinkling stars that carry the Seven Sacred Ceremonies of the Isaŋti Dakota, the same stars that are called the Big Dipper by the White people. The four stars of the bowl are also the Man Carriers that carry our departed Spirit down the Ghost Road—the Milky Way, to the Land Beyond, the Four Warriors who carry wounded relatives from battle.

"Ho! Grandfather Great Spirit, Spirits of the Waters, Medicine Bear, hear my prayer!" Matohota prayed in Dakota as he laid his paddle across the gunwales. "Pity and help our people in these desperate times. Watch over us on these waters to bring us safely to our family. Help us travel the Red Road to the north to be with the Free People. I ask you these things so our people will live. All my Relations!"

"Look!" cried Antoine excitedly twisting around and pointing up to the sky. "Grandpa Great Spirit has answered your prayer!" Looking up, Matohota saw that two rings had formed around the full moon—the Sign of the Medicine Bear.

TUESDAY, AUGUST 19, 1862

Śićuŋ of Geeshik

Their camp was in a stand of elm trees near the confluence of Stony Run Creek and the Minnesota River. The horses were left to graze on the nearby pristine prairie carpeted with big blue stem grass so tall the grazing horses could only be seen when they raised their heads to survey their surroundings with twitching ears. The tallgrasses were interspersed with towering spikes of prairie blazing star and clusters of sumac and lupine and filled with eastern meadowlarks and lark sparrows welcoming the new day with their songs and an occasional blue jay screaming its presence.

Wayuhi returned to the campsite from having ridden downstream for his purification bath, to recognize the Great Mystery and play the flute songs of Ćotaŋka for protection during the continuation of their journey. Kuŋśi and Ćaŋomnićawiŋ were busy shaking out and rolling up blankets that had been used for bedding as Wayuhi approached them with his bedroll, the smoke-tanned buffalo hide he had originally brought for Taoyateduta, with his flute strap slung over his shoulder.

"Nephew, there's some pemmican over by the tree," Ćaŋomnićawiŋ said. "Grandpa didn't want us to make fire since he thought there might be enemy lurking about."

"Iaśića?"

"Ojibway."

"Why does he think that?"

"He said he heard the sound of sandhill cranes echoing down the river this morning before sunrise. That's when he woke me and told me not to start a fire," said kuŋśi.

"Sandhill cranes?"

"He says his Medicine always warns him when the Ojibway are about with the sound of those birds. He said that their warning songs come from the Spirit World."

"Where did he go?"

"To look for their camp. He thinks they're near."

"Where's Ćaske?"

"He went to round up the rest of the horses."

Wayuhi laid his bedroll with the others and walked over to help himself to some pemmican and headed for a small knoll overlooking the river to watch for his grandfather—Ćetaŋiyotaŋka. He passed Wamnuwiŋ and her children who were busy loading the travois they had again tied to the white mare.

Sitting on the mound, he was joined by Ćaske as he saw their grandfather returning from upstream in that crouched run of his. He was bare-chested and dressed in a breechcloth, leggings, and moccasins with a single eagle feather in his turban and his long gray hair braided. He was carrying his flintlock Kentucky rifle and had a steel pipe tomahawk in his belt with brass-studded straps of a bandoleer bag and a powder horn crisscrossing his chest.

"Look, he runs like an antelope," said Wayuhi. "H*e* seems to flow without effort, without thinking about it."

"Those old people have a habit of doing that; always making us look bad. Aaaa!" said Ćaske respectfully.

"Grandsons," he said as he approached the boys who had jumped down onto the sandy riverbank to meet him. "Ojibway are camped about a mile upstream!"

"Wah!" exclaimed Wayuhi more impressed by the power of his Medicine than the threatening presence of the Ojibway.

"Ahhh, our rowdy neighbors to the north. They must have traveled by canoe down the Chippewa River," said Ćaske.

"How many?" asked Wayuhi, aware that his grandfather didn't seem to be winded from his run.

"Three."

"What will we do?"

"I recognized one of them. His name is Geeshik, a great warrior of many coups, many raids into our country, and many kills. So whatever we do, we must respect him since he is very dangerous."

"Grandfather, to count coup on a great warrior would be our Dakota way of showing him respect and, at the same time, bringing great honor to our people," said Wayuhi taking the initiative.

"Then we must go now, before they break camp," said Ćetaŋiyotaŋka knowing his grandson bore the Sacred Arrows and must go forward and could not turn back and knowing a pipe must be taken with them.

Wayuhi quickly turned to scale the riverbank and return to camp to prepare himself and his horse for battle as Ćaske began to follow him.

"Grandson Ćaske. One of us must stay with the women and children, to guide and protect them. We will meet you upstream."

Ćetaŋiyotaŋka returned to the campsite and retrieved his pipe bag. He called Wayuhi and they climbed the mound where his grandsons had waited for him earlier. The Minnesota River valley was studded with many such mounds, which were thought to be burial places of the Ancient Ones, and imbued with their magical power. He fitted his pipestone to the wooden stem and ceremoniously filled the bowl with seven pinches of caŋśaśa—tobacco mixed with the dried inner bark of the red willow, tamped the mixture down with a stick, and sealed the bowl with fat from the heart of a buffalo. He then placed the loaded pipe into his pipe bag to take with them on this day as was the Dakota tradition before war journeys when a warrior carried Sacred Arrows on his back.

Wayuhi and his grandfather rode silently toward the Ojibway campsite, which was located in a wooded area near a high granite outcropping adjacent to the Minnesota River. They stopped about fifty yards from the campsite as they could see movement. Wayuhi's spotted horse—Tataŋkayamni, with his tail bobbed for war, could sense the excitement in the air and was silently nodding his head in anticipation of a good wild run through the woods.

"Which one is Geeshik?" whispered the clear-sighted Wayuhi with the predaceous calmness of a falcon, his dream guardian, ready to stoop down upon its prey.

"He is the one with the otter skin headband with the grizzly bear claws strung around it. See him there?" grandpa said pointing with his chin.

"Hoka hey!" answered Wayuhi as he raised his eagle bone whistle to his lips and began blowing long shrill notes as they began their charge. With them was the cry of the Eagle, a call to the Thunderhawk of the Dakota for protection and help to overcome their enemy. The shrill sound echoed across the river and around the high granite cliff as even thunder from the hoof beats of their stallions was with them on this day bringing the advantage of confusion to the Dakota warriors.

The echoes made it sound as if an army of horse soldiers were attacking them. The explosion from grandfather's big calibre rifle billowed smoke as the heavy lead ball slammed one of the Ojibway to the ground. Another of the enemy emerged from the darkness of the trees as Wayuhi drew his powerful bow and released an arrow that pierced through the warrior's hair-pipe breast armor and deep into his chest as he fell forward onto the ground pushing the arrow completely through his body.

Entering the campsite at a full gallop, Wayuhi could see Geeshik leveling his long rifle toward Ćetaŋiyotaŋka. Applying knee pressure to his stallion, the horse cut sharply toward the Ojibway, who hastily fired the shot harmlessly into the air as Tataŋkayamni rammed him with his right shoulder, almost knocking the formidable warrior to the ground. Wayuhi struck the dazed Ojibway with his elk horn bow, not to kill him but to count coup. The bowstring snagged on one of the bear claws of the warrior's headdress yanking it totally off of his head as he rode by. Ćetaŋiyotaŋka was directly behind Wayuhi by now and counted a second coup with his rifle barrel as he sped by the hapless Geeshik.

They raced along the riverbank maintaining their rhythm for about half a mile upstream before slowing to a walk as Ćetaŋiyotaŋka rode up alongside his grandson who had stopped to water his horse in the river.

"Grandson," he said catching his breath as he excitedly slid off his bareback horse and landing with his rifle in hand. "You counted coup on a great enemy today!"

"So did you," he answered modestly.

"But the greatest prize goes to the warrior who counts the first coup and also captures something honorable. You captured his śićuŋ, his power."

"What do you mean?"

"Śićuŋ is what our Lakota relatives call that in a man which is spirit-like and guards him against evil, what I call his power."

"How does he get it?"

"In ceremonies or through other beings, especially animals."

"Animals?"

"Each claw on that headpiece has the śićuŋ of a Grizzly Bear and represents a coup he has counted against his enemies and was his śićuŋ or his power."

"But it was an accident. It got caught on my bow string," said Wayuhi feeling embarrassed for his fortuitous winning of such an awesome prize.

"There are no accidents! White Eagle Ghost guided you," said his grandfather as he poured powder into the long barrel of his upright rifle. "Your so-called accident would not have happened if you had not bravely stopped him from shooting at me."

"Hoka. Then his power is now my śićuŋ!" he shouted as he held up the red felt lined and quilled otter skin with its twenty Grizzly Bear claws rattling as if it were alive and confirming his claim. He could feel his body swelling with the Ojibway śićuŋ the power of Geeshik with each breath he drew as he quickly forgot his self-abashment.

"Among his Anishinabe People, only warriors of great deeds and the highest rank are allowed to wear that headpiece. So you should be greatly honored," he said as he pulled the rifle's ramrod out of its guides to push a patched .50 calibre ball down the octagon barrel.

"What will happen to Geeshik now?"

"Without his śićuŋ he cannot stay around here, it would be too dangerous."

"But what will he do?"

"He will bury his dead and paddle his canoe back to his village. He will have to explain to their relatives what happened on this day."

"Will he be dishonored?"

"He could be banished from his village. He has been humiliated and that is one event in a warrior's life that becomes unforgettable. He will make medicine to accumulate śićuŋ and return to seek revenge to regain his honor." Ćetaŋiyotaŋka slid the wooden brass-tipped ramrod back into its brass thimble-guides and stood smiling at his grandson with the deadly brass-studded walnut-stocked rifle cradled in his arms.

"But how will he know who I am?"

"He has your arrow. They are strong in their ways and can identify the spirit that a warrior leaves in his weapons like tracks that a wolf leaves in the snow."

The women and children sang a Strong Heart song as the two warriors rendez-voused with their relatives further upstream. As they rode up, Wayuhi held the headpiece of Geeshik high in the air as it was attached to the tip of his unstrung recurved bow while the women made tremolos as a tribute to the brave warriors.

"Our grandson showed himself well today," said Ćetaŋiyotaŋka as he again slid off of his bareback horse still cradling his flintlock rifle in his arms. "His great horsemanship saved my life!"

"What is that?" asked Ćaske pointing at the headpiece brandished by his brother.

"The śićuŋ of Geeshik!" proclaimed Wayuhi.

"Then he must be dead!" said Ćaske.

"Wayuhi honored the bravery of Geeshik by counting coup on him and leaving him alive. To show respect for a great enemy warrior in that way is an old tradition of our Isaŋti Dakota," stated Ćetaŋiyotaŋka proudly.

"Hoka! Then I saw grandpa strike a second coup on him!"

"You men did a great thing in stopping those Ojibway. They would have killed some of our relatives before this day was through," said kuŋśi.

Ćetaŋiyotaŋka leaned his rifle against a tree and retrieved his long porcupine quilled buckskin pipe bag and sat down cross-legged on the ground. He invited the others to join him in a circle as he removed the assembled pipe from the pipe bag. He then broke the seal of buffalo fat to smoke the pipe that he previously filled since the war journey was successful. Ćaske sat to the right of his grandfather and started a small fire of dried bark in the center of the small group with his fire-steel and flint.

After he lighted his pipe with a coal of fire, grandfather drew on the pipe, took four puffs and offered the mouthpiece to the four directions. He passed the pipe clockwise as each took four puffs and repeated the ceremonial offering of the pipe until it was returned. At the completion of the ceremony, Ćetaŋiyotaŋka cleaned his pipe, separated the bowl from the stem, and returned them to his pipe bag.

Ćaske sprinkled grains of cedar in the fire as Wayuhi passed the headpiece of Geeshik through its cleansing smoke four times. "The sacred evergreen used in a good way will purify any evil spirits or bad thoughts that may reside within you, " he said.

"Grandson Wayuhi," Ćetaŋiyotaŋka said. "Your coup today is of the highest honor for a warrior and, in our Dakota ways, you have the right to wear a single eagle feather, standing upright on the back of your head."

Ćetaŋiyotaŋka passed a center tail feather of a golden eagle through the cedar smoke and handed it to his grandson. "Since you already have the white feather of Ćotaŋka, I give you this feather to tie to the mane or tail of your great stallion, Tataŋkayamni."

"Big thank you, grandfather," said Wayuhi feeling honored for his buffalo runner and, now, his warhorse.

By late afternoon, they neared the Isaŋti Village of Mazaśa—Red Iron. The Southern Sissetoŋwan village was located on the southwest banks of the Minnesota River at its confluence with the Chippewa River. Riding along the ridge forming the Minnesota River valley, the travelers were met by a Red Soldier or camp guard of the Mazaśa Village. After recognizing them, the Red Soldier signaled the village of their approach with flashes from an elaborately decorated hand held mirror.

Ćaske and Wayuhi, with their faces blackened commemorating their recent battle, led the entry into the village. Tataŋkayamni pranced as if proud of the eagle feather tied to its forelock while Wayuhi sat like a prairie knight astride the stallion with his white eagle feather held vertically behind his head by a red headband and his long hair braided. With his unstrung bow, Wayuhi held aloft the headpiece of Geeshik for all to see.

Ćaske, with his colorful turban wrapped around his head, was astride his roan stallion and carrying his Indian trade rifle in a buckskin scabbard with long fringes and porcupine-quilled floral embellishment cradled in his arm. The three women followed with Wamnuwiŋ riding Wayuhi's mare with the colt trailing and the twins riding double on the mare with the loaded travois. Ćetaŋiyotaŋka, also wearing a turban with his face blackened, brought up the rear holding his

Kentucky Rifle vertically resting on his thigh and carrying his Medicine Shield of Uŋktehi on his left forearm.

"Red Iron is a farmer Indian but he has not become a Christian," said Ćaske as they rode into the village.

"Why is that?" asked Wayuhi.

"Because he won't give up his three wives. Aaaa!" said Ćaske.

"Aho! He's a good Indian!" laughed Wayuhi.

"And ten winters ago, the Indian Agent threw him in jail!"

"Why?"

"Because he wouldn't allow them to give our annuity money to those traders because he said they were nothing but thieving bootleggers!"

"Aho!"

"Then, four winters ago he went far to the east, to the village of the White man's chief, with many of our chiefs to sign a treaty but he was the only one who wouldn't wear white man's clothes or those stovepipe beaver hats."

"Why was that?"

"He said that even though we gave away our land like stupid jackasses, we don't have to look like stupid jackasses! Aaaa!" he answered as Wayuhi's stallion whinnied and reared as if he understood and both young men laughed uproariously.

Along the path to the heart of the village, women would often emit long shrill tremolos and men would blow whistles and dance in small circles in honor of the Ojibway trophy and the victorious warriors. The village of about a hundred lodges was made up of mostly traditional summer bark houses and several buffalo hide tipis as many of the younger people who preferred the chase to farming had recently returned from summer bison hunts on the western prairie. With dogs barking and children running along side the trotting horses in the late afternoon heat, they finally reached the traditional Isaŋti lodges of Mazaśa.

The chief was standing in front of his lodges with several men who were apparently members of his Soldiers Lodge. Mazaśa motioned for the travelers to dismount, as several young boys appeared to help with their horses. Ćetaŋiyotaŋka greeted his boyhood friend and proudly presented his two grandsons. Kuŋśi went to greet one of the three wives of Mazaśa as her daughters and little grandchildren began to untie the travois from the white mare.

Mazaśa invited his guests to sit under a shade in front of the lodges of his wives where he lit and passed his pipe to all in Dakota formality. Then helpers brought a pail of water with a buffalo horn dipper, followed by pails filled with buffalo meat, corn, and chokecherries that were passed to those present.

"Wayuhi," said Mazaśa while the food was going around and having been told that the young black-faced warrior was from the Otter Tail Village. "When my father was a young man like you, the Sissetoŋwan were one Tribe. But the White man's whiskey had caused so much trouble among us with our people killing each other that Standing Buffalo, grandfather of your present chief with the same name, moved his people far to the north."

"I didn't know that," said Wayuhi as he drank from the water pail.

"They settled at Otter Tail Lake and became the Northern Sissetoŋwan. We were under the leadership of my grandfather Blue Spirit and remained down around Swan Lake at Traverse des Sioux until we moved up here along the Minnesota ten winters ago. We became known as the Sissetoŋwan of the South," said Mazaśa while chewing his food.

"I wondered why we were split apart," said Wayuhi.

"Your father, Tiowaśte, is my nephew from way back then, so in that way, we are related," said Mazaśa in typical Dakota custom to establish relationships with other Dakotapi upon meeting.

"Ho!" exclaimed Ćetaŋiyotaŋka in agreement.

"Since that was a brave thing you have done against our enemy the Ojibway, and against the hated Geeshik, I am proud to call you my grandson."

"Ho!" exclaimed Ćetaŋiyotaŋka again in agreement.

"But whiskey is once again dividing our people," said Mazaśa.

"How is that?" asked Wayuhi. As he got up to carry the pail of boiled corn to Ćaske, he noticed two young women walking toward the river. One of them stopped and turned around as if someone had called her name. He could feel a lump in his throat as she looked at him for a moment then smiled, turned and continued walking toward the river with her friend. He almost spilled the pail of corn as he sat it in front of Ćaske.

"Ahhh, I saw that," teased Ćaske in a low voice. "Now you have finally seen a six-pony girl! Aaaa!" he said smiling with perfect glinting white teeth contrasting with his blackened face.

"The Lower Council has taken it upon itself to make war against the Americans without first asking the Upper Council," said Mazaśa as was common to refer to the Tribes of the Redwood Agency as the Lower Council and the Tribes of the Yellow Medicine Agency as the Upper Council. "They did not ask us since they knew that we would have forbidden any war, forbidden any killing of innocent people!"

"That is true, grandson," added Ćetaŋiyotaŋka. "Iŋyaŋgmani and the others in our village were surprised when they heard that it was the Mdewakaŋtoŋ and

Wahpekute that started killing the farmers. Since I had given them your warning from White Eagle Ghost, we were waiting to be attacked by the White men."

"There is honor in fighting a great enemy a great warrior like Geeshik but there is no honor in killing unarmed farmers, killing helpless women and children. That is the work of drunken cowards!" said Mazaśa as he passed on the pail of chokecherries.

"I was told that they were making war against the White traders and the Iaśića; that the Rice Creek Mdewakaŋtoŋ were going to rid our country of the evil whiskey and the people who make it and the people who sell it," said Ćaske.

"Messengers have told us today that that's what Red Middle Voice and his young warriors are doing and that they are getting ready to attack New Ulm where they make whiskey. But yesterday someone had fought and killed many soldiers from Fort Ridgely. Now the whiskey drinking is getting out of control and other blood-crazed groups are attacking the German settlements and killing innocent people," said Mazaśa.

"Now the Americans will send their soldiers with their big guns and we will all have to sing our death songs," said Ćetaŋiyotaŋka.

"They started the fight down there, now they can finish it in their own country and sing their own death songs! That's what I mean when I say that whiskey has divided us once again!" said Mazaśa.

"I thought that the Mdewakaŋtoŋ were fighting to be free like Standing Buffalo—following the herds and walking proudly in his own land. You people here have already surrendered and are captives on this little patch of earth that is no longer yours!" said Wayuhi.

Feeling frustrated and caught up in something he didn't understand, Wayuhi got up and walked toward the river. When he got there, he saw their horses standing in the shade, drinking and soaking their feet in the cool water. He looked up the path that followed the river upstream hoping to see the two young women once again, but they were nowhere in sight.

Hoka! What a beautiful girl, he thought. *What is this ache in my heart? Never before have I had such a strange feeling from just looking at a woman! It was almost as if she was feeling my gaze and hearing my thoughts!*

Knights of the Round Table

Lobo Amarillo was rearing back on his powerful rear legs awaiting the command to run. "Ah gentlemen," Luckenbach said to the twelve young officers who were standing on the adjacent viewing platform at the equestrian shooting range. "By usin a smooth sweet iron snaffle bit instead of the army issued curb bit, it's a might easier to guide a runnin horse with the reins held with yer teeth."

"Are those special reins, sir?"

"Only the piece that attaches to yer reins is special; it's made out of a new material called rubber and fits in yer mouth so y'all can hold onto the reins and still breathe through clenched teeth if need be."

"How's it work, sir?"

"Simply lean back slightly, turn yer head in the direction that y'all want to go," as he demonstrated on his standing horse. "It'll pull the neck rein to turn the mount in that direction," as he attempted to steady his horse.

"Where'd you learn that, sir?"

"When I was in the 2nd Cav in Texas. It makes absolute horse sense in combat since it frees both hands. Watch." Luckenbach said as he placed the fitting in his mouth, drew two of his Colt revolvers and put his eager mount forward.

A slight nudging in the ribs with his eagle head spurs and Amarillo was off at a gallop. The first set of two head-size watermelon targets impaled on six foot high poles appeared, one on each side, as the 1860 Army Colts bucked in his hands. As he immediately pointed the revolvers upwards to cock the hammers of the revolvers with his thumbs two more watermelons appeared one on each side as he again fired the Colts. Seconds later through the course two melons appeared on the right side followed by two appearing on the left side. Then he turned his horse forty-five degrees to the right with a target again on each side followed by a forty-five degree turn to the left with two melons on the left side, finishing the course.

He dropped the smoking revolvers into the pommel holsters over his saddle horn liking the smell of burnt blackpowder mixed with sweating horse and leather aromas. Grabbing the reins and pulling Amarillo to a stop, he turned the horse around and stood up in the creaking saddle to view the course. Seeing his trainees waving their hats and cheering from across the equestrian shooting range, he felt that he might have scored hits on most of the targets. As he put his horse back through the course toward the viewing stand, he saw that he had hits on all the watermelons except two, one of which had creased the top of the target. *Shoo-*

tin high, he thought. *As these model Colts tend to do.* Those that were hit were usually shattered into pieces with huge holes bored through them.

"Great shooting, sir!" exclaimed one of the young trainees holding his field glasses as the mounted captain approached the group.

"Don't forget," admonished the captain. "Johnny Reb is usually amovin and shootin at y'all with deadly accuracy. Takes a cool head to shoot accurately in a gun fight!"

"And great riding, sir!" said another as the rest nodded affirmatively and applauded.

"Well thankew, gentlemen," said Luckenbach. "Remember, always stand in the saddle soze yer legs absorb the movement of the horse."

"Do we have to use watermelons, sir!" laughed one of the officers.

"I like to use watermelons for targets since cavalry are still trained in sabre attacks to whack the melon or pumpkin heads of scarecrows oun courses similar to this one," said Luckenbach as he dismounted. "With .44 calibre pistols, the watermelons shatter with a direct hit givin a good dramatic effect and y'all can vary the distances of the targets to about ten yards or so from the rider, which y'all can't do oun a sabre course."

"Sir, seems like a man with a sabre can only whack one at a time, but we saw you out there shooting two at a time!"

"That's right," answered the captain. "And with the sabre, y'all have to be right oun top of or at least within reach of the enemy. With the Colts, y'all got a mite longer reach!"

"Are there any other questions?" asked the student leader.

"Yes sir. Who is the most formidable cavalry man, sir?" asked one of the young officers. "A Reb or an Indian?"

"Well that's a good question, Lieutenant," answered Luckenbach as he paused to think about it. "Most Indan boys cut their teeth oun weapons and are perfectly comfortable ausin em in warfare, the weapons that is. Oun top of that, Plains Indans and maybe Apaches usually been ridin bareback since they was knee high to a buffalo. Hell, a mounted Comanche with a bow can get six arrows into y'all faster'n y'all can reload a muzzleloader; oun top of that, they guide their horses with knee pressure—don't use no bits! Johnny Reb, oun the other hand, is usually comin from a farm or ranch and knows horses but don't know beans bout weapons.

"Indan boys are not only more adept at weapons but also, by bein inured to hunger, pain, and fatigue from cradle to grave, they learn military skills early in life. So, I reckon that the Plains Indan or Apache represents a more formidable threat than Johnny Reb, leastwise from a cavalry point of view. Hell, a Chiricahua can run further afoot in a day then a soldier astride a grain fed horse can ride!" concluded Luckenbach.

"How does the Union Soldier measure up, sir?"

"The Union Army recruits very inferior material from city slums back east and generally accepts anybody whose weight, height, and measurements meet official requirements. Hell, they don't even have to speak English!" The embarrassed young officer trainees stared at the ground and remained silent.

"All right. If there are no further questions, gentlemen, this afternoon's drill will consist of equitation with the new rein apparatus. Shortly after y'all hear the bugler sound 'drill call,' I'll expect y'all back out here again."

"Group, atten-hut!" called the student leader.

"Dismissed," ordered the captain.

Luckenbach tied his horse to the hitching rail outside the Gatehouse to Fort Snelling. As he walked toward the entrance he noticed that the area southwest of the fort had become a bustling army camp as conical four-man tents were being erected in anticipation of the appearance of the Renville Rangers being brought in by the Indian Agent Thomas Galbraith and others for basic and cavalry training. Entering through the Gatehouse and returning the salutes of the guards, he noticed that even the Parade Grounds were a bustle of activity as the newly formed Young Men's Guard and the Union Guard were being mustered into the Minnesota Volunteers of the Union Army.

After returning to his quarters, he freshened up and consumed a lunch left by his cook. He broke down the two Colts that he had fired, dropped both cylinders into a can containing a blackpowder cleaning solvent, then ran a solvent soaked rag through each barrel and laid them down on the table to soak for awhile. Then he went out to the Officer's mess room—a 20 by 40-foot room with a fireplace at each end, to find a newspaper to update him on current events of the war back east.

"Hey Luke! Come sit over here!" called Captain Buck Smith who was sitting at a large round table with several other officers.

"Afternoon, Buck! Y'all 'Knights of the Round Table' today?"

"We got us another war, Luke!"

"The hell you say!"

"Rumor is that Indians are killing people in Meeker County and at the Indian Agency on the Minnesota River!" said Buck.

"Well I'll be damned! Which Tribe?"

"All of them heathen devils—Sioux, Chippewa, and Winnebago! You name em!" said one of the officers.

"They say there're fifty thousand Indians out there on the warpath!" said another of the officers.

"Yeah! Then they say it's a damn Confederate conspiracy!" said another knowing the captain was from Texas, a confederate state.

"Rumor says the Sioux were induced to commit these outrages by Indians from Missouri, and secession traders from that state!" said Major Caleb Jones.

"Well that's right, Luke," said Buck. "They say that southern agents have been working to stir up the Indians, even brought them arms and cannon to open up a western front from here to Kansas with their Indian allies."

"Who the hell is 'they' that's atalkin all this stuff?" asked Luckenbach.

"A man named George Whitcomb from Greenleaf, over in Meeker County just north of Hutchinson, came in with a few other people this morning to inform the Governor. And that's where all the talk started; over in St. Paul," said Caleb.

"What have y'all heard from the Adjutant General's Office?"

"That's what we're waiting for. We've heard that Governor Ramsey is over at the Commanding Officer's Quarters now," said Buck.

"Yeah, you can see his buggy rig right over there in front of the CO's Quarters," said one of the officers leaning into the deep window well and looking out the window with the curtain parted.

"I imagine there'll be an Officers Call right quick," said another as he got up from the table. "So I'm gonna see about getting my field gear ready."

Most of the other officers got up from the table leaving Luckenbach with Buck Smith and Caleb Jones.

"How bout this Agent Galbraith who was acomin out here with fifty half-breeds from out thataway, sposed to be here this afternoon?" asked Luckenbach.

"Well we heard that Major Galbraith was stopped in St. Peter yesterday by a messenger from Redwood Agency and he headed back to Fort Ridgley with his recruits," said Buck.

"Major Galbraith?"

"That's right. Colonel Sibley gave his old Republican crony a commission for recruiting those breeds," said Caleb.

"Does that mean I can go back home now, Caleb? I was detailed up here just to train em people," said Luckenbach getting a laugh from his colleagues.

"Did he say fifty thousand Indians?" asked Buck.

"Yeah. But I doubt if there's ten thousand Indians left in the whole state of Minnesota—men, women, and children," said Caleb.

"Luke, what do you think about this notion of a confederate conspiracy with the Indians around here?" asked Buck.

"Hell, I think that's a bunch of bull! If'n these Sioux are anything like the Cheyenne or Arapaho, which I reckon they are, then they ain't got no use for any White man, regardless of his political persuasion."

"I suppose it's just a bunch of drunken Indians shooting up the place. Seems to happen every now and then," said Buck.

"Why just about three or four years ago, a bunch of Sioux killed about fifty people down in Iowa. Called it the 'Spirit Lake Massacre'. We never did do anything about it!" said Caleb.

"Well most Indans are like wolves. Peaceful at best and will usually run from y'all til they're hungry or y'all piss em off. Then look out!" said Luckenbach.

"I think that's what happened with these Sioux, especially with these Republicans grabbing everything that isn't nailed down. They're starving and been offended one time too many," said Caleb.

"I know one thing for sure. Both Governor Ramsey and Colonel Sibley have become rich men from their cheating of these Indians here in Minnesota," said Buck.

"How's that, Buck?" asked Luckenbach.

"Sibley was in the fur trade and represented the traders at the Sioux treaty negotiations of 1851—that treaty promised the Santee Sioux $495,000 in exchange for land," said Buck. "Sibley succeeded in claiming $145,000 of that amount as money due him for overpayments to the Sioux for furs! The Sioux objected to this obvious fraud, but none other than Agent Alexander Ramsey approved the claim."

"That's right," said Caleb. "A congressional investigator finally came out here in '61 and found evidence of outrageous frauds upon the Indians being perpetrated by the state's political elite!"

"Seems like I asked this question before, but where does President Lincoln stand with all that corruption?" asked Luckenbach.

"Well, these men are all loyal Republicans, high level political strategists who helped deliver the state for Lincoln in the election of 1860, and the new administration had to return the favor—look the other way in other words," said Buck.

"God knows what other kind of promises Lincoln made to these people to get their votes!" said Caleb.

"One thing I know is that last year, Senator Henry Rice managed to get a $24,000 federal payment for his role in Indian Removal after the Treaty of 1858!" said Buck.

"Then Senator Morton Wilkinson got the Lincoln Administration to make sure his political cronies got control of the Minnesota Indian Agencies, which gives them the first share in the Indian annuities!" said Caleb.

"Hell, everyone in Ramsey's administration has been lining his pockets with Indian money!" said Buck.

"Also, with Robert E. Lee kicking his butt in his own back yard, Lincoln gives comparatively low priority to the problems of a few lowly heathen redskins on the frontier," added Caleb.

"After all, it was Indians that killed Lincoln's grandfather!" said Buck.

"Well with the Sioux on the warpath, I wouldn't be surprised to see Sibley get a star out of this. Who else can they put out there?" asked Caleb.

"They could bring McDowell or McClellan out here since they got their butts kicked in Virginia," said Buck.

"Well I'm sure that somebody around here owes Sibley a favor."

"Dam," said Luckenbach. "I got sick to my stomach yesterday hearin bout whiskey drummin in Sioux country. But what y'all are sayin makes bootleggin sound like Sunday school!"

"Luke," said Caleb. "We believe that it's inept government officials, like Galbraith, who are ignorant of frontier conditions and Indian people, who spark Indian wars by making decisions that only exacerbate frontier tensions."

"That's right, Luke," said Buck. "It's those corrupt officials we call the 'Indian Ring,' formulating policies that promote the bureaucrat's self-interest, and undermining the welfare and safety of Indians, frontiersmen, and particularly us soldiers, who have to risk our lives picking up the pieces."

"The Army is here to enforce federal policy, but we vigorously object to civilian control of Indian affairs," added Caleb.

Damn, Luckenbach thought. *These hombres are no different than the people they criticize; they've never even thought about a little hablar de negocios con los Indios oun the nature of policy. They assume the same pendaho posture of knowing what's best for Indans and that their good intentions will excuse any resulting bloodshed!*

"Seems like y'all are only concerned with who will manage Indan policy, not what direction that policy should take," said Luckenbach.

"In a sense that's right, Luke," said Buck. "We as military officers don't quarrel with the ends of federal Indian policy, but we do debate the methods and management of that policy."

> *Come forth, and bring with you a heart*
> *That watches and receives,*

thought Luckenbach as he heard chairs scraping the wooden floor as the bugler sounded Officer's Call.

"Room! Atten-hut!" called the Duty Officer to the sixty-three officers in attendance at the Officers Call stood to attention.

"Please be seated, gentlemen," asked Oscar Malmros, the Adjutant General of Fort Snelling, as those having access to chairs sat down while many stood along the walls of the mess room of the Officers Barracks as this was probably the most highly attended Officers Call in anyone's recent memory.

"Gentlemen," said the general. "A short time ago the governor received the following dispatch from Fort Ridgley:

Commanding Officer at Fort Snelling:

Captain Marsh left this post at 10½ this morning to prevent Indian depredations at the Lower Agency. Some of the men have returned. I learn from them that Capt. Marsh is killed and only thirteen of his company are remaining.

The Indians are killing the settlers and plundering the country. Send reinforcements without delay. Respectfully,

Thomas P. Gere,
2nd Lieut. 5th Reg't Minn. Vol.

P.S.—Please hand this to Gov. Ramsey.

"Also received was the following dispatch from St. Peter:

Governor-

Sir: A second dispatch has arrived from the Fort. Capt. Marsh, on hearing of the fight at Red Wood, went with fifty of our company. Only thirteen came back. The captain was wounded and drowned.

The messenger is at the door, and I close. I leave in half an hour for the Fort, with fifty armed men.

N.K. Culver
1st Lieutenant 5th Min. Vols.

P.S. Five hundred men are needed.

"So gentlemen, in view of the reported Indian difficulties in the counties of Meeker, Brown, and Renville, calling for immediate interference of the Government, Col. Henry H. Sibley is hereby directed to take charge of a military expedition for their prompt suppression, and to restore the peace and quiet in those settlements.

Colonel Smith, commanding the place of General Rendezvous, at Fort Snelling, will forthwith detail four companies of his command to be placed under charge of Colonel Sibley.

Colonel Sibley will proceed without delay with said four companies to our frontier, and will collect in addition on the way such forces of mounted infantry, as he may deem available.

Colonel Sibley is hereby authorized to provide all necessary subsistence and transportation for the troops under his command.

Captain Webb will act as Adjutant to Colonel Sibley.

Mr. Mills is hereby appointed quartermaster for this expedition.

By order of the Commander in Chief, signed by myself
Oscar Malmros, Adjutant General.
"A roster will be posted, gentlemen, of all four companies affected by this order. In addition, Captain Luckenbach, as well as his training staff—Sergeants

Coker and Leddy, is detailed to this expedition to command any mounted infantry as may be recruited along the way. That is all, gentlemen!"

"Room! Atten-hut!" called the Duty Officer once again.

"Dismissed," said the general departing with his staff with the mess room erupting in anxious conversation.

Come quickly, King of Kings!

Astrid woke once again to the sound of a rooster crowing and sat up in her cot, only to find she was not in her room at all but on a bed of leaves under a pergola of fallen trees. She thought that like her the rooster must have escaped yesterday's onslaught and sought shelter in the forest. Looking east out across the creek, she saw a beautiful willow tree standing in the subdued light of dawn. It was a large, graceful tree with a thick trunk and furrowed bark with the light filtering down through its narrow leaves giving them a flickering translucent glow as they rustled featherlike in the morning breeze.

Is that eastward of Eden? she thought. *And is that the Tree of the Knowledge of Good and Evil? Are those the Wings of Anyels?* Feeling somewhat uncomfortable, she laid back down wishing that she had some of Olga's hot herbal medicine as she could hear her saying *Ja wohl, Astrid, an herbal tea,* as she closed her eyes and began to weep.

"Go back to the house and make sssome tea," she heard a strange voice whispering in the darkness of the shelter.

Looking out toward the stream, she saw a magnificent snake coiled in front of the opening of the shelter looking at her. The snake was large and golden with yellow diamond patterns outlined in violet, green and brown on its back and white scales on its belly. Its black eyes seemed fierce and piercing with a forked red tongue rhythmically flashing out of its mouth tasting the air. There was a strange, glowing lavender tinted aura that surrounded the serpent, which seemed to neutralize Astrid's fear.

"Who on earth are you?" she asked.

"I am the SSSerpent of the Garden of Eden," whispered the snake.

"Have you not been cursed by God who said that you will be more retched than the animals of the field?"

"And did He not sssay to you, woman, that in pain you shall bring forth children?"

"But it is that pain that affirms my humanness."

"And it is that sssame humanness that tempted Adam!"

"So to err and to feel pain is human?"

"Yesss! To feel pain is human!"

"Uff da!" cried Astrid jolted from her dream by a contraction in her stomach and a backache. She looked immediately to the opening of the shelter and, not seeing the snake, realized that she must have dozed off. *But it seemed so real,* she thought.

The serpent was the symbol of the Vikings she remembered Johannes saying. *Like the serpent, they were regenerative. They could make changes in their life and adapt to new circumstances as easily as a snake sheds its skin. The Norsemen were ambitious and tenacious and regarded obstacles in their path as wind in their sail to the fulfillment of their dreams of new lands and freedom. They emerged from those challenges transformed and renewed.*

You are like the serpent, he had said. *You are a Viking! You have a determined, powerful nature that thrives on periodic dramatic life changes and overcoming challenges.*

"Yohannes, what more dramatic life change could have occurred than where I find myself now?" she said as she surveyed her surroundings. "What greater challenge do I have to overcome than this?"

The morning was relatively quiet compared to yesterday when she could hear gunfire in the distance and Indians calling to each other in the woods. For a moment, she thought they had seen her tracks leading to her hiding place. She considered giving herself up to the Indians but she remembered Good Voice Woman's warning that it is very dangerous around here and she must think about the safety of her baby.

She ate some jerky and a turnip and drank some water from a glass jar that was in the bag Good Voice Woman had left with her and she had filled in the nearby creek. She could feel her baby moving. *How active he is,* she thought. *He just wants to be born at a time and place like this to make his grandfather proud.*

Her father-in law, Hans Mundahl, as most Haugians, regarded rural society as truly Norwegian. He regarded the urban community in Norway as tainted by its ties to Denmark and Sweden, which had successively ruled Norway for four centuries. Fed up with the pretensions of the official and clerical classes of Balestrand, Hans moved to the New World. Although her father-in-law's decision to migrate was primarily economic, leaving the problem of religious persecution behind and finding the promise of religious freedom in the new land were very compelling.

In Minnesota, the Norwegians took land in rural areas where they maintained their old ways that provided some continuity with the homeland. Mundahl, however, realized that they had to totally transform themselves to adapt successfully to the new land, which meant new crops, new language, and, more importantly, new ideas. That new land of the billowing prairie and lowlands as rich as the meadows of Goshen and access to the great Nile of America, the Mississippi, had transformed his ideals of a true Norwegian to become a true American and business was his longship to riches.

Since he was from a long line of whalers who had hunted the cold coasts of Greenland and fishermen who had dropped their nets into the Sognefjorden for five hundred years, establishing the Norway Fish Company was a natural for Hans. Born in Mundal, Norway in 1818, Hans had immigrated to Duluth, Minnesota in 1844 where he worked in pioneering the Norwegian commercial fishing industry along the north shore of Lake Superior. When rural land was made available by the Mendota Treaty of 1851, his distrust of the city and his desire to live a rural life led to his decision to bring his wife Karie and their three children including the six-year-old Johannes to the newly established Norwegian-American settlements and Haugian community of Arendahl Township in Fillmore County.

As Hauge had said—wealth was an expression of God's blessing and that the correct Christian understanding was not to let the material world blind you but to be a faithful and wise steward over what God hath provided, Hans Mundahl set out to acquire. He befriended the young Peter Peterson Hasleråd also from Norway who had found a natural spring and built a farm around his new limestone "Spring House" above the flood plain of the Root River. Hans had encouraged Peter to build a fish hatchery with the cold, clean water necessary for trout production from that remarkable spring which God hath provided and a partnership was formed. They soon had ponds dug and were well on their way to the production of yearling trout and their Norway Fish Company.

The Root River Valley lies in a part of the country largely untouched by glaciers of the last ice age allowing the river to carve deep cuts into the ancient rock formations. Great limestone cliffs provide sheltering walls of the valley as if protecting its uniqueness from the rest of Minnesota. It is warmer than the northern forests and wetter than the western prairies as it more resembles the Ozarks with its hardwood forests and the river teeming with smallmouth bass, walleye, catfish, and trout.

The Root River provided an outlet to the Mississippi on which they were able to import herring from Lake Superior and lutefisk—three finned Atlantic Cod preserved in lye, from countrymen in New York City for sale to the burgeoning Norwegian population in the area. "Wherever you have Norwegians, by Gud, you got to haf lutefisk!" Hans said to justify his venture to an investor in La Crosse. As more people came to settle in the community that became Peterson, the bearded Northmen were soon distributing fish to Norwegians in Arendahl and Norway Townships and as far south as the Hallingdal Norwegian settlements in the Spring Grove Township of Houston County.

With his newfound wealth, Hans built a fine home near Peter's farm and the Spring House that he believed was a little Temple of New Canaan and was able to send his three children to St. Paul for their schooling. Such was the world of the young Johannes Hanson Mundahl.

"Yohannes, I feel so alone and helpless without the beautiful brooch that you had given me! Like my Guardian Anyel, it too disappeared!"

How strange it was that Good Voice Woman came to help me yesterday, she thought. *She seemed like a Guardian Anyel. What on earth did she mean when she said that I would not see her again? And how does she know that someone will be here to help me today? How will that someone know where I am?*

Crawling out from under the shelter and carefully standing up, she slowly surveyed her surroundings and could see the forest of trees and undergrowth and the misty morning air filled with the cacophony of insects and birds with beams of light filtering through the green canopy of leaves from the sun rising on the eastern horizon. As she breathed the fragrant solitude of the wilderness, she had a feeling of total joy. Then she could hear the wild sounds of nature slowly transform to a choir of voices of what could only be Angels singing...

> *The King shall come when morning dawns*
> *And light triumphant breaks,*
> *When beauty gilds the eastern hills*
> *And life to joy awakes.*

Weeping as she felt her conversion to Christ, she carefully crawled back into her shelter that *was like a manger,* she thought. She could feel her baby moving and her water break as she also felt her conversion to motherhood.

> *Not as of old a little child,*
> *To bear and fight and die,*
> *But crowned with glory like the sun*
> *That lights the morning sky.*

"I have no doubt that Good Voice Woman was indeed a Guardian Anyel. I had prayed to God almighty that when I walk through the darkness in the valley

of death, He would send an Anyel of Mercy to accompany me! It is indeed God
that is working His mercy!"

> *Oh, brighter than the rising morn*
> *When Christ, victorious rose*
> *And left the lonesome place of death,*
> *Despite the rage of foes.*

Again feeling the contractions of her stomach muscles, Astrid could only lay
back and accept the pain. "I pray that a Guardian Anyel will come again for my
baby's sake! Good Voice Woman! Where are you?"

> *Oh, brighter than the glorious morn*
> *Shall dawn upon our race*
> *The day when Christ in splendor comes,*
> *And we shall see his face.*

"I had prayed to God almighty that He bless the children of the Bruners with
long life, happiness, and good health. Watch over them, dear God, that, in your
mercy, they have somehow survived!" she sobbed.

> *The King shall come when morning dawns*
> *And light and beauty brings.*
> *Hail, Christ the Lord! Your people pray:*
> *Come quickly, King of kings.*

Awakening in a sweat from her labor and the heat of the morning, Astrid had
no idea of how long she had been unconscious. She could no longer hear the
choir singing and thought that she must have been delirious. As she fully trusted
God to show his mercy and watch over her in her time of need, she remained
calm. She thought again of Olga and her belief that a healthy pregnancy should
be gentle, natural, and herbal and to trust in your natural God given body. She
thought that maybe if she got up on her knees and sat back on her heels, it would
be a more natural position for the baby to come.

As she began to get up, she looked out toward the stream and could see the
dark outline of a man standing on a fallen log. He was a large man with his back
to her, held a long rifle in his hands as he appeared to be looking for something.
She was about to call out to him when he turned and stepped forward into the
light. She could now see him clearly and at that instant he saw her.

"Oh my God," she cried out. "An Indian!"

Yellow Medicine

Matoȟota had sat watching the reflections of the bright golden topaz moon as the ripples on the Minnesota transformed it into a sparkling multifaceted gem. Because of constant gunfire and the yelling of desperate men from across the river throughout the moonlit night, he thought it best that he stand watch over his sleeping family. Even on his northeast side of the river near the mouth of Beaver Creek, he had seen bright fires from burning Iašića farms and heard wagons moving rapidly on the river road above.

His vigilance was intense since he knew that they were fair game for both intolerant Indians and vengeful White people alike. In the darkness before daylight, he quickly sprinted to the shore and pulled his canoe up a cut bank and into a thicket of undergrowth. He turned his canoe over and laid the paddles on the thwarts. With his newly acquired razor-sharp bowie knife, he chopped several overhanging branches from a nearby tree and laid them over the birch bark craft. With one of the heavily leaved branches, he returned to the shore and carefully covered their tracks on the beach and up the cut bank.

He went back to his family and saw that they were awake and rolling up their blankets. "We have to be away from here and into the forest before sunrise," he said.

Kuŋši hurriedly retrieved some boiled corn and pemmican from their pack and distributed breakfast to each before they gathered their loads to begin their trek. "Haŋhaŋnawotapi!" she whispered.

"We'll follow Beaver Creek through the woods all the way north to the prairie. Where the creek bends west, we'll keep going north until we come to Kaŋdiyohi country," said Matoȟota.

"When will we get there?" asked Waćiŋća.

"Maybe tonight or tomorrow morning, depending on how kuŋši feels. It's over twenty miles," answered his father.

Matoȟota could see smoke from at least two burning farms. It looked as if the farms were set afire the day before with the charred ruins still smoldering. If it was anything like what happened at the Redwood Agency, then he feared that the farmers and their families had been ruthlessly killed. As they crossed the bottomlands east of Beaver Creek and neared the river road, he could see a burning barn about half a mile to the east. He had his family members seek cover in a wooded thicket above the river road while he went to look for anyone still alive.

He was wearing a shirt of white trade cloth tucked under his breechcloth, worn buckskin leggings, and unadorned moccasins. He wore a weathered black army slouch hat still bearing the cavalry cap badge with the flat brim pulled down in front and an eagle feather stuck in a porcupine-quilled hatband. He had the huge stag-handled Bowie knife sheathed and tucked into his ceinture fléchée—his grandfather's hand-woven wool sash, and carried his brass-studded 50-calibre Kentucky Rifle cradled in his left arm. Crisscrossing his chest were the narrow worn leather straps of a rifle accoutrements bag and a powder horn.

As he neared the farm, he could see that the river road ran right through the farmyard, between what was left of the house and the barn and a few other buildings. Below the farm was a large cornfield that seemed to have been mostly harvested but left undamaged. From the tracks on the road, he saw that any livestock they might have had were herded off. He cautiously entered the farmyard with his rifle at the ready, as he could smell the stench of death in this place.

On the east side of the gutted house near the smoldering main entrance still standing was the grim scene of the tomahawked bodies of four family members—a woman and three young children, with several vultures flapping their wings and flying off at the sight of him. One of the small buildings near the barn was intact with the scalped, arrow-riddled body of the farmer lying in front of it. In front of the door were two crossed sticks each pounded into the ground; *an Indian way of saying, 'Do not enter here!* he thought.

Inside of the shed were the smashed components of a whiskey still—coiled copper tubing, and metal tanks of various sizes, which were common fixtures on Iaśića farms. *Why was this building left unburned?* he wondered. *Maybe it was their way of saying that whiskey is no longer tolerated here.*

He dragged the ripening corpse of the farmer to the house with the others and dug a shallow grave for the five family members and covered them with dirt. His work was interspersed with periods of vomiting from the sickening horror and stench of it all. He tied two sticks together in the form of a cross and pounded it into the ground at the head of the burial place; *a White man's way of saying, 'A Christian is buried here,'* he thought. *Strange how two signs almost alike can have such different meanings.*

He then stood before the graves and, wiping his sweating face with his shirt, respectfully said, "May their spirits return to their homeland where they will find peace! We are all related!" hesitant to mention the name of a God or Great Spirit that would allow such a heinous act to happen. He put on his shirt and hat, picked up his rifle and accoutrements and returned back down the road to his waiting family.

Walking northwest along the river road, they soon crossed the shallow Beaver Creek at a rocky ford and began to follow the stream north. Through the thicket of trees along the creek, Matohota saw a huge barn sitting on a rise and about a quarter of a mile to the northwest. Thinking it unusual that it wasn't burned, he motioned the column to a halt and pointed to it. He and Antoine approached the farm and saw that all of the buildings were left intact. They cautiously walked into the farmyard and could see no sign of human carnage or life.

The house was empty of people and miraculously had not been looted as food and dishes were still as placed on the dining room table the previous day. As they walked into the barn, they were surprised to find two milk cows in their stalls eating hay as if waiting to be milked. A third cow, Winnifred, began to enter the barn from the open back doors but mooed and shied away when it saw the two men.

Feeling that the farm was safe for now, Matohota asked his son to go back and bring the others. While Antoine was gone, he walked through the barn and out the back doors. Looking across a back hillside pasture and a small corral he saw nothing unusual and turned back to the barn. *What was that?* he thought as he turned and looked again into the corral. Opening the gate, he walked over to a shiny object that had caught his eye and picked it up. It was a beautiful brooch, a cut stone in an unusual silver setting. Thinking his wife might like it, he dropped it into his accoutrements bag. *Someone must have recently lost it* he thought, as he saw what looked like tracks of a woman walking across the corral and leading into the woods. *But she didn't seem to be in a hurry...*then, interrupting his thoughts, he heard his son calling him.

Returning through the barn and across the farmyard, he could see wagon tracks mingled with huge horse tracks. It looked like the attackers had loaded the family onto their own wagon and carted them off somewhere with their own team of draft horses. As he joined his family, they looked as bewildered as he was.

"Why was this farm spared?" Matohota asked of both the women in their Dakota language.

"Dey probably respect da family for some reason," said his wife Wahćaziwiŋ insisting on practicing her English.

"Grandson, from what you said those people at that other farm were most likely killed and their buildings burned because they made whiskey and were bootleggers."

"I know he didn't make whiskey here since we didn't find a still," said Antoine.

"He wasn't a bootlegger either," said kuŋśi.

"Who is he then?"

"He is an Iaśića named Max Bruner. The young men have always respected him as a brave man because he wouldn't allow them on his land. He would get mad and chase them off. We always respect a man who is brave and will defend his family and home place," said kuŋśi Okadawiŋ.

"What were the other farmers like?" asked Waćiŋća.

"Many were so afraid of Indians that our men could walk right into their houses and take something and the frightened farmers would do nothing."

"Son, our Dakotapi do not tolerate cowardly men," added Matohota.

"Dat is true, my son. Bravery is one of da, ah wowaśte topa," she said looking at her husband who shrugged his shoulders.

"Four virtues!" said the smiling Antoine.

"Ohaŋ, four virtues of our Isaŋti Dakota," said Wahćaziwiŋ.

"What are the others?" asked Waćiŋća.

"Respect, generosity, and wisdom," Antoine answered.

"I think that these Burners also have respect of our Dakota ways," said kuŋśi.

"How is that?"

"Bruner's wife, Olga, is a midwife among her people. She is trying to learn our language and is always asking us about plants, and how we help our women have babies. She says that our Indian babies are the healthiest she has ever seen."

"Have you been here before?"

"No, but I have often spoken to her. She knows that Medicine Man Ćetaŋhuŋka, and he and his friends have been here many times."

"Husband, he is da grandfather of dat little girl dat you save da udder morning!"

He raised his eyebrows with a look of surprise.

"That is true, grandson. It was his daughter Howaśtewiŋ that was killed by those drunken Iaśića, the one that you buried Sunday!"

"Mon Dieu!" he said shocked by the coincidence. "So he is the one who has done this?"

"He wanted revenge for his murdered daughter. He blamed whiskey and those who sell it."

"Husband, dere are many reasons why da lives of dis good family were spared. But power moves in mysterious ways and we must seek out da reason why da Great Spirit has brought us here."

Matohota thought of the brooch that he had found in the corral behind the barn. He retrieved the piece from his accoutrements bag and said, "Found this in the corral behind the barn," as he handed it to his wife.

His wife looked at it admiringly for several seconds then said, "Waśtedo!"— good one, in Dakota, forgetting about her need to practice her English as she handed it to kuŋśi Okadawiŋ.

Kuŋśi felt of the brooch and, looking at her grandson, said, "It is very old. It feels warm like it has life, like a Holy Man's ceremonial instruments."

"Where I found it there were tracks of a woman walking slowly toward the east, toward Beaver Creek."

"Then we must go find her! She is out there somewhere and needs our help!" said kuŋśi handing the brooch back to her grandson.

Matohota returned to the tracks of the woman and followed them out of the corral and into the wooded area toward Beaver Creek. His family followed in single file with Antoine again bringing up the rear. Upon reaching the creek, the tracks disappeared since the ground was littered with rotting tree branches, bark, and leaves. Following the creek upstream, he would occasionally find a footprint in open sand or a broken twig or an overturned rock that marked her passing.

Near a bend in the creek was an area with several fallen logs where he lost her trail. He motioned for his followers to stop while he began to scour the area for tracks. He followed the creek about fifty yards upstream and returned to the fallen trees. Climbing up on one of the logs for a better view of the surrounding forest, he carefully walked several paces up its inclined surface using his rifle as a balancing pole. Again seeing nothing, he turned to walk back down the log when he saw her. She was sitting under a sheltered area formed by several fallen trees.

"Oh my God, an Indian!" he heard her cry out.

In order not to frighten her even more, Matohota Stood frozen in his position on the log and said calmly, "Don't be afraid. We're here to help you."

"Who are you?" she pleaded.

"My name is Matohota Charbonneau. My wife and grandmother are near and will help you. Want me to call them?"

With tears running down her cheeks, she closed her eyes and nodded her head in a positive way as she inhaled the word, "Ya!"

As soon as the women appeared at the shelter, they could see that Astrid was pregnant and had recently lost her water.

"Husband, she's having a baby! Now! You must make a fire and boil some water!"

Matohota quickly started a fire with his flint steel while his boys went to gather wood. He then hung two kettles full of creek water from a rack that he had fashioned out of branches over the fire.

"Grandson, I need some pežutazi and I know you can find it around here," said kuŋśi as she gave him the large empty buckskin bag that Astrid had been given.

Matohota asked Antoine to come with him to find the plants. With their rifles cradled in their arms and walking east from the shelter, Antoine asked, "What is 'pežutazi'?"

"Pežutazi—yellow medicine, is what the White people call 'downy gents' or something like that."

"Like the river?"

"We call that river up north the Yellow Medicine because a lot of it grows around there."

"Is it yellow?"

"The roots are yellow."

"What does she do with them?"

"She uses the boiled flowers as sweet smelling cleansing water then she grinds up the roots and makes a tea."

"What for?"

"Eases the pain of the stomach muscles when a woman pushes the baby out. Good for snake bites too."

"What do we look for?"

"A little plant about as high as your knee with a hairy stem and shiny green narrow leaves in twos and purple bell-shaped flowers, usually in bunches at the ends of stems."

After they walked about a quarter of a mile, Antoine stopped and pointed at a thicket of tallgrass and prairie flowers. "Is that pežutazi?" he asked.

His father approached the plants and said, "Yes! And you must always be very respectful around these plants because they have mysterious powers."

"Respectful to a plant?"

"Our very survival depends on plants; they are part of our Sacred Circle."

"What do we do then?"

"Watch me," he said as he took a pinch of tobacco from a small buckskin pouch tied around his neck and sprinkled it over the plants as he prayed, "Grand-father Great Spirit, Grandmother Earth, Spirit of this plant. I am a poor man crying out to you for help. A woman bringing life into this world is in need of your powers. We are all related!"

He knelt down and made deep incisions into the earth around four of the plants with his bowie knife, then carefully pulled the plants out of the ground. While shaking dirt from around the roots he said to his son, "You must always pray to the Spirit of the plant, and then you must be very careful not to injure the roots."

"Why?"

"There is a story that kuŋśi tells about a man of our Tribe who was digging out one of these plants when he accidentally cut the side of one of the roots. A short time later a horse kicked him and he died. She says that it was because he wounded that plant."

Matoḣota placed the plants in the bag that kuŋśi had provided him thinking that the bag looked somehow familiar. He handed the bag to Antoine to carry but he was reluctant to take it because of the story his father had told him. "Don't worry," he said with a smile. "The plants like us!"

When they returned to the log shelter, his wife and grandmother were busy with Astrid. Kuŋśi opened the bag that contained the plants, broke the purple bell-shaped flowers off of the hairy stems, rolled them vigorously between her hands and dropped them into the boiling water of one of the kettles. "We made her walk around while you were gone, so now we are going to wash her with this sweet water and put buffalo grease on her," kuŋśi said as she and Waḣćaziwiŋ washed their hands with the hot fragrant water using the leaves as scouring pads.

As the women busied themselves with Astrid, Matoḣota ground the yellow roots between two stones and stirred the resulting mash into the boiling water. Waḣćaziwiŋ filled the glass jar with the tea and gave it to Astrid to drink. "Da baby is coming," she said to Astrid. "Dis tea will help you."

"I yust thank God almighty that you are all here!" said Astrid as she acknowledged the 'childish' omen of the Old Country by undoing her braided hair. "It is God working His mercy!"

"The baby's head will be out in a few minutes. That's when the pain will start," kuŋśi said in Dakota. Okadawiŋ could speak her late husband Jean-Jacques Charbonneu's French language and could understand English but was reluctant to speak it.

Having refilled one of the kettles with water and hanging it back over the fire, Matoḣota walked to the other side of the shelter where his two boys were sitting.

"What will we do now, father?" asked Antoine.

"I don't know," he answered. "She'll be too weak to walk very far."

"Aaahhh!" they could hear Astrid cry out.

"Nina patitaŋ, Astrid! Nina patitaŋ!" they could hear kuŋśi encouraging her in Dakota to push hard.

"These are crazy times," said Antoine. "All these people dying and here somebody is being born?"

"Where is she from?" asked Waćiŋća.

"I don't know but she must have lived on that farm back there."

"She smells like an Iaśića," said Antoine.

"They all smell like cow's milk," said Waćiŋća.

"Aaahhh!" they heard her cry out again.

"Push, Astrid! Push! Da baby is coming now!" said Waĥćaziwiŋ.

"We can't take her with us because she can't walk, but at the same time we can't leave her here," said Matoĥota.

"I think that we should take her to Fort Ridgley, to be safe with her own people," said Antoine.

"You're right. But I would have to take her to the fort by canoe and by myself," said Matoĥota. "Too dangerous for all of us."

"But you said she can't walk," said Waćiŋća.

"She should be able to walk from here to the canoe, but that's about all," he said thinking that they could make a litter if they had to.

"Then we could wait here for you," said Waćiŋća.

"No, you would be safer if you went on to be with the Gens Libre."

"Aaahhh!" she cried out again then Matoĥota heard her breathe a deep sigh of relief.

"Da baby is here, Astrid!" said Waĥćaziwiŋ as they could hear the baby cry. "It's a beautiful bald-head baby boy!"

Great Gift of Life

In the evening they were sitting around the small fire where the women had roasted some corn and had passed out some pemmican. Occasionally they could hear distant gunfire from across the river and thought that the fighting had moved farther south so Matohota had gone to scout the area. Astrid was sitting up after having slept for awhile and proudly nursing her newborn.

"What will you name your son den?" asked Wahćaziwiŋ.

"His name will be Arnt Yohannesen Mundahl," she answered thinking that Indians seemed to smell like cedar smoke.

"How does he get a name like dat?"

"We are Norwegians and that is the way that we name children."

"Among our Dakota, if first born is a son we name him Ćaske or chas-KAY, she said slowly enunciating the syllables. "And den if first born is a daughter her name is Winona or we-NO-na."

"Arnt is taken from the name of my father. Then Yohannesen is taken from the name of the baby's father, meaning the son of Yohannes. And then Mundahl is the town in Norway where many generations of my husband's family are from."

"Where are you from den?"

"We are from Arendahl, a township in southeastern Minnesota, not too far from here."

"So den you could name your son Arnt Yohannesen Arendahl?"

"I suppose we could, but in America we like to keep our names from the Old Country," she answered as she laid her baby down on her lavender shawl, wrapped him up and began to burp him. As she thought about it, though, she realized that it had never occurred to her that their last name could well be Arendahl.

"I name my first son Ćaske but when he got older, we change it to Antoine cause he look and act just like his grandpa Antoine, da fodder of the fodder of my children, who has not been heard from for many winters now."

"What is your udder ah I mean other boy's name?"

"We name him Hepaŋ because he was da second born, but his brudder start calling him Waćiŋća or Wa-CHI-cha which means cub because he look like his fodder."

"What does his father's name ah, I've tried but I can't pronounce it, ah Ma-toe-oak-da or something like that, what does it mean?"

"Ma-TOE-(guttural h)-da. It means 'Grizzly Bear' because he look and act just like one of dose big brown bears. Just look at him," she answered with a proud smile as Matohota returned and leaned his rifle against a log as he helped himself to roasted corn and pemmican.

"It looks like they took the Bruner's wagon to the ferry landing then across the Minnesota" he said to his family in Dakota. "They probably took them to Little Crow's Village."

"How long will we stay here?" asked Antoine.

"The moon will rise in about an hour from now," he said as he sat down at the fire. "When it sets around midnight is when we have to leave downstream for Fort Ridgley while it's dark and we have a better chance of getting there."

"How far is it?" asked Antoine.

"About fifteen miles as the crow flies," answered Matohota. "But the way this river bends and turns, it's probably closer to twenty-five miles."

"How long would it take you to get there paddling by yourself?" asked Antoine.

"About five hours," he answered.

"If I went with you, we could get there faster with two paddling," said Antoine.

"No. I want you both to stay with your mother and kuŋśi and take them to Kandiyohi. Then I'll meet you there in a couple of days."

"Well, anyway it's downstream, so at least you'll be with the current," said Antoine.

"Astrid, how did you get here den?" asked Wahćaziwiŋ.

There was silence for a long moment as the question awakened a deep psychological repression in Astrid as she laid her baby down and, staring at the ground, began crying almost hysterically. A cathartic release from the incredible stress of the last two days—of her perceived death of the Bruner's to her all night vigil of being alone in the dangerous forest to her baby coming and her not knowing what to do. All she had, her only comfort, was her enduring trust in God to work His mercy.

After a few minutes, Astrid began to compose herself and said, "Good Voice Woman came to warn me of...of the Indians killing the Yermans and...and brought me here! She gave me food and...and said that someone would soon be here for me!"

"Howaśtewiŋ!" said Wahćaziwiŋ in a shocked whisper as she looked at her husband.

"Yes!" said Astrid recognizing the Dakota name. "She said that I had to come with her for my baby's sake! She must have sensed that something bad was going to happen to my baby!" as she began crying again.

"There were tracks of only one person," Matohota said in Dakota slowly shaking his head and looking at the solemn faces of his family astonished by the thought of a ghostly return from the dead.

"But the Bruners!" she cried. "Were they all killed?"

"Astrid," said Wahćaziwiŋ. "Dey are all alive and taken captive to some place across da river!"

"But, but I heard shooting and…and screams!" she cried in disbelief.

"They were probably shooting to scare them since they knew that that brave man would try to fight them," said Matohota.

Astrid cried for several minutes in joyous relief sensing the presence of the Holy Spirit in the sparing of their precious lives. Then, while wiping her eyes, asked, "And how on earth did you know I was here?"

Matohota reached into his accoutrements bag and retrieved the amethyst brooch and handed it to Astrid. "I found this near the barn. Grandma said that you were out here somewhere and needed our help so we followed your tracks and found you. It must be yours."

"Ya!" said Astrid inhaling the word. In one epiphanous flash of understanding Astrid saw the coming together of Jesus Christ of the Haugians, the Great Spirit of the Dakota, and Odin of her Viking ancestors. She took the brooch and felt its healing radiance in her hand remembering the warmth of Johannes' hand on that cold winter night in Arendahl that seemed so long ago and realized that all of her prayers had been answered—that God had indeed shown His tender mercy. Astrid knew through this great gift of life that her conversion to Christ was now complete.

WEDNESDAY, AUGUST 20, 1862

Ways of the Isaŋti Warrior

The sun had risen over the eastern horizon as Wayuhi returned to the village of Red Iron where they had camped for the night. He removed the halter from his stallion and allowed him to join their string of horses standing in the shade of a huge tree near the river with their heads resting on each others backs and their tails swishing at flies. He laid his flute against a tree and was rolling up his buffalo robe when Ćaske came walking up from the river.

"Ahhh brother," he said. "That was a good fight that you had yesterday. Grandpa said that two of those Ojibway were armed with rifles and one had a shotgun."

"We had wokićiwaśte—advantage," answered Wayuhi as he tied the rolled-up robe with a rawhide cord and placed it with the others.

"What do you mean?"

"My father says that you should always strive to have wokićiwaśte, whether it's in fighting, hunting, playing or even arguing with someone."

"But how did you have wokićiwaśte in that fight?"

"They were camped on the river near a small butte so when I blew my whistle, it echoed all over the place and they couldn't tell where it was coming from. Then the echoes of the horses' hooves confused them even more."

"But what if you didn't confuse them?"

"Then we would have been shot," Wayuhi said with a sinister smile on his face as his brother tried to smile back.

"What other ways do you use wokićiwaśte?"

"Lots of ways," said Wayuhi as he retrieved his encased weapons hanging from a branch of a nearby tree. "When you attack an enemy, try to have the sun at your back since the enemy is blinded with the sun in his eyes. Or when you attack a village, hit them in the early morning and kill them in their beds." He paused for effect then said grinning, "Before they kill you."

"How do you use it in hunting buffalo?"

"The trick with buffalo is to chose wisely where you're going run them. A long flat dry treeless prairie to run on is your wokićiwaśte. But you want to get as close to the herd as possible before you start the running chase."

"How do you do that?"

"Usually I'll sit crouched down on my horse with a buffalo robe draped over us and let the horse graze downwind from the herd until we're close enough to start the run. Buffalo are very fast and you don't want to run your horse out before you even get to the herd."

"That's why you carry big buffalo robes with you?"

"Ho."

"But how do you know how to guide the horse when the herd is running?"

"Just let them go. They know how to run and the faster it is the better they like it!" Wayuhi said grinning.

"Aaaa!"

Wayuhi was wearing a long red breechcloth and moccasins and was bare-chested with the knife and quilled scabbard he had received from Mazamani hanging by a cord around his neck. He tied a bandana around his head and inserted the white eagle feather vertically centered on the back. His long black hair hung loosely and was still wet from his morning bath in the river.

"From what you said yesterday about those people down around the Lower Agency, the White man has wokićiwaśte," said Wayuhi. "That's probably what makes our people so angry."

"How is that?"

"That agent Galbraith controls the money and the food rations. If you don't do as he orders you, then you won't get your annuity payment and you won't get rations so your family will starve."

"That's why we still haven't received our money!"

"Ho! Galbraith is probably mad because a lot of our people won't give up our old ways and he calls us 'Blanket Indians.' He doesn't like it that the young Mdewakaŋtoŋ and Wahpekute warriors listen to Hoćokaduta and Iŋkpaduta and kill the bootleggers like you said because he loses too much money."

"So he has wokićiwaśte if we're all drunk and get the whiskey sickness where our stomachs get big and we turn yellow and scream in the night?"

"Ho! If you can keep the Dakotapi needing your whiskey, then you control them and pretty soon you have all of their land!"

"Brother, you carry Sacred Arrows and the great Thunder Bow of the west. What is the purpose of having them if you still use them to kill people?"

"There is a saying that weapons are instruments of the Black Road, despised by the Red Road. To use them only when unavoidable is the way of the Red Road."

"What does that mean?"

"The reason that weapons are instruments of the Black Road is that the Red Road is the way that gives life to our people, so something used for taking life is truly an instrument of the Black Road. So the saying has it that what contradicts the Red Road is despised."

"But it also said that to use weapons when unavoidable is also the way of the Red Road. What does that mean?"

"It means that life is sustained by death. The way of the Red Road is part of the Sacred Circle. The grasses are given life by the Earth Mother and grow fat and green during the Planting Moon. Then those grasses are eaten to give life to the great deer, elk, and buffalo nations. Then we kill a four-legged brother with an arrow to feed our people. So the arrow that has taken a life has given life. Then after a man dies, he is buried in the earth and his flesh and his bones feed the soil that gives life to the grasses, and the Sacred Circle is completed."

"But what about war and killing another man?"

"It happens that many people can suffer because of the evil of one man. So you can say that killing that one man can spare those many people of pain."

"Like killing those Ojibway?"

"The Ojibway raid into our country to kill our people. If we kill those Ojibway, then we bring life to those people who otherwise would have died. The purpose is that the weapon that kills is the weapon that gives life to our people."

"Why is the Pipe always carried with the Sacred Arrows?"

"To make sure that the use of weapons is unavoidable or in a good way. If the arrows are used to murder innocent people, the warrior and his family will suffer great misfortune or death."

"So Mazaśa has said that they are killing innocent people down there at the Redwood Agency. Does that mean that those warriors and their families will suffer great misfortune or death as you say?"

"Yes. And that is why we have left as White Eagle Ghost has warned us, because what is happening there is an evil war."

They left the village of Red Iron to continue their long journey to the northwest and hoped to make it to the mouth of the Lac qui Parle River by the late afternoon. Feeling wary even in familiar country, they climbed to the old buffalo trail that followed the sunlit ridge of the open prairie above the minacious ambuscading darkness of the wooded valley of the Minnesota. After riding a few miles along the ridge, they could see the Southern Sissetoŋwaŋ Village of Iśtakuźa—Sleepy Eyes, nestled peacefully down along the southwest shore of the river.

Those people down there seem to be as contented as spotted cows in the safety of their little fenced pastures and being hand-fed by the Waśićuŋ, Wayuhi thought. *They seem not to care that their freedom is lost and no more can they walk free and proud like buffalo bulls on the sacred ground of their ancestors. Why can they not see this, that they are prisoners in their own land?*

"Brother," said Ćaske as he rode up along side Wayuhi. "Are you thinking about that six-pony girl back there?"

"No, I was thinking about spotted cows."

"Lots of girls look like cows compared to her! Aaaa!"

"What's her name?"

"Her name is Timdokuota—Her Many Brothers. So she must have a lot of brothers but I've never known any."

"Where do you know her from?"

"I went to the agency school with her at Yellow Medicine. She's two winters older than me, the same age as you,"

"Where's she from?"

"She's from the Waȟpetoŋwaŋ Village of Wakaŋmani—Walks Holy, at Lac qui Parle, where we're going today."

"What do you know about her?"

"Only that she was taken from the Ojibway as a little baby and reared by a Dakota family there," said Ćaske as he pulled his mount to get back in line behind Wayuhi on the narrow path.

Timdokuota, he repeated to himself. His body remembered the feeling that he had as she looked at him for that brief instant. It was a feeling unlike any he had ever experienced in his life. Like thunder crashing and lightning striking him and awakening his manhood. *Was she the woman of my dream? With the beautiful Ojibway face painted black and white? But this time I was the one with the painted face, not her!*

His body also remembered the fear of the unknown, the excitement of the chase and the heart-pumping thrill of war. His father had always told him that when traveling in enemy territory or when traveling with women, children and elders to follow a rule of silence, to always keep his mind clear and to be wary. Death can strike in an instant. Only by maintaining an outer and inner silence can you hear the warnings of your guardian spirit. Only when you concentrate on your full field of vision can you be alerted to a lurking enemy—a slight movement in the shadows, the quick flash of sunlight on gunmetal, the silent flight of an arrow. When on the move, he said, use your side vision to achieve inner silence. Using your front vision will cause you to focus on things and your mind will carelessly wander and fill with distracting self-indulging thoughts.

I will empty my mind as my father has taught me. The Way of Silence is the first step to becoming a hunter and a warrior. It is the Great Mystery; the sacred silence that is the voice of Wakaŋtaŋka—the Great Spirit. Only through silence can you achieve the awareness of the hunter and the warrior to hear the voice of your guardian spirit.

He could see the wind race across the prairie as the big bluestem, Indian, and little bluestem grasses successively bowed and swayed to its presence. As the wind blew through his hair he could hear it whisper his name. "Wa-yu-hi!" Then it was gone down into the wooded valley of the Minnesota and he could hear it whistling through the trees and was aware of the leaves playfully dancing to its song.

Then another little wind rushed across the prairie with the grasses once again betraying its path. As the gamesome wind breezed by him he could again hear it calling his name but now daring him to the chase. "Wa-yu-hi! Catch-me-if-you-can!" he heard it whisper as he felt his arms becoming the powerful wings of a Peregrine Falcon and his primary feathers catching a thermal updraft and lifting his feathered body from the saddle and high up into the cyaneous summer sky. Through the telescopic brown eyes of the falcon he could see, far below, the Wakpa Minisota with its clear blue waters lazily coursing to the southeast.

Far to the northwest he could see the hazy curvature of the earth and the Lake That Talks—Lac qui Parle, with the Village of Wakaŋmani nestled along its southern shores. Following the old buffalo trail from the village to the southeast, he could see his own procession below him traveling single file along the path free of danger with his other self, his human form, in the lead.

With his wings curved like a bow, he hurled himself across the heavens with a spectacular display of falconine aerobatics and then, almost closing his wings, fell into a deep powerful stoop. With a backbone allowing little play and a breastbone arched to give strength to the bone structure, with even the underside of the feathers polished to a shiny surface to reduce friction, all were synergistically combined to give nothing less than great breath-taking speed to one of nature's most spirited aerial predators. Suddenly the frenzied dive exploded into a throw-up, a maneuver that would have broken the back of lesser birds, as he again climbed steeply and, in a heartbeat, disappeared without a trace across the endless sky as Wakaŋtaŋka whispered the promise of beauty and freedom into the wind that was heard by the awestruck Wayuhi.

The Isaŋti Waȟpetoŋwaŋ Village of Wakaŋmani was located near the mouth of the Lac qui Parle River to the west and the outlet of Lac qui Parle to the Wakpa Minisota to the east. The village was alive with activity as they rode in and made their way to the lodge of O'kdeśa—Redcoat, the brother of kuŋśi

Makadutawiŋ. After tending to his horses, Wayuhi went for a walk around the village of over one hundred lodges hoping to see again the beautiful Timdokuota. But even if he found her, he couldn't think of what he would say to her. *Six ponies*, he thought. *Where would I get six ponies?*

He noticed that this village was not unlike his own Otter Tail Village with the familiar smell and sound of horses, and comprised mostly of tipis, with very few, if any, of the Tipitaŋka—traditional bark lodges, as were used by Dakotapi farther southeast. *Buffalo hunters*, he thought. *And warrior horsemen*, since he saw many tipis with war shields displayed on small tripods in front with usually a fine treasured warhorse or buffalo runner staked out nearby for safekeeping.

He recognized several individuals who had joined Tataŋkanażiŋ in earlier raids against the Red Lake, Pillager, and Saulteaux bands of the Ojibway and even the Skidi Pawnee who were found hunting on the buffalo range of the Isaŋti Dakota and the Ihaŋktoŋwaŋna Nakota. Their lands extended from Lac qui Parle on the east to the James River Valley on the west and north to Mniwakaŋ—Sacred Water or Devil's Lake as called by the Wašićuŋ, including the Sheyenne River Valley, and south to the Minišośe—Missouri River, was the range of the Ihaŋktoŋwaŋ Nakota—Yankton Sioux.

In front of a few tipis, Wayuhi saw shields displayed with the war lances of the Napeśni. The lances were about ten feet long fringed with red trade cloth with twelve eagle feathers attached. The Napeśni—No Flight, was a society of elite warriors who made a vow to charge into battle and not retreat until either the enemy was defeated or they were killed. They wore buffalo horned headdresses with a trail of eagle feathers in addition to carrying the long lances. If one broke his oath, it was believed that lightning would strike him dead.

Following the river a short distance, Wayuhi reached its mouth at Lac qui Parle and sat on a gray log that had washed up on the sandy shore. The clear crystalline water was the color of the sky and its smooth mirror-like surface reflected the Land Beyond. Across the lake and above the wooded shoreline he could see the steeple of a Christian church and he could hear the faint pulse of a drum echoing across the water as if struggling for life.

The Napeśni, he thought. *Tataŋkanażiŋ has made a vow as a Napeśni. He is the embodiment of all things that are desired among warriors in our Nation. He is from a long line of chiefs, he is a fine horseman, he is a hunter who provides for his people, he is a great warrior who has counted many coups, and still he is a humble man of the Red Road! If someday I could be like him, I would bring pride and great strength to my people as he does!* He felt a compassionate emotion swell up in his chest and tears came to his eyes as he thought of the great suffering of his people as they travel the Black Road.

"I ask you these things so my people will live! We are all related!" he shouted as he stood and looked across the waters and could see the shadows of his people in the reflections of the Land Beyond upon the surface of the Lake That Talks.

In the distance, Wayuhi saw ripples on the lake coming toward him, as if a great creature under the water and near the surface was moving very rapidly and leaving a wake behind it. The movement stopped about ten paces out from where he was standing and, as the ripples settled, he could hear voices, like a man and a woman singing in perfect harmony, speaking to him.

"Wayuhi," the spirits said. "We have seen that you are becoming a fine Isaŋti Warrior."

"Who are you?" asked Wayuhi respectfully as he remembered that these mysterious waters were called the Lake That Talks.

"We are Uŋktehi, the Spirits of the Waters. Those who live in fear of life call us the Dreadful Ones."

"My grandfathers have spoken of you!"

"We see that around your neck you wear Isaŋwakaŋ, the consecrated Spirit Knife of the Isaŋti."

"You know of it?"

"It was hewn by the Ancient Ones from an ivory tusk of the Great Mammoth and the black fire stone of the Thunderbird."

"It was my grandpa Mazamani who gave this knife to me. And my grandpa Ćetaŋjiyotaŋka carries a Medicine Shield with your image on it."

"They are dauntless Isaŋti Warriors and have learned well the ways of the Ancient Ones."

"But why have you come to me?"

"We have come in answer to your prayer, your thoughts, to help you become the impeccable Isaŋti Warrior that is Tataŋkanażiŋ."

"My thoughts! You heard my thoughts?"

"Thoughts and prayers that come from the heart when you are sincere and truly humble yourself to these magical waters, this Lake That Talks, are always answered," they continued in perfect harmony.

"But why would you help me?"

"Because you want to bring pride and great strength to your people during these desperate times."

"How will you do that?"

"We have seen that somewhere you have learned Ćaŋku Ininayaŋka Kiŋ—the Way of Silence, the first step to becoming an Isaŋti Warrior. You have learned to empty your mind, the internal silence that catches the flowing life of the Earth Mother."

"I have had a good teacher. My father, Tiowaśte."

"Then we have seen that you have learned Ćaŋku Wihaŋmnaŋpi Kiŋ—the Way of Dreaming, the second step. We witnessed your dream of that masterful hunter of the skies, your thrilling demonstration of beauty and freedom."

"Wah! I thought it was real!"

"In a sense it was. But it was your dreaming body, your other self that was transformed. But now you must learn about the third step, Ćaŋku Tawaćiŋ Kiŋ—the Way of Intent."

"What is that?"

"Intent is the will, the spirit, the energy, the power that enables one to achieve the mood of a warrior and to perform acts impeccably. Intent is life itself!"

"But what do I do?"

"You must learn to trust your personal power!"

Wayuhi saw the great tenebrous form of Uŋktehi emerge from the depths of the lake. It stood looking at him with its big shaggy ears standing straight outward giving it the illusion of even greater size with water dripping profusely from its long curved white-ivory tusks as it raised its great trunk and blew water into the sky then emitted a deep infrasonic sound that Wayuhi could not hear but could feel in his bones. The sound created a circle of vibratory waves on the water emanating from the monolith that Wayuhi felt as soothing timbres of empathy, a feeling of pure deep love filled his body.

As the immense Wooly Mammoth turned and submerged back into the depths of the lake, Wayuhi saw the ephemeral image of the Ancient Ones who had taken the form of Uŋktehi as he heard them say, "These are the Ways of the Isaŋti Warrior, the true path to freedom!" When all was gone, he could once again see the reflection on the lake of the Land Beyond and the dark blanket-shrouded shadows of his people as they walked toward the campfires of the Wanaġi Taćaŋku—Ghost Road, called the Milky Way by the Waśićuŋ.

Wayuhi returned to the lodge of O'kdeśa anxious to speak with his grandpa about his extraordinary experience at the lake. Ćetaŋiyotaŋka was sitting with O'kdeśa on comfortable tanned buffalo hides and reed backrests in a tipi whose cover had been rolled up about knee high off the ground providing both shade and good air circulation.

"Grandson," said his grandfather gesturing to Wayuhi to sit down. "Something bad happened around here yesterday."

"What was that?" he asked knowing that it must be serious for his grandpa to even bring it up. He sat cross-legged in front of the smoldering fire and began to poke into the embers with a long fire stick.

"A Waśićuŋ missionary named Amos Huggins was killed at the Lac qui Parle School across the river."

"What happened?" he asked looking up as he laid down the fire stick. He knew the young peace-loving missionary who had often been to Otter Tail Village to talk of the Jesus Road to his Amdowapuśkiya relatives.

"All they know is that he was talking to two Dakota men when one of them shot him."

"Who did it?" he asked knowing that many young people around here disliked Waśićuŋ ways and had been aroused by the talk of war.

"He says it was a man named Tainŋa—Leather Blanket," said Ćetaŋiyotaŋka gesturing toward his brother-in-law with his lips.

"How do you know that he did it?" Wayuhi asked of O'kdeśa loudly as he was hard of hearing.

"A young boy named Tatekaġa—He Makes the Wind, saw him shoot the teacher but will not say why," said O'kdeśa loudly as was customary for people hard of hearing.

"Wah!" uttered Wayuhi, as he had to restrain himself from laughing when he heard the name of his childhood acquaintance that they used to call Fart. He knew him as a young man about his own age that had been touched by the Great Spirit and had many strange ways.

"They say that he lives in the Spirit World and talks with Waziya—the Spirit of the North, and can blow cold air out of his mouth while he blows hot air out of his ass," said O'kdeśa with a furrowed brow making the story even more unbearably funny to Wayuhi as he struggled to maintain a similar staid expression. "They say that he can change himself into a Great Horned Owl and hunt with silent wings on winter nights of the Hard Moon. Others say that he is a Heyoka—Contrary, because he does things backwards and likes to winter at Heyokati—Lodge of the Contrary, a big hill about ten miles west of here where he walks around naked. And then he is the grandson of Wakaŋmani, the Chief of our village."

"Do people believe him?" asked Wayuhi loudly making a mental note to tell Ćaske about the amazing feats of the flatulent Tatekaġa.

"Some say that he witched Tainŋa to kill that missionary because they were trying to force him to go to that Mission School," said O'kdeśa.

"What is Wakaŋmani going to do now?" asked Wayuhi.

"Yesterday, the Akićita—Soldiers Lodge, captured Tainŋa and his friend Hośiĥdi—He Brought the News, who was with him, to turn them over to the Big Knives. But after we heard about all the killings down at Lower Agency from Hośiĥdi, they let them go," said O'kdeśa.

"Where did they go then?"

"Back to the Village of Mazamani where they're from."

"Those Farmer Indians really got mad because they were released," said Ćetaŋiyotaŋka. "Most of them are Christians and live over there on the east side of the Minnesota around the old Lac qui Parle Mission."

"I saw their church a little while ago," said Wayuhi.

"There's been a lot of bad blood around here between the Dakota who want to keep the old ways and those Farmer Indians," said O'kdeśa. "Many Farmer Indians have been killed and their crops burned. A year ago they even burned that Hazelwood Mission to the ground and witched their bell so that it does not sing anymore. Then they burned all the crops on their big farm that they called the Hazelwood Republic."

"Many of our people across the river have become Christians and have come to be like White people," said Ćetaŋiyotaŋka. "They say the days of the Dakota are gone. They say we have to stay on the reservation like that Agent Galbraith orders us and no more can we hunt deer in the Big Woods or follow the buffalo on the western prairies."

"But how do they become like White people?" asked Wayuhi. "It is like telling an eagle to become like a chicken, a buffalo to become like a spotted cow, or a wolf to become like a dog! The Great Mystery has made us different from them!"

"They say that we must play the White man's game and that we cannot have any pride!" said O'kdeśa.

"Wah! What man would say such things! It is our pride that makes us Dakota!" retorted Wayuhi.

"Grandson, in the White man's game, only the White man wins. Our leaders found that out only after they had given away all of our land for the White man's whiskey. Soon the whiskey was also gone and all they had left were the swollen stomachs of the whiskey sickness."

"And no longer can we walk proudly if you take away our land, and we will no longer be free if we are chained to his fields like the pitiful Hasapa—Black Man," said O'kdeśa as he struggled to get up and hurriedly exited the lodge.

"You must excuse my brother-in-law, he is getting old and they can't hold it like they used to," said Ćetaŋiyotaŋka smiling.

"Ah, grandpa!" said Wayuhi loudly.

"You need not yell anymore, grandson. I can hear you just fine," said Ćetaŋiyotaŋka softly in his deep resonant voice.

Wayuhi told his grandfather of his experience of dreaming of a falcon that he thought was real and of his amazing experience with the Lake That Talks and then asked, "What did they mean by the Way of the Isaŋti Warrior?"

"The Way of the Isaŋti Warrior comes to our people from the Ancient Ones who, for some reason, took a liking to our Dakota people. The Way of the Isaŋti is the Sacred Circle, the Red Road. He who travels the Red Road lives for the happiness of his people, of love, and of making relatives. We have tried to live in harmony with the White man by making relatives with him as taught by the Red Road of the Sacred Circle and for many years it has worked. We have many relatives who are part French.

"But lately, with the Americans, we have learned that they walk a different road, the Black Road of greed and of war. For many years now the Americans have been taking our land and pushing our people farther and farther out of our homelands. They have brought their soldiers their sickness and their whiskey that have killed many of our people. Now they have brought their greed with the Indian Agents and the loving patience of our people has been stretched and snapped like a rope. The Isaŋti Warrior is one who must learn to walk both roads, to remain calm in the face of death, and yet not forgetting the possibility of sudden death during times of happiness. To learn to live in a world of war and a world of peace is the Way of the Isaŋti Warrior."

"Then they talked about Ćaŋku Tawaćiŋ Kiŋ as the third step to becoming an Isaŋti Warrior. They said that Intent is the will to achieve the mood of a warrior. What did they mean by that?"

"Intent is your personal power, something that is the outgrowth of your inner life that you must learn to trust. It was your intent to take the śićuŋ of Geeshik, not an accident as you said."

"I don't understand!"

"You said that the Dakota way to respect Geeshik was to count coup on him. But when you count coup on a man you strip him of his śićuŋ, his honor, his power."

"But what did they mean by the will to achieve the mood of a warrior?"

"The spirit or the fire within you is called the will. What comes out as a result is called the mood. The will is like the chief of a village, while the mood is his akićita—soldiers lodge. The will is within the village deploying the mood. If the mood rushes out too fast in defense of the village, it may be killed. Your will must restrain the mood so that it does not hurry."

"Like just now. My will was to be heard by O'kdeśa so my mood was speaking loudly. So after he left it was no longer necessary to speak loudly, as you reminded me, and my will had to restrain my mood."

"That is right! Intent is the will controlling the mood. The mood of a warrior is always under control, to remain calm even in the face of certain death, to kill only to bring life to our people."

"What did they mean when they said that the Ways of the Isaŋti Warrior are the true path to freedom?"

"It means freeing of the spirit. It means achieving the mastery of the Ways of Silence, Dreaming, and Intent to develop an inner spirit that flows like a river or the wind, like the Earth Mother who is always in motion. When there is the slightest feeling of fear of death or of attachment to life, the inner spirit loses its flow. Have an inner spirit devoid of all fear, free from all forms of attachment, and it is the master of itself. It knows no fear, no hindrances, no inhibitions, no stopping. It is free like the winds, like the rivers of the Earth Mother to follow its own course."

Wayuhi picked up his flute and walked to the nearby Wakpa Minisota. He sat in the shade of a huge elm tree and leaned up against its deeply furrowed bark. He could hear the flowing of the river accompanying the songs of Meadow Larks. He could feel the heat and humidity of the evening and the feeling of hunger pangs as he realized that he hadn't eaten all day. *Once again,* he thought as he recalled sitting under another tree near the Yellow Medicine. *Was that only three days ago?* he wondered.

His feeling of hunger mixed with the deep lingering feeling of love as his body remembered Uŋktehi at the Lake That Talks. He picked up his flute and began to play, not the Songs of Cotanka but the song of his inner spirit. The song merged with the melody of the river and the Meadow Larks, his will had looked into his heart and was commanding the mood of the warrior, the mood of impassioned love.

He laid down his flute and could feel the warmth of both the earth beneath him and the tree to his back, as if they too were relatives and would speak to him. *Anything could happen in this Wakaŋ place,* he thought as he awaited their agreement. He thought again of that day at Yellow Medicine when Siŋtesapedaŋ—the

Blacktailed Deer, had appeared as if by magic. *Hoka! Could it be that White Eagle Ghost had provided for me as he said he would?*

As he closed his eyes to empty his mind and practice Ćaŋku Ininayaŋka Kiŋ, he could hear the Medicine Songs of the Earth Mother the wind and the spirited falcon shrieking his songs of beauty and freedom from high in the darkening sky. He suddenly felt a powerful unity with all his relations—all those who have passed, all those who are here, and all those yet to come, when he heard the faint sound of a snapping twig.

"Wah!" he said softly as he rose and saw a young woman approaching from downstream. It was the beautiful doe-like Timdokuota!

Power of the Medicine Wolf

Fort Snelling was bustling with activity as the four troops of infantry began preparing for the march up the Minnesota River. Luckenbach had finished breakfast in his quarters, washed up and dressed in the uniform of the day. He thought about the orders of the previous day stating that he would be in charge of "…any mounted infantry that they recruited along the way." *Mounted infantry?* He thought of the absurd oxymoron. *No damn wonder these people don't know beans bout usin cavalry, referrin to us as mounted infantry. Why, hell! If'n we all had a real cavalry, we all would be out yonder by now savin lives.*

Luckenbach walked out into the crowded smoke-filled Officer's mess room with his cup full of hot coffee hoping to find a copy of the daily Pioneer & Democrat that was brought in from St. Paul about this time for an update on the Indian War. He saw his friends Captain Buck Smith and Major Caleb Jones sitting at a table with a newspaper and made his way through the crowd to join them.

"Good morning, Luke," said Buck. "Pull up a chair."

"Mornin, y'all," said Luckenbach happy to see his loquacious friends again. "The paper got any news bout the Indan fracas?"

"More news about our dear friend John," said Caleb. "It says that Captain John Marsh and thirty-seven of his company were killed, but it's still unconfirmed."

"Indans attacked Fort Ridgley?" asked the surprised Luckenbach since he had never heard of Indians laying siege to a fort while in Texas.

"Not yet, anyway," said Buck. "It says that John's company was fired on as they attempted to cross the Minnesota at the ferry landing near the Redwood Agency."

"Knowing him, he must have gotten a message about the killing going on at Redwood and was on his way over to stop it," said Caleb.

"They must have been sitting ducks out there," said Buck.

"They had no idea about how big this uprising is," said Caleb.

"How many Indans they talkin bout?" asked Luckenbach.

"Paper here says that a Mr. Dickinson estimated that at least a hundred and fifty Indians were engaged in the killings at the Redwood Agency," answered Caleb.

"Sure more than just a few drunks shooting things up," said Buck.

"Yeah, but it's a mite less than what someone was atalkin bout yesterday," said Luckenbach. "Fifty thousand Indans! Gawd damn!"

"There's something mighty strange about this here report," said Caleb Jones.

"What's that?" asked Buck.

"Well on the front page here, it quotes that same Mr. Dickinson as saying that when he got across the river from Redwood, he saw the Indian's firing into the trader's stores, and other buildings. He says that about forty men were firing into Merrick's store at once."

"What's wrong with that, Caleb?" asked Luckenbach.

"Hell, you can't see the traders stores from down across the river. You can't even see the Indian Agency buildings from across the river. Or from anywhere across the river for that matter, since all of those buildings are up over a steep wooded bluff from the Minnesota!"

"You sure?" asked Buck.

"Hell, I should know!" retorted Caleb. "I was garrisoned at Fort Ridgley for two years and climbed that steep hill many times."

"Why would he lie bout somethin like that?" asked Luckenbach.

"I'll be darned if I know," said Caleb. "Maybe he was also lying about the number of Indians he saw."

"You know, there's something else that's strange about that article," said Buck.

"What's that?" asked Caleb.

"Well, it seems that the annuity money that the Indians have been waiting for has miraculously shown up," said Buck. "It reads here that, 'The messengers, with the money to pay off the Indians, were at Fort Ridgley.'"

"Is that a strange coincidence?" asked Luckenbach facetiously.

"Well, the Sioux were virtually starving due to a crop failure and a delay in the arrival of annuities made matters worse," said Buck. "The hungry Sioux have been waiting at their agencies for nearly two months now."

"Damn, Buck!" exclaimed Luckenbach thinking there was nothing this new administration was capable of doing that would surprise him. "Y'all suggestin that some government official has baited the Sioux into an outbreak?"

"Well I think that if you keep a man hungry long enough and he sees his wife and children starving, at some point he'll resort to violence if need be to resolve that situation. I know I would!" answered Buck.

"You know, come to think of it, Lt. Sheehan, with two companies of the Fifth Minnesota Volunteers, was transferred out of Ft. Ridgely to Ft. Ripley. He left Ridgely on the morning of August 18th. Also, Gailbraith left for St. Paul with the Renville Rangers, a volunteer militia company, on August 17th leaving only two companies of volunteers on the Minnesota frontier. Was this a setting of the stage?" asked Caleb.

"Gawd damn!" said Luckenbach.

"So then the government brings in their soldiers and their canons to quell the violence and finally move those hostile Sioux out of Minnesota to Dakota Territory where they belong and, in the process, just happens to free up all that rich bottomland!" said Caleb. "And all with the support of the outraged American voters!"

"Well look for a minute at what else those crafty Republicans are doing," added Buck.

"There's more?" asked Luckenbach.

"Well, coincidentally, on May 20 of this year, Congress passed the Homestead Act," said Buck. "It offers settlers cheap land in the public domain, which means land ceded by Indian Tribes."

"Cheap land? Y'all mean someone has to pay for it."

"Only minimal costs, I suppose," answered Buck. "The settlers get 160 acres for $1.25 an acre after six months residence or, if people agree to stay on the land for five years, for a small registration fee of thirty dollars."

"Don't sound like a lot of profit to me."

"That's not where the profit is," added Buck. "The profit comes from providing all those new settlers with supplies—farm implements, guns, powder, mercantile goods, livestock, and the like."

"So it's the businessmen who stand to make considerable profit by a huge influx of White people into the state," said Luckenbach.

"Right! And most of those businessmen are Republicans, at least here in Minnesota!"

"So what else have those crafty Republicans done?" asked Luckenbach.

"Well less than two months later, July 1 in fact, Congress has also coincidentally passed the Pacific Railway Act authorizing huge cash subsidies and land grants for private businesses, also owned mostly by Republicans I suppose, to build railroad tracks across the continent."

"Gawd damn!" exclaimed Luckenbach. "Like I said, those Indans don't stand the chance of a rabbit in a wolf den!"

"Well Luke, anything that stands in the way of progress will be swept under the rug," said Buck with his eyebrows raised.

"Progress?" asked Luckenbach knowing that soldier's lives were sacrificed for this whole notion of progress and it infuriated military men; and the merchants tendency to ingratiate themselves with political leaders by arguing that the whole nation's interest would be served by such warfare only made matters worse.

"Well, the sense of Manifest Destiny justifies the greatest aspirations of American society and provides an overpowering rationale for sweeping aside Indians," said Buck.

"Luke, do you think for a minute that the rapid progress of civilization on this continent will permit the lands which are required for cultivation to be surrendered to savage tribes for hunting grounds?" asked Caleb.

"I like to feel that this is a free country still," said Luckenbach remembering his abolitionist father and his evening dinner table discussions of Rousseau. "For the Negro and likewise for Indans who are noble savages and should be able to live as nature intended."

"Well at least Lincoln may well agree with you," said Buck. "I hear he's coming out with an emancipation proclamation shortly to free the Negro slaves."

"How bout that! Lincoln is fixin to free the slaves at the same time that he's fixin to go to war with the Sioux who are fightin for their own freedom. Don't make any damn sense!" said Luckenbach setting his empty coffee cup on the table while pulling a pack of genuine Bull Durham out of his shirt pocket.

"You know," said Caleb holding the newspaper. "There's something else here that doesn't make any sense."

"What now, Caleb?" asked Luckenbach smiling while he sprinkled tobacco into a Riz La rolling paper curled in his fingers.

"In discussing the murders in Meeker County, it says that about one o'clock on Sunday last, seven or eight Indians in a bad disposition came to the home of Mr. Robinson Jones, in the town of Acton. So then he and his wife go to the home of Howard Baker, about a mile away, and were followed by the Indians. Soon the Indians start firing and four people are shot except Baker's wife and her child. So she starts down into the cellar with her child to hide when, at the head of the stairs, she falls and is knocked unconscious."

"Well what's irregular about that, Caleb?" asked Buck.

"When she revives the Indians are gone. She goes back outside, finds her husband still alive and puts a pillow under his head. He directs her to leave him and go to a neighbor's house about a mile away and give the alarm. Which she does!"

"Meanin that y'all thought it irregular that she finds her bleedin husband and all she does is put a damn pilla under his head and runs off for help?" said Luckenbach lighting his cigarette and dropping the match into his empty tin saddle mug wondering where she got the pillow.

"Yes! But, more importantly, she also leaves her two-year old infant there. Now I can't imagine a mother running off and leaving her baby in danger like that, let alone with her husband laying there bleeding to death, unless of course she was drunk!"

"Well I know that hothead Robinson Jones," said Buck. "I know that he and Baker were bootleggers and most likely consumed a good portion of their own evil brew."

"They probably were all drunk when those Sioux came by wanting some food or firewater knowing they were bootleggers," said Caleb. "Then they probably tried to run the Sioux off, which probably touched off the killing spree."

"It's like I said," said Luckenbach. "Nuthin worse than a hungry or pissed-off Indan!"

"By the way, what happened to that baby?" asked Buck.

"It says here that the people turned out and went to Baker's house only to find four people dead including Mr. Baker. The infant was found alive in the house."

"Well the sad thing about that is that only Mrs. Baker survived to tell us what happened," said Buck. "That's why that story seems irregular; she doubtless was drunk!"

Luckenbach exited the Officer's Barracks and walked west toward the hospital. In the space between the barracks and the hospital building he descended a stairway to the lower ground level providing access to the storehouse making up the southeast wall of the fort, the South Battery forming a corner, and a long building housing several small shops—blacksmith, carpentry, and the like, along the southwest wall. He noticed his friend the blacksmith waving him over for a visit.

The blacksmith was busy positioning an ox into an Ox Lift for shoeing. Since an ox can't balance itself on three legs, a stall-like contraption had to be built of timbers that could support the ox by two thick leather straps slung under its belly. Its head was held stationary by a wooden guillotine-like yoke around its neck as it bellowed in protest.

"Boozho, Capitaine!" said the blacksmith in the hearty Ojibway greeting that sounded like French to the captain. His name was Napoleon Bordulac who prided himself in both his French and Mashkiziibii Ojibwe ancestry. He was a bodacious man with powerful vascular arms, coal-black shoulder length hair, and a sparsely haired Indian moustache that curled around the corners of his mouth like parentheses. He had a high intelligent forehead with vascularity at the temples that stood out when he laughed or got upset and dark hairless coriaceous skin stretched over his long sinewy muscles that glistened in the sunlight from the sweat of his labor.

"Bon jour, Napoleon! How are y'all today?"

"Très bien, Capitaine. I am good usually. But I hear you go fight the Sioux?" Napoleon said as he slid one of the leather support slings under the huge animal.

"That's right, but it'll take bout a week to get everyone oun the road," answered Luckenbach as he moved to the other side of the Ox Lift and pulled the support sling through. He attached its chain attachment to a lintel-like structural member of the stall so that the sling fit snugly under the ox.

"Sacré mère! It be that Little Crow and his Kiyuksa and Kapozha Bands of those Mdewakato devils that be spilling German blood. He be a cruel evil sorcier, he be Satan that man!" he muttered as he passed the second sling under the bovine beast.

"So what do y'all know bout em people?" asked the captain grabbing the sling and attaching it to the lintel as he did the first.

"My Ojibwe people have been at war with the Mdewakato for a hundred of years. They be demons in the night," he said with the veins on his forehead dilating as he stared at the ground as if remembering some woeful experience.

"What do y'all mean?" asked Luckenbach knowing that Texians often referred to Kiowas and Comanches as demons. Even during the Mexican War, the Mexicans referred to Texas Rangers as Those Devil Texans.

"His name Little Crow befits him like the black-winged démon he be," scowled the fuliginous blacksmith. "Whispering wicked pitiless words into the ears of his starving Mdewakato people, witching them into this blood-crazed frénésie!"

With the discombobulated ox bellowing in his wooden stall, Napoleon untied his well-worn rawhide apron and tossed it onto the timber framework of the Ox Lift as he said loudly, "Come with me, Mon ami, I have something good for you."

Napoleon led Luckenbach to his shop at the south end of the long building. The shop floor was covered with coal ashes, a hot coal-filled forge as part of a huge brick chimney dominated the middle of the beam ceilinged room, and along the wall was a long workbench well lighted by three large windows facing northeast. He stoked his fire with a long overhead wooden handle that pumped a large bellows behind the fireplace then he went to the workbench and grabbed a small box that was sitting on a windowsill and blew the dust off.

"Mon ami," he said as he opened the ornately inlaid wooden box and sat it on the workbench. "Among our Ojibwe people, we have clans we call Dodaim. My dodaim be Myeengun—the Wolf. Some of our dodaim are responsable for leadership like the Crane and the Goose. Some are responsable for hunting like the Moose and the Deer. Then some are responsable for medicine like the Turtle and the Rattlesnake. My dodaim, the Wolf, be responsable for defense as be Noka—the Bear. After many years of defending our villages and our people, we have learned to make warrior medicine to fight the evil spirits the evil witching of the Mdewakato Dakota."

Reaching into the box he retrieved a small buckskin pouch that was attached to long braided buckskin cords as something to be worn around the neck. The pouch was elaborately decorated with blue and green porcupine quillwork with fringes as long as a finger and Luckenbach noticed the pleasant fragrance of cedar smoke as was typical of most Indian smoke-tanned animal hides.

Luckenbach had rolled a cigarette and lit it by scratching a match on the bottom of his boot. He put the foot up on a knee-high tree stump that supported a huge iron anvil as he leaned on his knee and attentively watched the blacksmith.

Raising the small flap on the pouch, Napoleon extracted a white pointed object about the size of his thumb. "This be the eyetooth of a Medicine Wolf, the huge white timber wolf of the northern woods. The wolf pack be highly organized and its rules must be obeyed, like your army. The Medicine Wolf be a great warrior, like you, and I want for you to have this," as he placed the tooth back into the pouch and handed it to the captain with his left hand as he offered his right.

Luckenbach hurriedly stuffed his cigarette into the hot coals of the forge and took the pouch in his left hand as he grasped the powerful right hand of Napoleon in the respectful Indian way of giving and receiving. "Well I sure want to thank y'all, Napoleon. No one has ever given me anything like this afore. I will treasure it dearly. But what do I do with it?"

"Wear it when you hunt the traîtresse Sioux. It will help you to see danger to see ambush, like the great mystérieux Medicine Wolf who can smell a Coureur de Bois and his hated wolf trap. You be hunting Satan and you can only do that with the power of wolf medicine!"

"Satan?"

"Oui! That be true, Mon ami. Remember Matthew 13,

> *He that soweth the good seed be the Son of Man. The field be the world, the good seeds be the sons of the kingdom, but the tares be the sons of the wicked one.*
> *The enemy who sowed them be the devil, the harvest be the end of the age, and the reapers be the angels."*

"Well thanks again, Napoleon. I guess I oughta be gettin over to see the Supply Officer afore he leaves," said Luckenbach feeling somewhat uneasy with the quoting of the Bible and the talk of witching and of the devil.

Napoleon once again reached up for the long wooden bellows handle and pumped it vigorously several times as he continued,

> *"The Son of Man will send out His angels, and they will gather out of His kingdom all things that offend, and those who practice lawlessness,*

The air from the bellows fed the hot coals as flames roared out and the coals shimmered into a bright reddish blue glow as if giving a pyrokinetic tenor to the quoted scriptures,

> *"And will cast them into the furnace of fire. Then shall the righteous shine forth as the sun in the kingdom of their Father.*

Gakina-awiiya!" said Napoleon with the Ojibwe phrase meaning 'We are all related' like a Christian ending a prayer with Amen. "And good hunting, Mon ami!" he said as Luckenbach exited the shop.

Luckenbach entered the storehouse and saw Lieutenant Meeker, the Supply Officer, standing at a podium-like desk doing paperwork in the darkness by the light of a candle since there were such few windows. "Good morning, Captain Luckenbach," he said. "You're up bright and early."

"Well I heard that y'all were goin over to St. Paul today so I hurried over."

"What is it that you need although I can probably guess?"

"I want to make sure that we all will have at least twenty of those 1859 Sharps Carbines, hopefully still in the boxes that we all can cart out west with us in a coupla days. Oh yeah, and plenty of those black powder paper cartridges in .54 calibre and number 11 caps."

"Captain, I thought sure that you'd be asking for some of those new Henry repeating rifles!" said the officer smiling.

"Now there's a fine rifle, Lieutenant. But it's a might unwieldy for use oun horseback."

"Well just fill out these requisition forms and that's all you should be needing for now. The rifles come five to a crate, so you'll be needing, ah lets see, four crates."

Luckenbach completed the requisitions and laid them on the supply officer's desk and headed for the door when he heard someone call his name.

"Hey Luke! Wait a minute!" said Jim Duncan, the Sutler, as he ascended a stairway from the lower levels.

"Well howdy, Jim. One of y'alls shipments come in?"

"Yeah, I just loaded the goods on the elevator down below and now I'm going to hoist it up here if my strength holds out," said Jim referring to the pulley operated elevator that allowed you to hoist cargo unloaded from boats and carted into the fort three levels down, and a short ways up from the Mississippi River boat landing.

"Were y'all wantin some help?"

"If you don't mind, Luke. By the way, I saw you talking to Napoleon Bordulac out there. Quite an interesting fellow, isn't he?"

"Yeah I reckon. He was tellin me bout how he believes that the leader of this Sioux uprisin is none other than Satan hisself."

"He possibly neglected to tell you that the Ojibway have been savagely mauling the Santee Sioux for many years now with iron axes and firearms received from the French."

"Didn't mention that."

"The Santee almost certainly have a different idea about who Satan is," Jim said as he pulled down on a heavy rope that was attached to a couple of large wooden pulleys as the cargo elevator below began to creak and groan its way up.

"So how have the Sioux fared against em?" asked the captain as he joined in the rope pull.

"The Santee survived but were gradually pushed westward," said Jim looking at Luckenbach as he paused for a moment to catch his breath. "Although the Sioux say that they moved of their own free will in pursuit of migrating herds, which I tend to believe." The elevator reached their level and Jim secured the elevator platform to the floor and opened a gate in the safety fence around the opening to the shaft for access to his shipment.

"Jim, I been ameanin to ask y'all bout an experience that I had the other day," said Luckenbach reluctantly since he felt they may have already hauled enough up from the lower depths.

"Is it about elephants, Luke?"

"Yeah, it is," said the captain as he related his mysterious encounter at the deserted Indian village on Nine Mile Creek.

"I had thought that something like that had happened to you when you mentioned elephants the other day. As I had said, not many people around here know about the Wooly Mammoths let alone the Medicine Dance of the Mdewakaŋtoŋ Santee's."

"So I did see somethin?"

"I believe so. Those ceremonies of the Santee's were, and most likely still are, very powerful. Some of the ceremonies performed by these Holy Men allow them to see or even actually be in the future. From what you describe, it seems that your entry onto a sacred ceremonial ground was coincident with an ancient Mdewakaŋtoŋ ceremony from God knows when."

"Y'all mean that that ceremony happened oun the same location only at some day a loung time past?"

"Exactly! From what you describe, I don't think they had ever seen a White man before let alone a horse. Imagine their amazement!"

"I feel I can well imagine that! But how bout when he handed me that pipe and when I reached for it, it all disappeared?"

"I don't think he was handing you the calumet. I think that, as a Holy Man, he was bravely holding it abreast with both hands to protect himself and his people from what he saw as a very frightful apparition or as a harbinger of death and destruction that is now about to be vengefully unleashed against his Mdewakaŋ-toŋ people!" said Jim as he removed his glasses from a shirt pocket and twirled them by one of the temples.

"Usin an Indan pipe to protect hisself?"

"Exactly. And it worked because you and your warhorse disappeared, at least until now. And they had their glimpse into the future, the prophetic vision of things to come," said the luciferous Sutler as he put on his wire framed spectacles and began to unload his cargo.

"Well I'll be damned!" said Luckenbach as he stepped out of the darkness of the supply building and into the bright late morning sunlight. He reached into his shirt pocket and retrieved the buckskin pouch. He removed the polished eye-tooth of the Medicine Wolf and held it in his clenched fist and thought about Comanche, Dakota and Ojibway Medicine Men and the Pennsylvania Dutch Hexenmiesters of his early youth. He thought of what a great mysterious world this is as he remembered his father reading Wordsworth…

> *Come forth into the light of things,*
> *Let nature be your teacher.*

"Well I'll be damned again!" he said smiling.

Sacred Child of the Harvest Moon

It was shortly after midnight with the moon setting on the southern horizon. Matohota had left his wife and grandmother under the able protection of his two strong young sons and had instructed them to leave at daybreak for Kandiyohi to be with the Gens Libre. Carrying his Kentucky Rifle at the ready with Astrid following him with her baby wrapped in her lavender shawl, they followed a deer trail along Beaver Creek until reaching its mouth at the Minnesota River.

Except for the sound of a deep-throated drum like a strong pulse of the Dakota throbbing from somewhere across the river and the peaceful harmony of crickets, all was quiet with no echoes of distant shooting or people calling out as the night before. Astrid was exhausted after their mile or so treks through the dark forest and sat down to rest and nurse her baby. Matohota had uncovered his hidden canoe and carried it down to the river's edge. He tipped the craft into the water on both sides for a few minutes since the hull of an Indian canoe likes to be wet as the birch paneling and black spruce root lacing expands making the craft more watertight.

The moon had gone down and the night was now dark with a canopy of stars. Being time for their journey to Fort Ridgley, Matohota assisted Astrid into the bow of the canoe and when she was settled on the cedar floorboards he carefully handed her the bundled baby. He sprinkled a pinch of tobacco onto the river for safe guidance. He then placed his dangerous loaded rifle carefully into the canoe making sure that there was powder in the flash pan then pushed the craft out into the current and jumped into the stern. His hornbeam paddle cut silently into the water as they were finally on their way.

Matohota was happy to be on the river again. A place where he felt he belonged, where his strength was an asset, where his skill in crafting birch canoes was sought by many, where he felt in touch with his Dakota and French ancestors who believed that knowledge of the rivers and creeks of the Upper Mississippi Watershed was essential to their survival. He knew that many of his Isaŋti people were now looking to the west to the way of the horse and following the buffalo. But he preferred the old ways of his Isaŋti Mdewakaŋtoŋwaŋ, the way of the canoe and the Hahawakpa—Mississippi River, the great mysterious waterway of his youth, and the way of the chase, hunting and trapping in the immense forests of the north.

As they approached the ferryboat-landing site at Redwood Agency where several soldiers had been killed earlier, he slowed his canoe and approached the area cautiously by staying on the eastern side of the river. In the darkness with the tall reed grass, cattails and wild blue indigo growing in abundance along the shore, he couldn't see if the bodies of the soldiers were still there. But as he got nearer, the stench of decaying human flesh indicated that they indeed were.

"Uff! What on earth is that smell?" whispered Astrid.

"Many soldiers were killed here Monday."

"Maybe someone is still alive!"

"All been killed and scalped."

"Oh merciful God," prayed Astrid. "They were so young and may not have been prepared to enter into eternity so hastily, have mercy on them and accept their souls into the Kingdom of Heaven."

Matohota noticed that the pulley rope for the ferryboat had been cut and the boat had drifted about a hundred yards downstream and beached on the western shore pulling the severed rope behind it. Shortly after passing the grounded boat, he felt the bow of the canoe hit something, not a log but softer like a deer or a human body. Carefully guiding the canoe around until he could see the object in the dark water, he saw that it was the body of a soldier. And from the captain's bars on his gold shoulder straps, he was an officer!

Since he couldn't hold the body and paddle at the same time, he hurriedly turned the canoe around and paddled back upstream to the ferryboat.

"What on earth are you doing?" whispered the concerned Astrid.

"There's a dead man in the water. Can't leave him there."

"But where are you going?"

"To get some rope."

"Rope? What on earth for?"

"You'll see," he answered as he found the rope that was attached to the ferry floating on the river like a water moccasin and pulled an adequate length into the canoe and cut it with his bowie knife.

Going back downstream he found the floating corpse, tied the rope under his arms and tied the free end of the rope to one of the canoe thwarts. He paddled to the eastern shore, jumped out into the shallow water and pulled the bow onto the beach with Astrid sitting there with her baby. With the rope in hand, he pulled the body of the soldier across the water and up on the beach.

"How did he die?" asked Astrid attempting to get up out of the canoe with her baby to help but deciding not to.

"I don't know. Don't see any gunshot wounds anywhere; he must have drowned while trying to escape since he wasn't scalped."

"Do you know him?"

"Seen him before. Name was John Marsh," said Matohota noticing that, as he had hoped, the captain had a waist belt with cap and cartridge boxes and a holster attached. Across his chest was a narrow strap attached to the belt and supporting a sword scabbard at his left side but the sword was gone. *He must have lost it in the river*, he thought. Removing the pistol belt, he opened the flap on the holster and was pleased to find a handgun. He drew out the revolver and could see that it was a nickel-plated 1851 Navy Colt.

"Mon Dieu!" he said holding the well-balanced weapon. Poking a twig into the chambers, he found that all of the rounds had been fired. *Now if he just has some caps and balls*, he thought as he opened the wet leather boxes. In the small box he found several copper coated fulminate caps that he hoped would still fire while in the other larger box he found water logged paper cartridges with .36 calibre lead balls.

"We're in luck," he said. "I can reload this gun with my own black powder!"

"But why on earth do you need a gun?" asked Astrid. "I have prayed for our safe deliverance and it shall be so."

"Good! But just in case, it doesn't hurt to have a little bit of hell around," he said as he began to dry the revolver off with his shirttail. He noticed that it was a beautifully engraved pistol with carved ivory grips. There was lettering on the barrel that he couldn't read, not just because of the darkness but also because he couldn't read English. He attached one of the fulminate caps to a nipple on the back of the cylinder, turned the cylinder to firing position, pulled the hammer to full cock and pulled the trigger. A small popping noise and flash emanated from the revolver as Matohota breathed a sigh of relief. "The caps still work!" he said to himself amazed at how the Great Spirit provides for you when in need.

He loaded the revolver as best he could in the darkness by estimating the amount of blackpowder in each chamber from his powder horn. In true Indian fashion, he used kinnikinnick branch shavings that he carried in a buckskin pouch to wad his rifle to likewise wad the chambers and prevent flashover. He rammed the six lead balls down on the wadding of each of the chambers, then fitted the dried caps on to the nipples on the back of the cylinder, set the hammer carefully down on a safety pin between chambers and slid the Colt into his ceinture fléchée.

"I'm going to dig a shallow grave for the soldier," Matohota said as he returned to the canoe for his hornbeam paddle.

"You are a very good person, Grizzly Bear," said Astrid unable to pronounce his Dakota name. "And I yust want you to know that I am very much in appreciation of what you are doing, both for that poor solyier, and us," said Astrid with her baby nursing under her shawl.

Matohota hurriedly dug the shallow grave with his paddle and dragged the body of Captain Marsh over and laid him carefully in it. He covered the body with the rich black bottom soil and made a cross from driftwood tied together with a strand from his rope. He pushed the cross into the soft earth at the head of the grave, looped the black waist belt with its holster, leather boxes, empty sword scabbard and brass officer's belt plate over the vertical member of the cross, hoping that someone from the fort would find him for a proper burial.

He removed his tattered hat and looked solemnly into the night sky and prayed, "Grandfather Great Spirit, Four Winds, Medicine Bear, hear my prayer! The spirit of this good brave soldier chief is coming to you. He died in a good way trying to protect his people. Help all of his relations during their time of mourning. His people like to honor their fallen warriors with flags, bugles, drums, many gun salutes, and good words of his brave deeds. I am a poor man and have none of these things and only the Four Winds can speak of his bravery on this night.

"Oh Grandfather Great Spirit, help my Dakota people during these terrible times. Guide my family to be with the Free People. Guide us safely on this night to the soldier fort with this new life, this sacred child of the Harvest Moon. I ask you all these things so my people will live! All my relations!"

Matohota returned to the canoe and gently pushed it back out onto the river while Astrid and her baby slept. He marveled at how quiet the baby seemed to be since he had not heard him cry all night, like Indian babies who know when danger is lurking about.

As they ventured further down the river, Matohota could hear a drum and sporadic distant gunfire and shouts coming from the south and was concerned for the safety of his passengers. And especially with the river twisting and turning like a snake they could easily come around a bend and right into a hostile camp of either Whites or Indians. *What would they do if they saw us?* he wondered. *I must remember to tell Astrid to pull her shawl up over her head so she looks like an Indian woman. But what if we came on a White man's camp! Mon Dieu!*

As he paddled silently along wondering what grand-père Jean-Jacques would have done in a situation like this, he noticed flashes of light in the northern sky. At first he thought that it was a storm coming, but then realized that it was Mahpiyataŋiŋ—the Northern Lights.

"Grandson, remember the campfires of the Hahatoŋwaŋ!" he heard a familiar voice whispering.

"Grand-père, I remember!" he whispered back. "I remember you telling us when we were children, that those lights were Hahatoŋwaŋ—Ojibway, campfires. And you warned us that whenever we saw them, we had to get into our lodge quickly since the Ojibway like to steal little Dakota children. But then you were just telling us that to make sure that we would come in at night."

Campfires, he thought. *Mon Dieu! Maybe if I look for the glow of campfires I could have enough time to do something before we were seen. Maybe we could portage around their camp or something.*

"Merci, grand-père," he said feeling his grandfather's presence on the rivers. He was amazed again at how the Great Spirit was watching over him and providing for his needs by bringing Maȟpiyataŋiŋ and Jean-Jacques Charbonneau on this night.

But then maybe it was Astrid's prayer, he thought. *She said that she had taken care of all that with her prayer and that it will be so! Where does she get her strength, that woman?* Astrid was awake as he could see her moving her baby around then leaning her head back and looking up toward the stars.

"I yust heard someone talking," she said quietly as she turned and looked back. "Did you hear them?"

"It was me talking to myself," he whispered then thought maybe he shouldn't have said that as she looked at him for a few seconds then turned forward again.

Never before have I seen such a strong willed White woman. She accepts her fate like an Indian woman and sleeps peacefully with her baby even with the sound of war drums in the night as if there were no dangerous people lurking around here. She has prayed for our safe deliverance and believes like a preacher man that her God will take care of us. 'It will be so!' she says. Mon Dieu! She is strong in her ways like an Indian!

As the river wound its way to the southeast, Matoȟota was entranced by the beauty of the night—the reflection of the starry sky on the wide river contrasted with the dark foreboding shadows along the shore, the sounds of crickets and bullfrogs, which seemed to imperceptibly speed up until a climax was reached and then slow down again, and accented with the occasional splash of a fish jumping out of the water. The slow rhythmic beating of the drum was perfectly synchronized with the diminuendo and crescendo of the songs of the night, proving that the Dakota are as much a part of this wondrous place of the Wakpa Minisota as the sparkling universe of stars and singing creatures of the night.

Coming around a bend in the river, Matohota caught a glimpse of the faint flicker of a fire through the trees near the west shoreline. He immediately guided the canoe to the west shore and under the overhanging branches of a cottonwood tree. He stepped out of the canoe and pulled its bow up onto the beach.

"What is happening?" asked Astrid in a whisper.

"I saw a campfire downstream."

"I told you I heard voices."

"I'll be back shortly," he said laying his hat in the canoe and, after removing his powder horn, accoutrements bag and white shirt, blackening his face and shoulders with mud.

Matohota turned and moved silently through the darkness of the trees and shrubs of the riverbank. Nearing the small fire thirty yards downstream, he saw two men sitting around the embers but was concerned that others may be nearby. One of them threw some wood on the waning fire and he could hear the crunching of coals as a column of sparks rose and disappeared into the night. As the light from the fire increased, he saw that they were Indian and recognized them.

He circled around the camp area and could see three others bedded down and five picketed horses. The horses sensed his presence and began to snort and nervously stomp their hooves. One of the men stood up, picked up a rifle and cautiously took several steps toward the horses then stopped as if expecting a hungry wolf or, worse yet, a grizzly bear to be lurking in the darkness. After scanning the shadows for several seconds, he returned to the fire sitting with his back to the river and continuing to watch the uneasy mustangs.

Matohota silently returned to his canoe with Astrid, startled by his ursine aura not unlike the nervous horses, waiting in the darkness.

"What did you see?" she asked in a whisper.

"Five Indians with guns and horses."

"Do you know them?"

"One is a Wahpekute Chief called Iŋkpaduta."

"What on earth do we do now?"

"We can get by them since I don't think they're watching the river."

"But what if they see us?"

"Chance we have to take since it'll be daylight soon," he said knowing there were no options since Iŋkpaduta had no love for White people or farmer Indian breeds.

Matohota cut two long leaved branches from overhead and attached them to the starboard side of the canoe. He pulled the craft into the water and leveraged himself back into his kneeling position in the stern. He guided the canoe to the far, east side of the river about a good stone throw from the campers yet still in the current allowing them to noiselessly drift past their campsite. As they entered the area of the river lighted by the flickering campfire, Matohota ducked his head behind the leaves of their camouflage, as did Astrid.

Drifting past the campsite, Matohota, peering through the leaves, could see one of the men walking toward the river and standing on a rock in the shallow water of the shoreline. At that moment, Astrid's baby let out a whimper. He reached for his rifle as he watched the unarmed man who looked directly at them for a few seconds, then looked up and down the river and, seemingly satisfied that the noise was from an animal of some kind, squatted down and began splashing water on his face, apparently to stay awake during his watch.

Matohota realized he had not slept for two nights and hoped he would be up for whatever lies ahead of them. As they were safely past the Indian camp, he discarded the cottonwood branch cover and began paddling. He knew they had little time before daybreak as he saw An'pao Wićaŋḣpi—the Morning Star, shining brightly above the eastern horizon.

Valley of the Nations

Astrid was wide-awake after the tension of their floating chicanery at the riverside encampment. She realized that her experiences of the last few days had been unlike any in her life. As she recalled Johannes saying that she thrives on periodic dramatic life changes, she also realized that her most dramatic life change thus far has been her unexpected association with the Dakota Indians.

They are a people of extreme contrasts, she thought. *On the one hand, some are on a violent rampage to kill all of the Yermans. Then, on the other hand, others did everything they could to help me in labor while one is risking his life to protect ours. It is like the extreme contrast between devils and anyels.*

Our church elders have said that devils are anyels who have fallen out of grace with God. Devils are only different from anyels in that their nature is morally corrupt. Devil is the opposite of anyel as evil is the opposite of good. Satan, the leader of the devils, is the opposite not of God since He can have no opposite, but of Michael the Archanyel.

I am sure that Good Voice Woman is a Guardian Anyel since I could feel the presence of the Holy Spirit in her. I wonder why the family members seemed so concerned last night when I mentioned her name? she wondered. *They yust looked at me wide-eyed and talked to each other in their language but told me nothing about her. I pray that she has not come to harm!*

And that man, Grizzly Bear! What a fine person he is to yust leave his family to see to our safety. I had prayed to God to send another Guardian Anyel for my baby's sake. Is he that Guardian Anyel? Is he Michael the Archanyel whose yob is to protect the children of God from physical and spiritual danyers?

> *The pow'rs of death have done their worst,*
> *But Christ their legions has dispersed.*
> *Let shouts of holy joy out-burst.*
> *Alleluia!*

What yoy this is! Astrid thought in tears as she could once again hear the choir of Angels. *Never have I had such a wondrous experience of being so close to God—the smells of the river, the sounds of the night, the feel of my newborn baby as he finds nourishment from my breast, and to lean my head back and see the wonderful star filled universe of His creation! And is that Christ rising?* she wondered as she saw Venus shining brightly above the eastern horizon.

> *The three sad days have quickly sped,*
> *He rises glorious from the dead.*
> *All glory to our risen head!*
> *Alleluia!*

Come onto me, all ye that labor and are heavy laden, and I will give you rest, she remembered from Matthew. *I was truly in labor and heavily laden with fear and now I am fully rested and full of life, as if I have been reborn. I am aware that I have become my Higher Self. I must now fulfill my mission on earth, a mission of discipline and service to others that they may also find conversion and come to faith.*

> *Lord, by the stripes which wounded you,*
> *From death's sting free your servants too,*
> *That we may live and sing to you.*
> *Alleluia!*

Astrid looked for the first light of dawn in the eastern sky as she brought her baby up to her shoulder and began burping him.

"Astrid," she heard Matohota whisper.

"Yes," she whispered back as she turned in the canoe to look at him.

"About a mile now to the fort."

"How long until we get there?"

"Should be there before daybreak."

"What will we do then?"

"Not sure. The war drums getting louder. Can you hear the singing?"

"What on earth does that mean?" she asked as she realized that she could also hear the singing echoing upriver that she might have thought was the choir of angels.

"It means that they're gathering to attack the fort!"

"Oh merciful God in Heaven!"

"We have to think about how to get you and the baby through those Indians and safely to the fort."

Astrid knew that the only way to gain safe passage to the fort was with the protective white light of God. *We must pray to God to send his legion of angels to place their protective shields around us as we walk through the valley of the nations.*

DAY OF PLENTY

Matohota could see the Morning Star still shining brightly over the horizon and hoped it was a sign that all would be well. *Kuŋśi Okadawiŋ said that among our Dakota, the Morning Star represents knowledge,* he recalled. *The ignorance of darkness is overwhelmed by the knowledge of light that comes every morning with its rising.*

Then why is it that our people are doing this? This killing and destruction! Is war the ignorance of darkness that will change to peace with the knowledge of light brought by the Morning Star?

Matohota could hear the deep resonance of the drum and the singing getting louder as he paddled the twisting river and neared the stretch of riverfront adjacent to the fort. *It seems like our very life is always in flux, like things are always changing between wicked and good influences—pain and pleasure, fear and happiness, death and birth. In the wintertime, we face starvation. Then during the summer, there is great abundance. Do our people not understand that this day of plenty, of our looting and burning the farms of the Iaśića and killing of the Big Knives, will be followed tomorrow by the death of many of our people, the destruction of our villages, and the banishment of survivors from these lands of the Wakpa Minisota forever?*

Kuŋśi has said that it is only through our ceremonial ways, through sacred ritual that harmony can be achieved and our world restored to its proper balance. Why have so many of our people forsaken those ways? I walk the White man's road but I am still strong in the ways of the Red Road, the ceremonial rituals of our people!

As they neared the Fort Ridgley area, Matohota was unsure of what to expect. *In trying to make it to the fort, we could be killed by the Indians! While if we made it to the fort, then the soldiers could kill us!* he thought shaking his head at the gruesome reality of the dilemma. He decided to beach the canoe and scout the area ahead hoping they could loop around any Dakota massing near the river and, with his shirt as a white flag, gain safe entry into the fort.

Matohota guided the canoe onto the northeast shore of the river and, jumping into the cool knee-high water of the shoreline, pulled the bow of the craft up onto the sandy beach. Astrid rose with her baby in her arms and stepped out of the craft onto dry ground for the first time since their departure several hours earlier.

"Are we finally there, Grizzly Bear?"

"Just about."

"What do we do, now then?" she asked then sat down on a large rock with her back against a tree.

"I'm going to take a look at what's over there. To see if we can make it to the fort."

"IF we can make it?" she asked.

With his rifle in hand, he climbed the steep cottonwood treed bank of the river to the prairie above. He sprinted across a small open field and up onto a small knoll. Crawling to the top of the hill and parting the little blue stem and sage, he had a good view of Fort Ridgley about a mile distant. The fort-with-out-walls sat on a spur of high prairie tableland about 150 feet above the valley floor with undulating grassland sloping to the west.

Cut into that grassy slope southwest of the fort was a deep treed ravine with drainage to the river and about half-a-mile from his location. In that ravine he estimated there to be at least two hundred warriors visible in the dim light around campfires with more groups and individuals arriving from across the river. Since he couldn't see that many horses, he assumed most of the men were afoot. The war dancing, he could see, had increased in fervor throughout the night with war whoops and the firing of guns into the air by warriors who considered it honorable to die in battle now preparing to lay siege to the fort.

Matohota could also see that, as it would be daylight soon, any approach to the fort would be in plain view of the Indians in the ravine. Also the few horses they had available were being used for groups patrolling the perimeter of the fort in hopes of stopping any reinforcements from entering, assuring that attempts by them to reach the fort unnoticed were impossible.

With dispirited news, he made his way back to Astrid.

Path of Light

Sitting alone with her sleeping baby waiting for the return of Matohota, Astrid was wondering what her father would say in this situation with Indians rising like the tide and engulfing settlers and soldiers alike in a sea of blood. *My father is a compassionate man of the Bible who always recites Scriptures to express his interpretation of things:*

> *Like fish taken in a cruel net, like birds caught in a snare, so the sons of men are snared in an evil time, when it falls suddenly upon them.*

Then he would probably say that the Dakota are not possessed by demons nor do they have evil hearts, but, rather, are caught up in evil times.

And these indeed are evil times. With brother killing brother in a bloody Civil War in the east and our men going off to die in that war for reasons women will never understand. With the black Africans in the south taken in the cruel net of slavery and the red Indians in the west caught in the land hungry snare of the rapidly advancing European immigrants.

My father had often spoken kindly of the few Dakota people he had known. It was while hunting one winter near Forestville on the South Branch of the Root River that he had found an old deserted Indian village. Then, during the following summer, he found that several Dakota families made pilgrimages each year to that village from the Redwood Agency where they had been moved after the Treaty of 1851.

They said that their Dakota people had occupied the village for many generations because it was on hallowed ground. It was the Spirit of the North who dwelt there in a cave that made it so. To prove it, the Indians had taken father to the west side of a craggy limestone hill where the warm waters of the South Branch disappeared into the ground. Then, after taking him to the east side of the same hill where the river reappeared, father was shocked to find that the water was now very cold, about thirty degrees colder than when it submerged.

The Dakota told him that it was the Spirit of the North, whose breath is the frosty North Wind, who breathes on the water making it cold as it passes through her lodge. The Indians said that the Spirit of the North is an elderly woman whose surly temperament must be appeased each year through ceremony else never-ending blizzards and glacial cold will once again engulf the land. Father was very taken by those intensely spiritual people who often gave him tanned hides as well as sharing their wild game—bison, venison, wild turkey, and goose. Father would often reciprocate by giving them barrels of lutefisk, which they politely refused saying that they preferred the fresh trout of the Root River, but they did like lefsa with butter.

When we were older, father would often take us children camping there and tell us the stories that were told to him about the mysteries of the Root River valley. But the Indians had stopped their pilgrimages there for unknown reasons and for years father would go there each summer hoping to find them again. He said it was yust like a band of golden eagles landing in a tree and bestowing the landscape with an air of regal dignity and beauty then flying off again leaving only a memory.

"Astrid," she heard Matohota calling softly from the top of the riverbank.

"Yes! I was yust beginning to worry," she whispered back while rocking her whimpering baby after having replaced the soiled sage leaves in his makeshift diaper—a bandana that Waȟċaziwiŋ had given her. Astrid was grateful that he had announced himself remembering how he had startled her earlier with his sudden dreggy appearance.

Matohota descended the wooded bank and leaned his rifle against a tree and sat on the ground near Astrid as he said, "I don't think we should try making it to the fort."

"Why on earth not?" Astrid asked knowing that if your belief is strong enough, then anything is possible.

"It's going to be attacked today. Even if we made it there, you and the baby wouldn't be safe if it was overrun by Indians."

"I don't believe that it will be overrun!"

"Why?"

"Because a choir of angels has told me that Christ has dispersed their leyions!"

"Leyions? What's that mean?"

"It means that the worst is over. Most of the evil has already been done!"

"So what do we do now?"

"Go to the fort, of course!"

"It's still too risky!"

"But isn't it riskier to be caught out here in the open?"

"I spose but..."

"Then we must go! And we must go now!" she interrupted as she could see the dawn breaking on the eastern horizon giving their situation a sense of urgency.

"And how are we going to do that?"

"God will light our way if we but ask him!" she said feeling a strange sensation overcoming her. It was a feeling of renewal that she attributed to the manifestation of her Higher Self, of intense clarity of mind and senses where the colors of the early dawn were vibrantly alive. It was also a feeling of extraordinary lightness, like having wings and being able to glide across the prairie and soar up into the heavens.

Astrid watched Matohota as he stood, walked to the river, primed his rifle and laid it carefully into the canoe. She watched him turn to the river and sprinkle something onto the water as she heard him say in his native tongue, "Mitakuye owasu!"

I have heard others refer to Indians as heathens, as lazy and good for nothing savages, she thought. *But like my father, I have grown to have a deep respect for the spiritual genius of these people. Grizzly Bear is very kind and a man of prayer, but true to his name, seems extremely dangerous. He carries the trait of his people, a people of extreme contrasts.* Standing with her baby and also walking to the river, she looked upstream and then turned to look downstream.

"Which way we going?" asked Matohota as he readied to push the birchbark craft back into the water.

It was then, in the darkness of downstream, that Astrid saw a white point of light hovering over the water and pulsating like a star. She knew it was a sign; it was God pointing the way.

"We must go downstream," she pleaded.

"Alright," he answered as he inhaled deeply and waited to assist her back into the bow of the canoe. "But it's very dangerous down there. I saw a couple hundred Dakota with more coming in all the time."

As they began the last leg of their journey, Astrid realized that throughout the morning she's felt a strange urgency to get to Fort Ridgley. There, somehow, she could feel the presence of Johannes. *But how could that be?* she wondered. *He is far away in a confederate prison.* She remembered occasions when she had similarly sensed his presence and ran to the front door of her parent's Arendahl home only to see him climbing up their front stairs. As the sound of the drums and the singing grew louder, Astrid grasped her amethyst brooch and felt its reassuring warmth.

"How far do you wanna go?"

"Until we get a sign."

"Alright," he answered doubtfully shrugging his shoulders.

Watching the pulsating point of light ahead of them, Astrid began to pray for divine help. She knew that according to God's laws, heavenly representatives might not intervene into humanly affairs unless first asked to do so. *When God created us,* her church Elders would say, *He gave us free will and expects us to use it.*

Without free will, we wouldn't be able to experience the good and bad results of our decisions; we wouldn't be able to grow from the lessons of life.

"Oh Father in Heaven. Thank you this morning for allowing us to see the light of thy Kingdom shining on this river of life. Please send thy Anyels of Mercy, oh God, to protect us as we walk through the valley of the nations. Allow us to see the light of thy face shining on us to light our path that we may be saved. Thank you this morning, oh God, for sparing the life of my dear husband Yohannes. Please bring him home safely to see his new son who, with thy Devine blessing, was born strong and healthy.

"Oh God. Thank you for delivering me from evil by sending thy Guardian Anyels. I pray that the soul of Good Voice Woman will have life everlasting in the Kingdom of Heaven. I thank you for sending this fine young man, Grizzly Bear, and that you watch over him and return him safely to his family and that he finds them in good health. I pray this for all who have accepted thy son Yesus, to whom you have given power to become the children of God. I den Hellige namn Gud Fader, Son og den Hellig Ånds! Amen."

Alleluia, Alleluia, Alleluia!

Hearing the choir of Angels again, Astrid could see the point of light ahead of them growing in size and intensity. As Matohota paddled nearer they entered into the field of light where she could see the faint images of winged angels bearing shields standing along the shore. A short distance ahead of them, she could see the large ball of light now shining from the top of the riverbank of the northeast shore. As they got nearer, she could see standing in the light, the image of a majestic angel in shining armor with a winged helmet and a brilliant sapphire-blue cape. In his right hand was a sword of blue flames, the sword of Michael the Archangel.

"There's the sign!" she whispered loudly as Matohota slowed the canoe and paddled to the shore.

Matohota leveraged himself out of the canoe and into the knee-high water of the shore and pushed the bow up onto the sandy beach. He helped Astrid with her baby out of the canoe and then reached for his rifle.

"Grizzly Bear, do you see the brilliant light and the angel?" asked Astrid thinking that, being a mystically gifted person, he should be able to see into the world of spirits.

"Yes!" he answered in apparent astonishment.

"Then you must lay your weapons down! You must absolutely believe in the protective power of the Holy Spirit!"

Matohota laid the long rifle back into the canoe. Hesitantly, he removed the Colt pistol and his sheathed bowie knife from his belt and also placed them into the canoe. He hurriedly put his shirt back on as well as his hat, pulled the craft into a nearby thicket of tall reed grass and covered it. He returned and stood before Astrid holding his hornbeam paddle with one end resting on the ground.

"Grizzly Bear," she said looking both puzzled and amused. "You're bringing your oar?"

"Didn't Moses walk with a staff?"

"Very well then," she said after a moments thought. "Can we get under way?"

Astrid carrying her baby followed Matohota to the top of the riverbank. He stopped when he reached the top and seemed to marvel at the portal of light, which was a gateway to a tube of blue ethereal light as round as a spread eagled man could reach and shimmered over a golden glowing pathway. When Astrid reached the portal, she could see the tube of light that led from where they stood at the prairies edge and up the sloping prairie tableland a half-mile to the fort.

"Grizzly Bear," she said in reverence. "Do you see it? God has provided His path of light!"

> He broke the age-bound chains of hell;
> The bars from heav'n's high portals fell.
> Let hymns of praise his triumph tell.
> Alleluia!

Astrid heard the choir of angels again as she stepped over the threshold into the tunnel of light as the sound of the Dakota drum and the singing stopped abruptly, as if she had entered into a totally different dimension. She turned to see that Matohota seemed reluctant to enter. She held up her hand and motioned for him to follow her not sure that he would be able to hear her voice from another dimension. Matohota, with his paddle in hand, stepped into the lighted passageway and began to follow her.

As they passed near the Indian encampment, she noticed that the Indians went about their activities totally unaware of their passing, although she could see all of their actions through the wall of light devoid of sound. As they passed near a large group of men who were seated on the ground in a circle, she noticed that one of the men suddenly stood up and looked their way. He was a tall man with splashes of red paint on his thin body, wore a buffalo horned headdress and carried an eagle wing fan in his hand. He stood there for a long moment then started walking slowly toward them as if dancing.

"He sees us!" said Matohota.

"Who is he?" asked Astrid.

"His name is Ćetaŋhuŋka. He is a Medicine Man from Little Crow's Village, the father of Good Voice Woman."

"Then that's why he sees us. He lives in the spirit world."

"Don't worry; he won't try to harm us."

Ćetaŋhuŋka stopped a few paces from Astrid and Matohota, touched the earth with his fan, raised it toward the rising sun, and then motioned toward them with the eagle feathers four times as she could hear him praying in his language. He reached down and grabbed a handful of earth, held the hand out in front of him and let the dirt fall into the breeze then turned and slowly danced away as he continued praying. Then she could hear the voices of the choir of angels.

> *The strife is o'er, the battle done;*
> *Now is the victor's triumph won!*
> *Now be the song of praise begun.*
> *Alleluia!*
> *Alleluia, Alleluia, Alleluia!*

Afterword

Wayuhi returned to the Otter Tail Village with Timdokuota and his relations. Not long thereafter Tataŋkanażiŋ, fearing retaliation from the Americans for the Minnesota War of 1862, took his Amdowapuśkiya band of Northern Sisse-toŋwan out onto the western prairies of Dakota Territory and southern Manitoba. After several years of smallpox, starvation and being chased by American soldiers, Tiowaśte, the father of Wayuhi, led several hundred of his people to the newly-built Fort Totten near Devil's Lake in Dakota Territory in 1867.

Wayuhi and Timdokuota lived out their lives near the community of Tokio, a short distance from Mniwakaŋ Ćaŋte where he made his Vision Quest, on the Spirit Lake Dakota Reservation in what is now North Dakota. They finally made it to the Center of the World since, near there, in Pierce County, North Dakota is the Geographical Center of North America. Tataŋkanażiŋ, called the last of the great Sissetoŋwan Chiefs of the buffalo days, died as a true Napeśni in Montana in 1871, but that's another story.

Capt. Wolfgang Luckenbach stayed on at Fort Snelling to help organize and train the 1st Minnesota Regiment Cavalry "Mounted Rangers" for frontier duty against Indians. From there he had a hand in the development of a new Union Cavalry, a cavalry of blue pistoleros flaunting its new tactics with revolvers blazing as they thundered toward Appomattox.

After the war, Luckenbach returned to the Blanco River country of south Texas where he took over his family ranch. He lived out his life not too far from a Texas town that bears his name; a town established as a trading post and was reputed to be one of the few never to break a peace treaty with the Comanche Indians with whom they traded.

Astrid Arntsdatter Mundahl's keen intuition about her husband's presence at Fort Ridgley turned out to be true. The Confederate Army agreed to release the captured soldiers of the 3rd Regiment Minnesota Infantry, United States Volunteers, if they agreed to return home and not participate in military activities against the south. The State of Minnesota immediately deployed the Regiment to Fort Ridgley to aid in the Minnesota Conflict. Johannes arrived there in October 1862 only to be joyously greeted by his wife and his new Säugling.

Today, on the windswept prairie of Camp Township of Renville County near the Minnesota River, is a small white church behind which is a beautiful wrought iron sign identifying Hauges Cemetery arching over the entrance. In that cemetery is the lonely grave of Johannes Mundahl who died in 1878. It is not known what happened to Astrid after the death of her beloved Johannes. Some say she helped found the Hauge Synod Seminary in Red Wing. Others say she went on to fulfill her mission on earth, a mission of discipline and service to others that they may also find conversion and come to faith, by founding a home for unwed Scandinavian mothers in St. Paul.

Matohota Charbonneau was treated as a hero by the soldiers garrisoned at Fort Ridgley for bringing in Astrid and her newborn baby. That very day the soldiers repelled attacks by Dakota warriors with deadly cannon fire. The pow'rs of death had indeed done their worst since, from then on, the successes of the Dakota in their violent quest for freedom quickly deteriorated.

Matohota returned to find his family well accepted and taken in by the Gens Libre. They lived with the Free People hunting buffalo and living a wonderfully free life until the slaughter of the great herds ten years later. With his boys well grown with families of their own, Matohota took his wife to the pristine Boundary Waters Country of northern Minnesota where he lived out his life hunting, trapping, and fabricating birchbark canoes. Always in the back of his mind was the hope of someday finding his father, the powerful hunter-trapper-warrior Antoine Charbonneau, and the man who the Isaŋti Dakota respectfully named Pahayużataŋka—Great Scalp Taker.

The Minnesota Conflict of 1862 was the beginning of the Sioux Indian's fight for his lands and freedom that ended tragically at the Wounded Knee Massacre in 1890. By the end of the Minnesota Conflict in September 1862, General Sibley and a five-man commission had sentenced 303 Dakota to be hanged. President Lincoln intervened and issued an order allowing only 38 of the planned executions to ultimately take place. The political pressures of the on-going Civil War and the upcoming elections made the President reluctant to alienate his allies in Minnesota by stopping the executions altogether.

Thus, in Mankato, Minnesota on the day after Christmas 1862, 38 condemned Dakota Indians were hanged marking the largest mass execution in America's history. Among those hanged was Hepaŋ, the husband of Wamnuwiŋ, who told her of his vision that he would not see his family again; the enigmatic Tatekaǧa who lived in the spirit world and talked to Waziya; and Ćetaŋhuŋka, the Medicine Man who set out on a wokićize wakaŋ—holy war, to rid the Wakpa Minisota of whiskey, those who made it, and those who sold it to avenge the brutal murder of his daughter.

It was said that as the 38 condemned men mounted the scaffold chanting their death songs, a steam locomotive entering Mankato sounded a shrill whistle as Shakopee, a Mdewakaŋtoŋ Chief, pointed to it and said, "As the White man comes in, the Indian goes out!"

Appendix

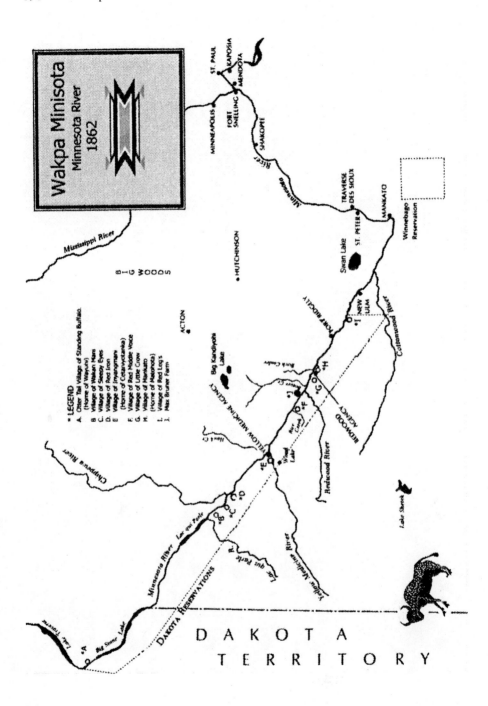

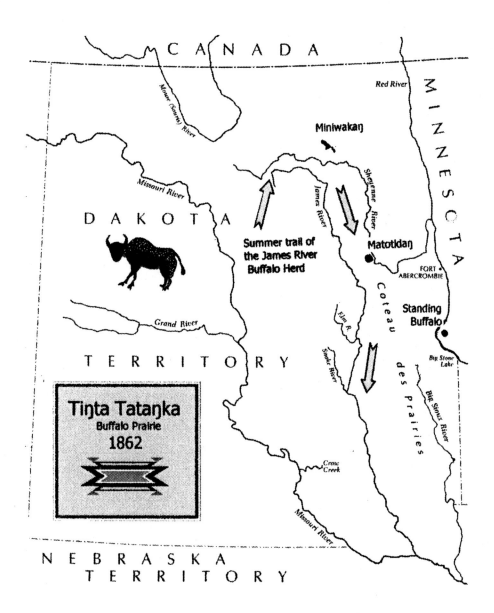

978-0-595-34992-0
0-595-34992-7

Printed in the United States
41675LVS00004B/233